VERY SPECIAL FORCES

LEXI GRAVES MYSTERIES

Camilla Chafer

ALSO BY CAMILLA CHAFER

CHAPTER ONE

"I'm hit!" I gasped. My fingers, snug in thick, padded gloves, moved down to the red patch currently widening over my heart. Any moment now, my life would expire and that would be it. Game over. I dropped my head back in the grass where I landed at the impact of the bullet and stared up at the blue sky, so peaceful and still, nary a cloud drifting past. A second later, a face loomed over me.

Lily pulled back her protective goggles and grinned. "Gotcha!" she said just as the buzzer across my breastplate sounded. "You're dead!"

"We're on the same team, Lily!" I yelled.

Lily wrinkled her nose and knit her eyebrows together. "Dammit," she muttered, a confused look spreading across the parts of her face not covered by the protective mask. "I knew I missed something crucial in the game plan." She dropped onto the grass next to me and sighed.

Pushing up with my elbows, I sat upright and tapped the breastplate until the incessant buzzer stopped sounding. It continued to flash red, alerting the controller that another player was off the field and ensuring that both my opponents and teammates knew there was no point wasting their paintball cartridges on me since I was officially dead.

"I really thought we would win this," I said. "I thought we nailed the game plan. We would have, if you'd only paid more attention to it."

"I had my mind on other things," said Lily. She looked down and pulled a face. "Do you think this jumpsuit makes me look fat?"

"No. Even fat couldn't make you look fat."

"You say the nicest things." Lily frowned again. "Although I'm struggling to get my head around that one."

"Would being fat be the worst thing in the world?" I asked. "So long as you feel good, that's the main thing."

"Nope, it's not the worst. I just want to feel confident in my mom body. I want to feel like the woman who used to dance on tables until two in the morning."

"You felt like that last week," I reminded her. "We were asked to leave, remember?"

"Oh yeah!" Lily giggled. "In that case, I feel great and I didn't even have a hangover afterwards."

"Winning at life," I said as we fist-bumped. I looked around, wondering where the rest of our team was, but did I really care? Paintballing was not my idea of a good time, even if it were fun to run around a fenced-in pitch, shooting the opposite team.

A yell shattered the silence followed by other manly grunting noises before two camouflaged men appeared from behind a small hill. All their breastplates flashed red and one was covered from head to toe in paint splatters. He pulled off his goggles and laughed as he walked towards us, closely flanked by the other men. Before they reached us, Lily's breastplate began to flash green.

"Uh-oh," she said, staring down at it. "What did I do?"

I shook my head. "You won," I told her. "You're the last woman standing."

"Unbelievable," said Solomon when he reached us. He held his hand out to me and tugged me to my feet before pulling up Lily. After he kissed me, he asked Lily, "How did you win? What was your game plan?"

"Stealth tactics," she said, her face now serious. "Solid game plan. Nerves of steel."

Solomon looked at me. I nodded. "That's exactly what happened," I lied.

"And it had nothing to do with me sitting here while you guys shot each other up," Lily added.

"Thought so," said Solomon. He pointed to his paint-splattered jumpsuit and glanced toward the sniggering trio behind him. "Your brothers thought it was perfectly fair to team up against me."

My three older brothers, Garrett, Daniel, and Jord, pulled off their goggles and laughed, clapping each other on their backs and never looking one bit ashamed.

"You're on our team, Jord," I reminded the youngest of the trio and also Lily's husband. "You shot your own teammate!"

Jord shrugged and slung an arm around Lily's shoulders. "It was worth it if only to get the drop on Solomon."

"It'll never happen again," said Solomon. "Plus, we still won, thanks to Lily's tactics that left her as the last player alive."

Lily grinned. "Let's go get that trophy!"

"And pizzas," added Jord, "and beers."

"We have a baby to get home to," Lily reminded him.

"Baby? We have a baby?" asked Jord, pretending to look puzzled. He checked the imaginary watch on his wrist. "I think we have plenty of time left for fun."

"Mom and Dad will love any extra time they can get with Poppy," I told them. "Take advantage of it and enjoy yourselves. Anyway, you know Victoria loves playing with Poppy. Poppy is the only member of the family smaller than her."

"I don't need to be told twice. Do you?" asked Jord.

"Lead the way to the bar," replied Lily and they scooted off hand-in-hand with Garrett and Daniel following behind.

I looked around for my colleagues at the Solomon Detective Agency, spying Fletcher, Flaherty and Lucas waiting at the gates to the enclosure. Only Tony Delgado was missing and that was because he was currently on his honeymoon with my sister, Serena. They got married a month before but had to delay their honeymoon slightly due to a combination of work commitments and Serena's fussiness about where they should vacation. With Serena's daughter safely ensconced at my parents' house for ten days, they headed to white sand and blue seas, their exact location unknown.

"This was fun. Lily enjoyed it even if she's not an official crimefighter," I said, slipping my hand into Solomon's as we followed our team to the exit.

"She's one of the family," he replied. "This was much better than just holding a team building day for the private investigator squad. We should do it more often."

"Maybe next time we could have more padding." I winced as I breathed audibly, certain I would wind up with a bruise or two by the morning. "Fun as this was, I don't want any bruises when I wear my wedding dress."

"Duly noted. Only two weeks until the wedding." Solomon smiled. "Are you sure you don't need any time off? I don't want you to feel rushed with the planning or overwhelmed by the job."

"I'm fine," I told him, and I truly was. Having smugly wrapped up my latest case, a simple desk job, mainly running background checks on a department store's employees after a wave of thefts, I was satisfied. It didn't take long to ascertain that one long-standing staff member incurred a bad gambling debt after several bereavements and felt compelled to resort to theft in his effort to solve it. I recommended the staff member be moved to a position of less responsibility, more monitoring, and provided with counseling as well as any reasonable measures the store manager was amenable to. I was feeling more than a little proud of myself for my compassionate response. "I need to do something or I'll just get in Francesca's way," I said, referring to our wedding planner. She picked up the bulk of the wedding work once we decided what we wanted and how we expected our wedding day to play out. Now it was merely days away, and all I had to do was avoid getting into trouble before the happy event. How hard could that be?

"Then I'll expect to see you in the office at nine sharp tomorrow," said Solomon. "I'm sure we can find something for you to do that doesn't involve chasing down lunatics or getting shot at. Until then, I could use a cold beer, a hot shower and a home-cooked meal. I can cook it."

"You sound like you're married already. You'll make a terrific husband."

"Best compliment you've paid me all day," he said, stopping to kiss me again. Behind us, someone cheered.

~

"Nine sharp," I said. I tapped my watch as I pointed to the clock on the wall. Solomon and I entered only a minute earlier, the first to arrive in the PI's shared office. We both made for the small boardroom where we held meetings and I looked around. "Where is everyone?" I wondered as I moved to the window and looked down at the street below.

"Some of us don't carpool with the boss," said Fletcher, yawning as he walked in. Pulling out a chair, he slumped in it and yawned again. Usually he looked stony, like the hard ex-CIA agent he was, but not today. Today, he looked like he needed to go back to bed.

"Some of us have to because he makes breakfast," I pointed out. "It would be rude not to carpool. Why are you so tired?"

"I didn't go to bed until three am, thanks to your brother and sister-in-law insisting that I do shots until the wee hours."

"There was nothing to 'insist' upon," said Flaherty as he strolled in, a box of donuts under his arm. He dropped the box on the table and Fletcher's hand moved towards it automatically, his fingers feebly attempting to flick open the lid. "I'm surprised Fletch can move."

"Practice," groaned Fletcher. He dragged a donut from the box. "Reflexes."

I grabbed the back of a chair and pulled it out before dropping into it. "How come you look so awake?" I asked Flaherty. Matt Flaherty was a former detective and long-time friend of Solomon's. He'd been relegated an invalid after being shot in the line of duty but seemed content to work for the agency rather than enjoy an early retirement.

"I went home at a reasonable hour and didn't imbibe like the world's alcohol was becoming a scarce resource," explained Flaherty. "Not all of us want to look like gnarled, old PIs."

"I definitely don't," I agreed. I glanced down at my pink pants, cream blouse and darling two-tone heels. I couldn't be further from a gnarled PI, which was exactly why Solomon initially hired me. Our targets never suspected me.

"Anyone know where Lucas is?" asked Solomon. He stood at the head of the table, his arms folded, waiting.

"Here!" said Lucas as he hurried in, raising his hand and sliding into the chair next to Fletcher. "What happened to you?" he hissed, taking one look at Fletcher's bleary eyes.

"Seriously?" Fletcher raised his head wearily. "I'm the only one with a hangover?"

We all nodded and he slumped even further into his seat.

"Let's get to it," said Solomon. "As a caveat before we start, Lexi and I are both reducing our workloads in the run-up to the wedding; so anything that looks time-consuming will be handed over to you guys."

There was a small chorus of 'you got it, boss', 'we can handle it' and 'does that mean extra donuts if Lexi wants to fit into her dress?' The last one I took particular offense at. Like I could leave anyone my allotted share of donuts! I reached for a jelly-filled donut dusted with powdered sugar and stuck out my tongue.

"Glad we're all up to speed," continued Solomon without defending me on the donut issue. He began to hand out a sheaf of thin files. "We have several cases in this week. There's a neighbor problem a realtor has asked us to look into. Something to do with a boundary line potentially being illegally moved. I know, I know. Not riveting stuff but you never can tell when small cases like these can end up generating a big lead later."

"I can cover this in an hour or two," said Lucas. "It's easy to look up property records."

"Great. When you have the boundary lines confirmed, Fletcher can head out to the property with a measuring tape and confirm it old school-style. Then you can go home," Solomon added with a pointed look at Fletcher.

"Thanks, boss," said Fletcher, not even pretending to argue.

"What else do we have?" asked Flaherty.

"The register at Dollar Donuts has been coming up short for the past month. The owner wants us to find out who's behind it."

"On it," yelled Flaherty as he reached for the file.

"You don't know all the details yet," said Solomon.

Flaherty gave a smug smile. "I know all there is to know. Stake out the donut shop. Pretty much my life's dream. Anything else?"

Solomon shook his head. "That's about it," he agreed. "Don't spend more than a couple days on it. There's a new employee and the assistant manager is apparently behaving oddly. Check them both out and then put surveillance in place. Dollar Donuts doesn't have any cameras so there's no video footage to examine. Next up is a divorce case. Suspected hidden assets, disgruntled spouses. Lexi, do you and Lucas want to team up on this one?"

"What kind of hidden assets?" I asked.

"Property, investments and bank accounts. The marriage reportedly lasted a heady forty-three days before the husband suspected that the wife was just in it for the money. He's accusing her of being a gold-digger. She's adamant she's not. The lawyers have agreed to team up to find out what the situation is and who's telling the truth. The information is in the files. It should be mostly desk work."

"I can do that," I said, "but I'll need to defer to Lucas for any trickier financial angles. There are limits to my talents." Unless we were talking cocktails, cake, and getting into trouble, for which there were no limits.

"Perfect." Solomon consulted the files that were left. "The first of the last two case requests involves a missing person but since it's only been forty hours, I'm going to pass that one back to the Montgomery Police Department; and the other is a family squabble. Something about some coins, one that most likely needs a lawyer to really shake that money tree rather than private investigators." Solomon tucked both files under his arm. "No walk-ins for the past two weeks unless someone forgot to mention one?" he added, looking around as we shook our heads. It had actually been very quiet in the office for the past couple of weeks, which was not a bad thing. Usually, I would have been searching for something to do but now that the wedding plans were in the final stages and the big day only a couple of weeks away, I was glad of the quiet time. If I were lucky, it would continue and Solomon and I could get married in peace before embarking on our honeymoon with nothing more to concentrate on than each other. Each other and the sun, the sand, the ocean, and the entire cocktail menu.

"Lexi?"

"Hmm?" I looked up and blinked, disappointed that I was still in the office and not on the honeymoon that so briefly occupied my thoughts.

"Are you okay to get started, or is it too much?" asked Solomon.

"It's perfect," I assured him.

"You don't have any dress fittings or other wedding preparations scheduled?"

"Not today. I'll get started on these and let you know when my report is ready," I said as I stood up and collected the file.

Lucas waved as he left the office before disappearing upstairs to the upper floor of the detective agency. Fletcher and Flaherty were on his heels, reminiscing about the paintball wars, leaving Solomon and me as the last participants to depart. The phone in Solomon's office began to ring and he jogged over to answer it. A moment later, he strolled out again just as I sat at my desk, holding his jacket in hand. "I have to head out," he said. "I might be gone all afternoon. Do you want to go out for a bite to eat later?"

"Can we cook at home? I promised Lily I would meet her at the gym after work. We're taking a new class."

"What kind of class?"

"Lily calls it strengthening and core work with a touch of dance."

"Okay," said Solomon, his eyes glazing over. "Just don't get injured."

I held back a snort of derision, primarily because his advice was good and Lily had been slightly sketchy about offering any details of the class. She convinced me on the principle that it would be a good way to get fit since we needed to find a new regular class after becoming so scarred from the spin class we used to take. That, coincidentally took a murderous turn, and since the once ultra-fit Lily had delivered a baby, I was finding it harder than ever to get enthused or motivated for any kind of fitness efforts. Only the thoughts of looking back on my wedding photos could manage to spur me on.

"You too," I shot back pointlessly; Solomon remained a wall of muscle that rarely got injured. However, he'd only recently recovered from a gunshot wound that nearly killed him so I was well aware that he wasn't completely indestructible.

Solomon simply smiled, dropped a kiss on my lips, didn't argue when I prolonged it, and promptly left, leaving me alone in the office.

"I could literally do anything in here and no one would ever know," I told the empty room. I jumped when the phone in Solomon's office rang at that very second. "Who's watching me?" I asked out loud while crossing the floor and reaching for the phone.

"Solomon Detective Agency," I answered.

"That you, Lexi?" asked Jim, the doorman who monitored the building's front entryway.

"Yep," I said.

"There's a lady down here asking to see someone. She says she doesn't have an appointment or any identification with her. Shall I send her up or tell her to call for an appointment?"

"Did she say what it's about?" I asked, wondering if the woman might be connected to one of the cases Solomon had just handed out.

"Just that it's a case she wants to discuss very badly and she really wants to talk to someone now. I asked her if you'd already taken it and she said no."

"Send her up. I'll take her to one of the meeting rooms," I decided. The work Solomon assigned to me could wait the thirty minutes or so it would take to talk to the woman. Plus, a walk-in was always intriguing. A lot of clients preferred to make an appointment in advance. A walk-in was still deciding whether or not they needed a PI. They gravitated to the office before they could talk themselves out of it.

"You got it," said Jim before he hung up. I replaced the handset, then jogged to my desk. Checking my pockets for my cell phone, I grabbed a pen because they invariably went missing from the small meeting rooms we used for new clients. In practice, any employee of the agency had access to the rooms so they were often used for meetings or quiet work. Smartly located away from the two main offices that encompassed the agency's working environment, there were no guarantees that things wouldn't be moved around a little.

The woman that exited the elevator was taller than me, hitting around five-foot-eleven in her flats. Dressed in a nice pair of navy pants and a pale pink t-shirt that was not quite business casual but definitely chic, her nails were manicured and her black hair had been blown out recently, possibly before work. She obviously took pride in her appearance. She looked me over, albeit barely perceptibly, and smiled.

"You must be Lexi Graves," she said, stretching out a hand to shake mine.

"That's correct. And you are?"

"Jas Kapoor. Thanks for seeing me. I'm sorry I didn't make an appointment but I was walking past your office and I thought I'd just take a chance that someone was free to see me."

"Come through and you can tell me what's on your mind," I said, indicating she should follow me to the meeting room. The first room was empty and the door already stood open. Jas followed me inside and I shut the door while she took a seat. She set her purse on the floor and crossed her legs, her face suddenly pensive. I pulled out the chair opposite and sat and waited.

"I don't know where to start," she said after a long pause. "If I tell you, I'm sure you'll say it's nothing."

"You must think it's something," I pointed out.

"Yes, yes, I do, but it's the strangest thing. I'm not sure I can even tell you what the problem is."

"Is it personal or professional?" I asked.

"Personal. Not my personal issue, as such. It's my best friend. There's something wrong. Something really wrong and I think she might be in grave danger."

CHAPTER TWO

"What makes you think your friend is in some kind of danger?" I asked. "Has she been harassed? Perhaps received a threatening message?"

Jas shook her head and her shiny hair tumbled around her shoulders, giving me a case of hair envy. "Oh no, nothing like that. This is where you'll think I'm crazy. I couldn't even tell you why I think Julia's in danger. She has a great life. I know I should be happy for her. I am happy for her! But there's something wrong. I have a terrible feeling. Do I sound crazy?"

"No, you don't sound crazy. How long have you known each other?"

"Five years. Julia moved into my building and we struck up a friendship. We realized we had so many things in common and were hanging out all the time. She even introduced me to my boyfriend although we split up a few months ago." Jas looked down and sighed, an ebb of unhappiness emanating from her. "I mentioned my concerns to a couple of friends in our group and they seemed to think I want her to be unhappy too."

"In what way?"

"I mean because I'm single now, they think I'm jealous that she's happily attached and I should be thrilled for her. She got engaged two months ago and they're getting married next month. I want to be happy for her but there's something wrong."

"You mentioned the feeling of something wrong several times. Do you know what it might be?"

"I think so," she replied, nodding slowly. She met my eyes and dropped them again and I had to wonder if it was a flash of shame I saw crossing her face. "It's her fiancé, Bryce. Bryce Maynard. They've only been together seven months but in the last six months, she's changed and I think it has something to do with him. She's not the same as she used to be." Jas pulled a photo from her purse and handed it to me. "This was taken a couple of months ago."

"Could it be that she wanted to change in some way?" I asked as I looked at the photo of the smiling couple. It wasn't rare for a person to change a bit to impress their new partner or for some other undefined goal.

Jas shrugged. "Well, I guess that could be the case. She dresses better now. Not that Julia was ever a bad dresser, but she's that little bit more chic now. She spends more money on clothes. Manicures and blowouts too. She joined a gym and works out a lot. I know, none of that sounds terrible! I even encouraged her but it's her personality that's changed. She's shyer, I think, and there's an insecurity about her that wasn't there before. She always defers to whatever Bryce wants and if we're together, she doesn't answer without looking at him first. She cancels our plans." Jas stopped. "I know I sound jealous but truly, I'm not."

"There's something you're not telling me," I said, sensing there was still more to the story.

Jas nodded. "A couple of months ago Julia had a big bruise on her arm. She said she fell but I'm sure I saw deep finger marks. I didn't see her for two weeks after that and by then, it was gone. It seemed like she was avoiding me."

"Do you think her fiancé did it?"

"I wasn't sure and I didn't think much more about it until I saw her coming home from work last month and she was limping. She had her ankle in a bandage and said she sprained it while jogging but the night before, I heard a crash in her apartment. We live right next door to each other. I mentioned the noise and she went all red and said no, she knocked over a lamp. I thought back to when she had the bruise on her arm and I felt suspicious. She's not accident-prone at all."

"Did you ask her again?"

"I tried to but she shut me down. She said she had a lot on her mind and she'd been a little clumsy lately and told me not to think anything of it. The day after that, I buzzed in a flower delivery guy and discovered that Bryce had sent her a beautiful bouquet."

"Was that unusual? Did he make gestures like that often?"

"Oh, all the time. There was pretty much a bunch every week since they started dating. Not just cheap flowers either! Only lovely, hand-tied bouquets, all different kinds. We all thought that was terrific at first. Bryce was so sweet and thoughtful."

"But you thought it was a guilt bouquet?" I pressed.

"I did, and I feel bad for thinking that. Julia said he just wanted to cheer her up. All our other friends thought it was adorable. One of our group had just been hospitalized to have a baby and all her husband did was bring her a McDonalds Happy Meal to celebrate the baby's arrival."

I couldn't help it; I laughed. "Did she at least get a milkshake with it?" I wondered.

"No, he got her a Diet Coke," said Jas. Her shoulders shook with laughter. "Some men are clueless."

"But not your friend's fiancé. What else does he do that's nice?"

"Oh, lots of things. He takes her out for meals. He might even drop in with a surprise lunch picnic to her workplace. He'll supply the wine and cook them dinner at her apartment or his. He buys her beautiful, thoughtful gifts for her birthday and it's never anything generic like chocolate. He took her to Hawaii for a vacation and paid for everything. His proposal was straight out of a movie. There was even a carriage ride and a string quartet waiting for them at the end."

"That all sounds pretty nice," I said.

"It is. All our friends love him. His friends too. It's not a party without him. He's always arranging some kind of get-together, or a night out, or a boys' weekend away."

"Is there anything you can think of, excluding your suspicions about physical violence, that add to your distrust toward him?"

"No. He's so damn perfect, it's hard to ever find fault with him." Jas blew out a breath and shifted uncomfortably in her seat.

"What do your friends think?"

"That I'm a little jealous of Julia and Bryce's happiness and they assure me I'll feel better once I start dating again. It's not true though. That is, I am a little unhappy. I do miss my ex-boyfriend but I would never want someone else to feel unhappy just because I am." Jas paused and sighed. "Perhaps it is nothing. Perhaps I'm just being overly cautious but I'm sure something is wrong and I think the changes in her personality are directly because of him. Do you think you can help me find out if Julia is okay? I can pay you. I'm not rich but I have some money put away and I think protecting my friend would be making the best use of it."

"I'd like you to fill out some forms," I told her. Turning in my chair, I reached for the client forms that we left in the room. There wasn't a single pen around so I was glad I'd brought my own, which I handed to her. "I'm not promising anything but if you can tell me as much information as you have, I'll think about how and if I can help."

"Thank you! Thank you so much!"

"I want you to add a timeline of events as you've noticed them too," I added. "When they met, where and how, everything you can think of up to now, including when you first noticed a change in your friend's behavior."

"So you do believe me?" Jas asked, looking up from the forms I placed in front of her.

"I believe that the bruise and the injury could be a cause for concern but the other things you mentioned don't raise any immediate red flags. I also believe that you don't want your friend to be unhappy and that you're not jealous." By the time I finished speaking, Jas had already picked up the pen and was steadily working her way through the document.

I leaned back in my seat and gave her time to finish while I thought about the case. Concerned friends had come in before so it wasn't unusual but they generally had more serious issues that validated their worries. A missing person, for example. Jas Kapoor didn't have that. It sounded like, mostly, she just had a hunch. I had learned not to dismiss hunches. Trusting my gut was important in my business.

"I think that's everything," she said almost ten minutes later. She laid the pen on top of the pages and pushed the small pile towards me. "I need to get back to work but I really appreciate you meeting me at, well, no notice at all."

"It's not a problem," I replied as I reached for the paperwork. "After I review the information you gave me, I'll be in touch."

Jas pushed back her chair and stood, but hesitated before leaving the table. "What should I do until then? We're going to a gym class later—Bryce is out of town for the night—and we live next door to each other."

"Go about your life as normal," I told her. "Take the gym class. Hang out. Do whatever you would normally do."

"No, I mean, do I say something to my friend? Do I tell her that I'm worried?"

"Have you told her before that you're worried about her?"

"Yes, and she dismissed my concerns."

"Unless something terrible happens, don't bring up your worries for now. Just be a good friend and remain observant. If there is something wrong, you don't want to alienate her when she might need you. And if there really isn't anything wrong, insisting that there is could end the friendship," I added. There was no telling how a person might react, plus, there was always the possibility that nothing was really wrong, or that there was something wrong which was entirely unrelated to the relationship. Jas's hunch might have been correct but aimed in the wrong direction.

"I'm not going to mention that I was here."

"I think that would be wise."

Jas stuck out her hand and I shook it before escorting her to the elevator. "Thanks again," she said as the doors slid open. "You can call me anytime if you need more information, or if you make a decision. I really hope you can help me find out if Julia is okay, one way or the other."

I nodded and smiled as she stepped inside and the doors closed behind her. When I was sure she'd gone, I made my way back to the PI's shared office and dropped into my desk chair, spreading the paperwork in front of me. I gave the first pages a cursory glance. Jas had written down all her contact details, as well as those of Julia and Julia's fiancé including their home addresses and places of work. The next page had a list of reasons why she wanted to engage the agency's services but there was nothing glaringly upsetting. To her knowledge, there hadn't been any police involvement, her friend had never complained of any poor treatment by the fiancé, and Jas hadn't witnessed anything appalling. All I had was a strange feeling that something wasn't right.

I knew what Solomon would say about it. That there was no indication of anything wrong at all. Unless I could come up with something to corroborate Jas's ill ease, it was unlikely we would take this case.

"What the hell," I said, reaching for my laptop. "My actual case can wait for another ten minutes."

Using the information Jas gave me, I plugged Julia Atwater's name into the search engine. She was a social media junkie. Facebook, Twitter, Instagram, a music sharing account. I scrolled through each for a minute. Facebook hadn't been updated in a while unless she locked down her privacy settings, but there was a nice profile shot of Julia and a man. They had their arms around each other and were beaming at the camera. I clicked on the comments and read a slew of "gorgeous couple!" and "relationship goals!" and other compliments. Twitter hadn't been updated in a month and Instagram was a nice selection of baking and outdoors shots of places Julia visited. Most of the latter photos were captioned with "Bryce and I at the farmer's market" or "Bryce and I out to dinner" or "surprise flowers from lovely Bryce." Julia looked happy in the selfies. The only thing different I noted was less of her friends appeared in the photos of the last couple of months. They were replaced by more with Bryce but maybe that was because they were in their happy love bubble.

I also noted Julia's appearance had changed slightly in the past few months. Gone was the tumbling, wavy hair to be outdone by a chic, collarbone-length cut. Her clothes had smartened too. The color palette remained mostly the same but her clothes were a little more fitted and a couple of very nice purses were noticeable in the background shots. Again, there was nothing wrong with that. Lots of women indulged in updating their wardrobes when they found a partner they wanted to impress. It could even be as simple as her tastes had matured or she wanted to impress a boss at work.

Without closing the pages, I searched for Bryce Maynard. He had an Instagram that was unpopulated although there was a small profile shot of him, artfully shot. Facebook was more revealing. Another solo shot of him served as a profile photo and there was a banner photo of a group of friends all wearing shorts and holding beers next to a pool. He provided the occasional update and there were a couple of photos that he and Julia were tagged in. A slew of comments praised how happy they looked and what a great couple they were. Somebody commented that Julia was "a serious upgrade!" I wondered what the commenter meant by that.

I grabbed a slip of paper and made a note of my findings, then closed the file. There was nothing that raised my suspicions during this cursory glance into their lives but I needed a little time to think about the next step. A hunch was still a hunch and Jas knew both parties far better than I did. Of course there was still that accusation of jealousy. I hadn't gotten the impression Jas was jealous of her friend but a few minutes of plundering her life wouldn't hurt.

I returned to Julia's page and tapped Jas's name into the friend's list, ensuring I could find her quickly. Her profile was locked down but there was a nice ream of comments on her profile photo including one from Julia, dated just two months ago. It was as nice and friendly as any exchange Lily and I might have. It wasn't a true indicator of no jealousy though. Jealousy could often be dressed up as friendship. All the same, I still didn't get that impression from Jas.

I closed the browser pages on my laptop and pushed the new case file to one side. Solomon had given me a case I was actually being paid to do and that had to be my focus. I would think about Jas's case later.

The marriage between Steve and Faye Wendell lasted just forty-three days. Not exactly shocking, but hardly something to boast about. The husband was a wealthy man and several clippings were included about how he'd made his money. Apparently, he wasn't much of an academic but rather gifted in mechanics. After barely graduating high school, he'd gone to work at a local auto shop and, within five years, he owned it. He acquired two other auto shops in Montgomery in the next two years and then several more in the state. Now, at age forty-two, he owned one hundred and seventeen Wendell's Auto shops nationwide, all proudly bearing his name. I'd heard of him. His auto shop serviced my VW and made me a loyal customer. I never felt like his staff talked down to me, even though my knowledge of cars was minimal, and not once did I ever feel ripped off.

Faye was a different type of person. She graduated high school with a 4.0 grade average and attended a good university to study history on an athletics scholarship. Although she'd won a few heats during her studies, she hadn't been a consistently outstanding athlete. When she graduated, she was scouted for modeling. A few years of working in Paris, Milan, and Tokyo followed before she took up a master's degree in business administration that she was eager to put to use. Sensible with money, she invested her modeling fees into a property that she still owned as well as a small number of other investments. She was ten years younger than her husband and they were introduced through a mutual acquaintance.

I couldn't see the issue for either them. They seemed to have the right mix of brains, beauty and business acumen that complemented each other. Yet, somehow, it had fallen apart in a mere forty-three days.

Steve Wendell initiated divorce proceedings on the grounds of fraud. In a longer statement, he asserted his wife had known how much money he made and targeted him deliberately. Hopelessly swept up in the romance, he provided generous gifts during their courtship. They were engaged after six months with a fifty thousand dollar-diamond ring and married two months later. He claimed an argument about money had revealed her true intentions. According to him, she no longer wished to work and instead, expected him to finance a lifestyle they never agreed upon. She claimed she could "get everything" since they were legally married.

Faye also provided a counter statement saying she loved her husband, the money was inconsequential and that if he would just talk to her, he would understand the truth. She didn't want a divorce.

Apparently, the judge was refusing to sign a divorce without hard evidence of any wrongdoing and both parties concurred the Solomon Detective Agency was the right way of finding it.

As far as statements went, Faye really hadn't grasped the concept of defending herself. Nor, however, had she asked for anything. All she wanted to do was talk. I rested my chin in my hand as I stared at her statement. Was talking things out the action of a money grabber? Why hadn't she demanded anything?

Finding hidden assets in a divorce was one thing, but proving someone was solely after money was a much more difficult affair. There would be no paper trail, which meant a deep dive into their finances wouldn't help. I could try to prove the wife had dire financial circumstances that she hadn't made her new husband aware of, and the money he insisted she was after would cover that. Lucas could find any hidden financial issues, which left me with the job of tracking down Faye and asking her what was going on. With both parties in agreement to hiring the agency, she had to be waiting for someone to make contact and clearly, she wanted to talk.

CHAPTER THREE

Faye Wendell was staying at the Newbury Hotel. It wasn't the most expensive hotel in Montgomery but one of the top five, occupying what had once been a rundown historic home. Since its acquisition, it received a sympathetic, and costly restoration, which also included a very fancy spa in a former outbuilding. If I intended to lick my wounds anywhere, I would definitely choose here.

I asked for Mrs. Wendell at the reception desk, giving my name and agency title and was assured she would be with me very soon. Taking up a position on one of the large leather couches in what had once been a parlor and now served as a waiting area, I observed my surroundings. Big windows overlooked a lawn that stretched down to the street where a valet waited to take the patrons' cars to a hidden parking lot. The parlor walls were covered in a delicate wallpaper of wildflowers and the woodwork was either perfectly preserved or so well restored that I couldn't tell the difference. The furniture was old and heavy and I was pretty sure I didn't want to accidentally smash any of the vases or lamps.

"You must be Lexi Graves," said a voice from the doorway.

I looked up, assessing the woman quickly. She was tall and willowy as befitted a formal model but instead of an extravagant outfit, she wore simple blue jeans, a pink button-down shirt and flat pumps with jeweled bows. Her hair was jaw-length, white blond and her cheekbones looked like they could cut ice. Her eyes were red and angry. She was a beautiful woman; it was a shame she looked so dejected.

"That's right. You must be Mrs. Wendell," I said, getting to my feet and handing her a business card. It was still a novelty to hand those things out but then again, it's funny what makes a person feel successful as a grownup. Previously, I thought I'd reached the adult threshold when I managed to save the deposit for my home rather than blowing it on fashion.

"Faye, please. I didn't expect you quite so quickly. Have you spoken to my husband yet?" she asked while staring at the business card like it might offer her more than my name, title, and phone number.

"No, not yet. Is there somewhere we can talk?"

"We can go into the garden at the back. Conversational privacy isn't the top priority around here." Faye turned and I followed her through the lobby to the rear of the hotel. We stepped out into a small, paved courtyard scattered with garden furniture but she didn't stop there. Instead, she continued across to the paved path and we walked in silence for a couple of minutes until we reached a bench in the shade of a massive oak tree. Faye sat and crossed her legs at the ankle.

"Your husband and you both chose to hire a private investigator to look into your affairs," I started. "Your lawyers both agreed to appoint my firm."

"Correct, although I'm not sure what you can possibly prove or disprove. I told Steve that I wasn't after his money. What more can I say?" she asked. Her shoulders dropped and she sighed.

"Did you sign a pre-nup?" I asked.

"No, neither of us asked for one."

"Was there a reason for that? According to the statement from your lawyers, you both have assets."

"I can't speak for my husband but I went into this marriage assuming I would stay in it." Faye nudged the pavers with the toe of her pumps and sighed. "I didn't think there was a need for a pre-nup. It just never came up."

"Your husband's statement says that you no longer wished to work and expected him to finance a lifestyle not agreed upon," I said, recalling the wording and hoping I got it right.

"I read his statement. He's right, I do want to give up work but not forever. I like my job! I'm happy doing it because I'm good at what I do. I just wanted to know if he would support me with some time off. I don't know why he leapt to conclusions that weren't accurate but he went ballistic when I suggested it."

"Are you sure you have no idea?"

"Well, one of his close friends is getting a divorce after four years and his wife has asked for a huge alimony payout, and another friend just broke up with a girlfriend whom he said turned out to be a gold-digger. I don't know how true that is but perhaps those relationships were on his mind, but I don't know what they have to do with me!"

"What do you think your husband meant when he claimed you said you would get everything?"

Faye rolled her eyes. "I didn't say that. I said I *already* had everything I would ever need. Steve was so furious by that point, he wouldn't even listen to anything more I had to say. If he had, he would have..." She trailed off and closed her eyes for a moment.

"Are you okay?" I leaned forward as Faye took a couple of deep breaths. "You look a little green."

With her eyes still closed, Faye nodded. "Sorry, I haven't been feeling too well." She took a series of deep breaths and opened her eyes again. "I didn't even mean support me financially."

"What did you mean?"

"I meant emotionally. Look, can I talk to my husband? My lawyer says I can't but if I can talk to him, I can explain myself directly."

"I'm only here to prove one way or the other what the angle is regarding finances."

"You mean whether I'm a gold-digger or not."

That was true, but it was hardly polite to be so direct about it. Plus, she looked depressed enough without me making it worse. She pushed her hair back behind her ear and I frowned. Something valuable was missing.

"Mr. Wendell says he bought you an engagement ring. Can I ask why you aren't wearing it?"

"I haven't sold it, if that's what you think," she said, reaching into her shirt and pulling out a delicate, silver chain. Suspended on it were two rings, one a fat diamond, the other an elegant, gold band. "My fingers are a little swollen and I was worried my rings would get too tight."

"If you wanted to take time off, why didn't you ask for financial support?" I wondered. "Why only emotional?"

"I don't need my husband's money. I never have. When I started modeling, my parents made sure I had a financial adviser to help me. We all heard stories about girls in the industry who earned a ton of money, burned out or got too old to get work, and left with nothing. They didn't want that for me and neither did I. I paid off my student loans, invested in my future and one of those investments eventually paid off. I own a thirty percent stake in a friend's start-up and she just floated the business on the stock exchange. I'm going to make more money than I even know what to do with. More money than I'll ever need in a lifetime."

"That's great!"

"Yeah. Terrific." Faye laughed. "You know, the funny thing is, if we did get divorced right now, my husband stands to get a better payout from me than I do from him. It's ironic he's the one who wants to divorce me."

"Can you prove everything you just told me about the investment?" I asked.

"Well, sure."

"My email is on the business card I gave you. Please send the information to me as soon as you can. I think it will be instrumental in proving you had no intentions towards fraudulently marrying your husband. I'm going to talk to Mr. Wendell; then I'll file my report."

"Do whatever you need to do," said Faye. She sighed again. "I just want this to end."

"The marriage?"

"The stupidity."

"Just to be clear... do you want your marriage to end?" I asked.

Faye shook her head. "No. I want my husband. I love him and I can't imagine life without him."

I said goodbye and left her alone on the garden bench. The valet delivered my car to the curb and I drove off after plugging in the address for Steve Wendell's head office. The meeting with Faye Wendell hadn't been exactly as I expected. Like her statement, there was no great defense but she did appear to have irrefutable proof that she wasn't a gold-digger. If the evidence came through, it flipped the situation. The question was: did Steve Wendell know about his wife's new money? Did he expect a payday? Without appearing too obvious about it? By filing to divorce his wife for fraud, perhaps that wasn't the case but I couldn't be sure. If he was really all about getting money for himself and jettisoning his wife, why would he hire us? It didn't seem like the actions of a guilty man unless he thought he were smarter than us. No, if he knew Faye was wealthier than he, how had he gotten it into his head that he was being used for money? It didn't make any sense.

Many national businesses wanted glossy offices downtown where they could be seen, but not Steve Wendell. The head offices for Wendell's Autos occupied the two floors over the auto shop business that bore his name in a small industrial complex that also housed a parts supply shop, a kitchen showroom, and a lighting store. I walked up the narrow staircase and asked the zebra-print-wearing receptionist for him. She took a long look at me and raised one very over-plucked eyebrow. "What's the nature of your business?" she asked in the strongest Jersey accent I'd ever heard.

"It's a private personal matter. He is expecting someone from my firm to contact him," I said as I handed her my card.

"Is he?" She didn't move for the longest moment but finally picked up her phone and jabbed the numbers with the end of her pen. "Boss, there's a Lexi Graves from the Solomon Detective Agency to see you. Okay. Sure." She dropped the handset and pointed to the corridor behind her. "He says you can go in. His office is at the end of the corridor."

"Thank you."

"You're welcome," she drawled. The phone began to ring again and she turned to answer it, forgetting me instantly.

I skirted the desk and walked to the office, politely knocking and waiting to be called in.

The man sitting behind the desk didn't need to tidy up his strawberry blond hair so much as to have someone tell him three days of beard stubble was not a look that suited him. His open-necked shirt was rumpled and his eyes were bloodshot, like he'd indulged in one too many beers the night before. Either that, or he'd been crying too. Not exactly the sign of a man who was happy to be getting a divorce or gleeful at a sudden windfall.

He stood up and held out his hand, giving mine a fast shake before he gestured to the chair on my side of the desk. "I'm Steve. Thanks for coming," he said. "I wasn't sure when to expect you."

"I picked up the case this morning," I explained. "I wanted to come and see you as soon as I could. I understand this is a difficult time for you."

"Let's be real. It's a crap time. My wife just shattered my life."

"Did she?" I asked as I sat down.

Steve Wendell rocked back in his chair and for a moment, I thought he might pop his feet on the desk. Instead he swiveled a bit, barely a few degrees from one side to the other. "She doesn't want to be married to me. She wants my money. Helluva lot of money for forty-three days 'work'," he said, adding air quotes.

"You wrote in your statement that your wife asked you for money to finance a lifestyle. What did she say exactly?"

"Something like she wanted to take time off to focus on other things and she would need support. She said she was worried it would be a lifestyle change and she didn't want things to get too hard."

"That doesn't sound like a demand for money."

Steve huffed. "It started that way for my best buddy, Al. His wife wanted to be a homemaker so she gave up work when they married. Not sure what she did to maintain their home since they had a housekeeper and she was always out spending his money. I have never known a woman to shop like that. Don't think I ever saw her wear the same thing twice and Al isn't exactly making the big bucks."

"I understand your wife has a job she likes and has no intention of giving up."

"Well, she can't now her meal ticket is gone. Big B's girlfriend thought she'd pull that too. She was a lawyer but turns out she was just plain crazy."

"Big B?"

"Sorry, a buddy of mine. He's tall, hence Big B."

"Okay. I'm looking into both of your finances and I understand your wife is independently wealthy."

"She's got some money. She was pretty sensible with her modeling income. She owns a house."

"And there isn't a pre-nup?"

"No. That was a dumb move."

"Why's that?"

"I thought Faye was marrying me for me. If I'd realized it was for my money, I'd have insisted on an ironclad pre-nup." Steve waved his hands around his office. "I barely graduated high school and started out as an apprentice on the shop floor. Now I own a bunch of shops with plans to franchise more nationwide as well as taking over another business that's got the locations but not the management. I've made a lot of money, and I stand to make more, and I've been smart with my assets. I own this business entirely."

"Has she requested any alimony?" I asked.

"No."

"Or a payout of any kind?"

"Well, no..."

I paused and watched him for any signs of guilt. "Don't you think that's strange?"

"She did ask for money when we were arguing. She mentioned something about putting a hundred grand in a trust fund but I said there was no way I was just handing over that much money. That's when the fight started."

"A trust fund? Not her own account?" I was missing something, something I could almost turn into an idea.

"That's right."

"Huh. I understand Mrs. Wendell isn't staying in the family home any longer."

"No, I told her to get out. I don't even know where she is." Steve played with a pencil, tapping it against the desk. He didn't look at me when he asked, "Is she okay?"

"She's okay," I told him. "She's staying at a hotel. Has she requested any money since you told her to get out?"

"No, not a penny. I figure she's waiting to hit me with a demand through her lawyers. The tension is getting to me."

"Do you have any evidence of fraud on your wife's part?" I asked.

"Nothing that I can put in front of a judge. My lawyers already told me that; *he said, she said* isn't going anywhere. That's why we agreed on hiring you to find the evidence one way or the other."

"What happens if I don't find any evidence?"

Steve shrugged. "I don't know."

"Mr. Wendell, do you want to divorce your wife?"

He took a long moment before he tossed down the pencil and looked me directly in the eye. "No, I don't. I love my wife but I don't want to be married to someone who doesn't love me back and sees me as a meal ticket."

I thanked him for his time and left him to whatever he'd been struggling to concentrate on when I arrived. As I drove away, I knew I needed Lucas to do some digging into the couple's financials. So far, I hadn't come up with anything that suggested there was any kind of marital fraud. Quite the opposite; they both gave every appearance of loving each other, so what went wrong?

It was close to the time to meet Lily at the gym when I reached the office so instead of going up, I sent Lucas an email from my phone asking him to deep dive the Wendells' finances, and try to corroborate Faye's investment story. I couldn't wait to see what he came up with. That done, and my gym bag already in the trunk, I headed for the gym, thoughts of the couple still puzzling me.

Lily was waiting for me in the locker room, looking fabulously fit in shiny, black hotpants and a hot pink bra with a criss-crossed back. Her blond curls were tamed into a high ponytail and she looked fit to burst.

"Someone looks excited," I remarked as she bounded over to me.

"Someone got a whole night's sleep," said Lily. "Eight whole glorious hours! I feel like I can conquer the world. I feel like there's nothing I can't achieve."

"Is this class going to make you more energetic? Or strip you of the last ounce of energy you have?"

"I have no idea. Let's find out. Quick. Get changed!" Lily spun me around and gave me a push towards an empty locker.

I dropped my bag onto the bench and quickly swapped my day clothes for stretchy black leggings and a lilac singlet. It wasn't as sexy hot as Lily's outfit but it was comfortable and I had a brief moment of fear that one day "comfortable" would be high on my fashion requirements. I shucked my shoes and pulled on my sneakers, then added my padlock to the locker.

"You didn't get the memo?" asked Lily. She gave my outfit a long, cool look.

What had I missed? "Memo?"

"I said wear something sexy." She waved a hand at my attire and shook her head.

"This is sexy." I looked down. It was form-fitting, flattering, and in very chic shades of black and lilac.

"It's not stripper sexy."

"I'm not a stripper!"

"Oh, yeah. I thought it was implied. Do you have anything else with you?"

"No."

"This might not work." She waved a hand over my outfit again. I looked down, wondering exactly what was wrong with it. "You might fall off. I guess we'll find out." She turned around and pulled the door open, skipping towards the workout rooms.

"Wait! What?" I yelled after her. "Fall off what?" Lily didn't turn around so I hurried after her, a slightly sick feeling building in my stomach. What exactly had Lily signed me up for? And why the fudge hadn't I checked the small print, or asked if there was small print? In all the years Lily and I had been friends, I really should have known better than to blithely go along with her suggestion of a new gym class but I'd operated under the impression marriage and motherhood had chilled her out. Silly me. A nuclear bomb couldn't chill Lily out.

I stepped through the door into the workout room a few seconds after Lily and immediately halted. This was no dance class. At least it wasn't the hip-hop, salsa, Zumba, cardio-toning-hybrid-whatever class I envisioned. No. The room was fitted out with a dozen floor-to-ceiling poles, each currently being claimed by women in booty shorts and tiny bra tops. No, scratch that. There was one man and his thighs were the tautest of all, catching more than a few envious glances.

The front of the class was wall-to-wall mirror with a sound system stacked in one corner. The woman currently bent in half and tying her sneakers stretched, flexed more abs than the average six-pack, and began to fiddle with the portable audio speaker in her fanny pack.

A cold feeling washed through me. I hurried over to Lily who was clutching a pole in the middle of the class. "Grab that pole," she said, jabbing a finger at the one next to her.

"Is this..." I gasped, hardly able to bring myself to utter the words. "Pole dancing?" I squeaked finally.

"Hell, no," snorted Lily. "This is vertical dancing with core workout. It has a fancier name but I forgot what it is."

"Pole dancing," I squeaked again.

"No—" Lily wrinkled her nose "—it's definitely vertical dance something."

"There's a pole and no one is wearing more than ten inches of spandex. That's pole dancing."

"No, that involves lingerie and not a lot of it."

"Potato, *potahto*."

"No carbs until after the wedding," said Lily. "We can grab a salad after or a green smoothie at the gym's smoothie bar. Lots of nutrients. Your wedding dress, here we come!"

I gulped.

"Lexi?"

I stilled. Someone behind me had not only recognized me but broken the sanctity of my gym time and announced it. Even worse, whoever it was probably thought I'd willingly signed up to learn how to pole dance. No, wait, they must have also signed up for it so they couldn't judge me. I turned, already inwardly cringing. "Jas?" I squeaked as I saw my client from earlier in the day. Gone were the business chic clothes, replaced with running shorts and a pristine white crop top that shone against her brown skin.

"Hi," she said, smiling in a bemused sort of way. "Have you done this class before?"

I shook my head. "First time. Lily signed me up," I said, pointing an accusing finger at Lily. Lily beamed.

"Us too," said Jas. "This is my friend, Julia." She waved to her friend at the pole next to her. The woman placed her water bottle and towel at the base of the pole and jogged over. "Julia, this is Lexi. She's an old acquaintance of mine."

"That's right," I agreed readily.

"Hey," said Julia, smiling and holding her hand up for a finger wave. "I'm not a member of this gym but Jas persuaded me that it would be fun to try some new classes and here I am."

"If you like this, twerking for beginners is on Sunday morning," called Lily. Unfortunately, she wasn't joking.

"I go to church on Sunday," said Julia.

"It's very early so if you're Catholic you can ask for forgiveness right after," said Lily. "It's very popular."

"It sounds like fun," said Julia, a wistful edge to her voice, "but I'll be spending all weekend trying to find a new venue for my engagement party." She waggled her hand, flashing a very large diamond ring. Lily and I made the appropriate admiring cooing noises and Julia beamed.

"When's the party?" asked Lily.

"It was supposed to be on the weekend. We originally wanted Lily's Bar but we couldn't get the right date so my fiancé and I settled for Jewel's downtown but their kitchen had a fire and now they've canceled all bookings."

Lily straightened. "You wanted Lily's?"

"Yes, my fiancé loves it there. He says it's the best bar in all of Montgomery. Just our vibe."

"Then you're talking to the right person," said Lily. "I'm the owner, Lily, and I happen to know there's a cancellation on Saturday night. The room is still available and you won't have to spend all weekend scouting new venues. Why don't we talk after the class?"

"Oh my gosh! Really?" Julia's face lit up. "Are you serious?"

"Absolutely!"

"I think you might have saved my life," gushed Julia. "Bryce will be thrilled! Isn't this great news, Jas?"

Next to her, Jas smiled. "Fabulous," she agreed. "Why don't we all meet up in the bar after and get to know each other?" she added with a pointed look to me.

I got the message. This was the perfect opportunity to get to know her friend better without alerting her that Jas had asked me to look into Julia's relationship. I still wasn't sure if I would take the case but this could help me work that out faster than poring over the client file later.

"Okay, ladies," yelled the instructor as a thumping bassline started up. "Let's warm up, then grab those poles!"

CHAPTER FOUR

I slumped into the chair in the gym's smoothie bar and winced. The hour-long class had been every bit as terrifying as I anticipated when I walked in, along with the side bonus of being absolutely exhausting as well. My abs screamed. My upper arms felt hot and sore and my thighs were ready to collapse. Even my hair couldn't summon any enthusiasm to look cute.

The way I saw it, I had three choices. I could keep going with an overly-enthusiastic Lily to this class for the next two weeks and potentially die, or I could keep going, suck it up and potentially look amazing on my wedding day with some extra moves that would probably break Solomon on our honeymoon. Or I could excuse myself from all classes and do some half-hearted exercise that would leave me looking and feeling reasonable, combined with the unfailing ability to walk down the aisle without my legs begging to buckle. Clearly, I had a hard decision to make.

"Drink this," said Lily. She pushed a large plastic cup filled with dark green liquid towards me.

"No more punishment," I said as I rejected it with my forefinger, the only bit of me that didn't currently hurt.

"You can't be in that much pain."

"I am. I am broken."

"Wait until you feel it tomorrow," snorted Lily. "Don't drop anything tomorrow. You'll need those mechanical grabbers elderly people use to pick things up since you'll be too sore all over to reach for anything."

"Yay," I spluttered weakly. I forgot about the post-exercise days when I had to wobble up and down stairs on unsteady legs, and when even pressing the gas pedal down seemed like torture.

Lily pushed the vile liquid towards me. "This will help your body repair itself with a great combination of protein powder and nutrients."

I leaned in and sniffed. "Why does it smell like feet and death?"

"Why can't you smell normal things like normal people?"

I thought that was rich, coming from Lily, who didn't do very much that people would consider normal but I was saved from summoning up a sarcastic answer when Jas and Julia joined our table. Their smoothies looked like they had just been milked from unicorns; all delightful shades of pink, lemon and dairy-free cream; and the aroma was delicious. "I want that smoothie," I whimpered, barely refraining from adding it's not fair.

"I wish I had your commitment to healthy consumption," said Julia as she looked at the green smoothie. She dropped her gym bag at her feet and slid into the chair next to me, pulling off her headband. Her hair swung around her chin in an impossibly chic way. Jas took the last chair between Julia and Lily, completing our foursome. "Bryce has really helped me commit to my fitness goals but there are some things I just can't do," she added, giving my green smoothie a pointed look.

"Totally understandable," I agreed, taking a surreptitious sniff of the smoothie. Definitely feet and death.

"Lexi is getting married soon and I am making sure she looks amazing on her wedding day, no matter what it takes," said Lily.

"She's starving me into my dress," I said and Jas and Julia laughed. Except I wasn't joking. I would rather have starved than drink the smoothie.

"You're engaged too? We should talk weddings," tattled Julia happily. "Isn't wedding planning so much fun? I never thought Bryce would be into it, but he insists on getting involved in every aspect. He has such an eye for detail. He's made all kinds of suggestions for the flowers and the church and the reception venue. I know it will be perfect. And now we have the perfect venue for our engagement party, I can only see that as an auspicious start to the rest of our plans!"

"Lexi had her engagement party at my bar too," Lily told her. "It was magical. I have some photos on my website of it, and other parties we've hosted. If you like any of the looks, we can recreate them, but if you'd rather have something personal, you can decorate the private room yourself or we can work with your decorator."

"I would love to see that..." Lily and Jas swapped places and Lily pulled out her phone to show off some of the event photos she used to entice new clients.

"I'm glad we ran into you," said Jas softly. "Have you had a chance to think?"

I cast a quick glance to Julia. "Still thinking," I replied just as softly. I hadn't had much of a chance to observe Julia during the class since it was loud, fast-paced, hard work, and some of it we spent upside-down, or at least, tried to. What I did notice was Julia seemed to be having fun, the look of concentration on her face interspersed with high-fives, laughter, and some light-hearted moaning about screaming muscles. Nothing about her persona said she was in trouble, afraid of anyone or anything. She didn't appear to be bruised or injured in any way either. Her workout clothes were nice and neat, definitely not of the stripper variety but a smart pair of hotpants in a thick, stretchy fabric and a sleeveless tank. Her hair was just long enough that she needed to wear a headband to push it back although several strands had escaped to frame her pretty, makeup-free face. Yet, every so often I caught her with a blank expression, like she was deep in thought.

Now I had the opportunity to assess her again. Flushed cheeks after the class, a towel slung around her neck and happily sipping on her unicorn smoothie while talking to Lily about cocktails. The decision of whether they should have tapas dishes spread across tables or waiters circulating with canapes was yet to be made, and what did Lily think of the idea of bringing in their own DJ since they had already booked him and Bryce "just loved his style!'"? She looked happy, animated, and entirely carefree.

So, why was I concerned about those blank moments?

"She isn't always like this," said Jas softly. "He's been away on a business trip for two days. She'll make decisions and then he'll convince her to change them. She wanted a small wedding, he wants two hundred guests. She wanted wildflowers in her bouquet, now she's getting red roses. She's right that he wants Lily's bar for the party but whatever decision she makes about the decor or the food won't meet with his approval."

"That's not exactly indicative of something wrong," I pointed out. "Lots of couples like different things and later compromise."

"I know but do all the compromises have to go his way?"

"Let me think about it some more."

"What are you two talking about?" asked Lily. "You look serious."

"Just some work stuff I thought Jas could help with," I said dismissively, knowing I had to change the topic quickly before Lily or Julia asked exactly what it was. "Not nearly as interesting as what you're talking about. Is it settled? Are you having the party at Lily's?"

"Yes!" beamed Julia. "I texted Bryce right after class finished and he just texted back to say 'Book it!', and we have. I am so excited! I'm going to tell all our guests tonight that there's a change in venue and the party is going ahead after all."

"That's terrific news."

"Drink your smoothie," said Lily. She reached across the table and nudged it towards me. "Don't worry, you won't turn green."

"I hope not," I said, staring at it. Something about it triggered something in my mind, I thought I couldn't quite grasp. What was it? I glanced at Jas then Julia. Nothing about them. Something earlier today.

That was it! *Faye Wendell!* In a sudden burst of mental clarity, I knew that all the clues had been there. I just hadn't connected them until now.

"Excuse me, I have to make a phone call," I said, wincing in pain as I stood and grabbed my cell phone from my jacket pocket. "I'll be right back."

I hurried outside through the rear exit that led to a small area where outdoor boot camps were held. Fortunately, no one was out there. I dialed Faye's number and she answered. I asked her the question that suddenly popped into my head and after a long pause, she confirmed my suspicions.

"I'll set up a meeting," I said. "Please don't worry about a thing."

After I hung up, I went back inside but instead of our full table, only Lily remained. "Where did everyone go?" I asked.

"Julia wanted to get started on the last-minute preparations for the party and your friend said she had to head home and would catch up with you soon. How do you know each other anyway? I'm not sure I believe you when you said you were talking about work."

"We were talking about work. Jas came to see me earlier about a case."

"Really? Why didn't she say anything? Is it super confidential?" Lily asked.

"All my cases are confidential."

Lily leaned her elbow on the table and propped her chin in her hand. She took a long suck on the straw in her smoothie and waited.

"I can't tell you!"

Lily shrugged one shoulder. "I can wait."

"I really can't! I don't even know if I'm going to take the case." Why would I? There didn't appear to be anything there except that niggling feeling about Jas's concerns and those moments when Julia's face had been so devoid of anything.

"Julia never mentioned it. Oh, is it because she doesn't know? It must be very important then to not tell your best friend about unless it's... oh! Oh! That's it, isn't it? It's about Julia." Lily's eyes widened. "I knew it! What did she do? Should I not have taken her booking? She already paid the deposit by bank transfer from her cell phone. Should I cancel? I'll feel bad about it unless... is she psycho? Does she steal stuff? Set fire to things? Is that why Jewel's had that fire?"

"No, nothing like that." I restrained the urge to roll my eyes, which was a shame because my eye muscles didn't hurt and it would probably have been a really satisfying eye roll.

"So it is about her!"

"Julia hasn't done anything wrong, that's all I can tell you," I said. There was no point denying it. Lily knew and she would keep prying. "You don't have to cancel her reservation."

"Good to know. I will sleep easier knowing she isn't going to destroy my bar. So, are you investigating her?" Lily prodded gently.

"No! Not her exactly. Maybe something involving her but I haven't decided if I'll take the case yet. I need to get more information."

"Why don't you work the party?" Lily suggested in a feat of outstanding ingenuity. "You can get close to her and she won't think anything of it since she already knows we're friends. Then you can decide what to do."

I sat up a little straighter and promptly regretted it. My core muscles hated me and made it known. Lily was right; I was going to hurt in the morning. "Could I? It would really help."

"Sure. I can always use another set of hands especially when there's a private party going on; plus, I know you have plenty of experience as a cocktail waitress. Will it really help?"

"Yes," I nodded, certain it would. It would give me the perfect opportunity to get closer to Julia and Bryce and the people in their life. Family, friends, and colleagues were guaranteed to be there. Plus, in my server capacity, I could easily listen in on conversations. If anyone else voiced a suspicion about Bryce that would confirm what Jas said, I could find out. If it just appeared that they were any other couple, and showed no signs of anything untoward, I would politely decline the case. "Thanks, Lily."

"Anytime. Drink your smoothie."

"Absolutely not."

By the time we left the gym a half hour later, I had drunk half the smoothie and found it not quite as unpleasant in taste as it smelled. I wasn't convinced of Lily's enthusiastic claims about its wonderful properties but what didn't kill you made you stronger and drinking it hadn't killed me. Drinking two might have so I was determined to be the one to order smoothies when we next hit the gym's bar. Thinking of the bar made me briefly sad. Where had the days of drinking beers and eating burgers at O'Grady's gone? How had we grown up into two bona fide adults? One married person with a baby and a business to run, and one almost married person with an actual fulfilling career. "Damn," I said to myself as I fished my car keys from my purse. "We're grownups."

"Unfortunately," agreed Lily, "but one real night out —no babies, no partners—and we can smash anyone's assumptions of that."

"What if someone sees us?"

"Most of town has seen us do something stupid at one time or another," Lily reminded me.

"True, but we're law-abiding citizens now."

Lily snorted. "No, we just don't get caught. Enjoy your sexy dinner with sexy Solomon." She waved as she hopped into her car and pulled out of the space. I walked three cars down and raised the car key to beep the door open but before I could do so, the hair on the back of my neck rose. Someone was watching me. If I had any doubts about gut feelings, I didn't now. I slipped my hands into my jacket pockets looking for a weapon but it hadn't occurred to me to bring my gun to the gym and I didn't have anything handy like the Swiss Army knife my mother had given me or even a can of mace. I did, however, have my phone. I unlocked it, scrolled for Solomon, my thumb poised over his name.

"Whoever you are, step out into the open," I called loudly over the pounding of my thumping heart. They didn't know it was a phone in my pocket. It could be anything and truly, it was a weapon of sorts. Solomon would come to my aid the instant I needed him and good luck to anyone who tried to hurt me.

There was a rustling behind the trees, then a thickset African-American man in a black jacket, the collar turned up, stepped out. "How did you know I was there?" he asked in a gruff voice.

"I smelled you," I said, which wasn't true but would certainly give him something to think about.

"I told you," said a second male voice. A slightly taller and similarly attired Caucasian man stepped out from behind the first. He had a knit cap pulled low over his forehead and his hands were thrust into his pockets. "I told you that you splashed too much of that stuff on. You smell like a teenage boy who just got his first bottle of aftershave."

"I do not. It's nice stuff. My wife bought it for Christmas."

"Where from? The Dollar Store?"

"If you ever shopped anywhere else, you would know that some things cost more than a buck."

I sighed. I would know this bickering anywhere. I just hadn't heard it in a long time. "Luke Harris and Jesse Kafsky," I said.

The pair stepped forwards, quietly now. "It's Sergeant Major Kafsky to you," said the taller of the pair.

"Ignore him. I'm Captain Harris now. He has to do what I say."

Kafsky made a rude noise.

I looked between them, wondering how they had got through Army bootcamp when I hadn't. "Amazing. Which idiot promoted you two?" I teased, thrilled to see them after so long.

The pair glanced at each other and grinned. "Same idiot. How's civilian life?" asked Harris.

"It was okay until you two showed up. What did I do to deserve this?" I asked, holding back the smile that was threatening to burst from my lips.

"You don't write, you don't call..."

"I do!" I protested.

"You Whatsapp photos of small animals on skateboards and ask our opinions on shoes."

"The shoes question was meant for my best friend, Lily."

Kafsky leaned in and said softly, "I still say go with the lilac pumps with the bows. Chic yet edgy."

"Very manly," said Harris. "This is why you wear a uniform; otherwise you might pick stuff like that."

"Not for me," sniffed Kafsky. "Lexi asked our opinion. As a friend, I gave it."

"Okay, enough!" I called out. My muscles were tired —I was tired—and I wanted to head home for a shower, then a relaxing evening of carbohydrate consumption, kissing, and dodging my mother's group chat messages about my wedding. "You didn't come all this way to hide out in the trees near my gym to talk about my messaging problems. How can I help?"

"Actually, we haven't come far. We're stationed in Fort Charles for a couple months."

"And we remembered you live nearby. It didn't take long to track you down," added Harris.

"How did you track me down?" I wondered.

"We're elite soldiers. We have skills," said Harris.

"We saw you as we were driving around and followed you here and waited," said Kafsky.

"You're both so weird. You could have just asked me for my current address."

"Regardless, we need your help. You're a PI now. You find stuff."

Instantly, I was on alert. What the hell kind of problem did they have? "What have you lost?"

"It's only a little thing..."

"Very little," agreed Kafsky, widening his thumb and forefinger slightly. "Just a teensy problem."

"Hardly anything!"

"Out with it!" I yelled.

"We lost a tank," said Harris. "And we need you to get it back before the Army finds out it's missing."

CHAPTER FIVE

I paced beside the long windows that overlooked the street. Several floors up, everything seemed peaceful. There were no worried friends, no over-anxious mothers checking for the seventeenth time if I'd confirmed my choice of wedding dress because I was crazy to think any dress could be altered in a week, and no friends from long ago who had misplaced a tank. A tank! Not just any tank. A military tank!

"Take a seat," instructed one of the lawyers, an older lady named Marianne Lewis. She arrived with Steve Wendell a few minutes ago, after my request to the couple's respective legal firms. Steve appeared tired and irritated. The lawyer looked like she was ready to send everyone a bill and do something more interesting.

"Sorry," I said as I took a seat.

Steve checked his watch. "She's late," he said.

"Not yet," said his lawyer, "there're five more minutes. Ms. Graves, can you give us a hint as to what's inside the document?" She nodded to the brown envelope I placed on the table, deliberately out of reach.

"I think it would be fairer to wait for the other party."

"I'm paying for this!" huffed Steve. "I should know what's in it."

"You're both my clients and as such you get the information at the same time," I reminded him.

"I don't see why she has to be here," said Steve and then he fell silent when the door opened and his wife's lawyer stepped through, followed by his wife. She raised a hand to give a small wave to Steve and his eyes fixed on her empty left hand. His tired expression became thunderous and he turned his head away. Faye glanced at me and gave me a small, sad smile.

"Thanks for coming," I said to them. "If you'd like to sit, we'll begin." We exchanged brief pleasantries as Faye and her lawyer took positions opposite Steve and his lawyer, then both teams settled around the table and all heads turned to me.

I had a brief moment of enjoying my status at the head of the table with all the information. Plus, if it didn't go well, I sat nearest the door and was wearing flat pumps. I could be out of here faster than I could say "Settle your bill with my boss!"

"You both instructed me to find out for certain if there was any financial motivation for this marriage to take place," I started. "I have learned that there is not. In fact, Mr. Wendell, if you were to continue with your divorce you would receive, not pay, alimony."

Steve's head shot up. "What?"

"Basically, she's saying I'm richer than you," said Faye. Instead of looking happy about it, she seemed sullen.

"So you didn't marry me for my money?" he replied incredulously, his voice rising.

"How many times do I have to tell you I never wanted your money?" Faye yelled back. Her lawyer placed a calm hand on her wrist and shook his head, causing Faye to fall silent. I held back a smile at the display of pique that had probably been a long time coming with her pig-headed husband.

"But you wanted to give up work and be a kept woman!" he yelled back. On his side of the table, his lawyer repeated the same calming motion.

"You asked me to expose any financial motivation in this marriage and I believe there was," I said.

"Hah! I knew it!" huffed Steve. "What did she do?"

"You're a jerk," said Faye.

"You're both jerks," I said. "If either of you learned how to communicate, you wouldn't be in this mess."

"What?" I wasn't sure who spat that question but all heads turned to me again.

"Mrs. Wendell did make a request for support. Emotional support for herself."

"She asked for money," butted in Steve.

"Not for herself. She wanted to set up a college fund. She explained everything to me," I said calmly although I really wanted to bash their heads together.

"A college fund? She's been to college! She has a master's degree!"

"Not me, you moron!" yelled Faye, standing up and leaning across the table. "I wanted to set one up for our baby but the moment I brought up the subject of money, you wouldn't let me get a word in. You ranted and raved before you threw me out!"

Steve shot to his feet. "You asked for... wait! What?" He stood a little straighter, frown lines etched deeply across his forehead. "You're... pregnant?"

"Yes, I am! And I wanted to talk about college funds for our baby and taking some time off work so I could be a mom."

"Why didn't you tell me?"

"I tried! You wouldn't listen!"

"But you've been gone weeks!"

"You wouldn't take my calls. What was I supposed to do? Drop you an email that you wouldn't even read?"

"I... I..." Steve stuttered, knowing he was cornered.

"I've had to live in a hotel, being sick every morning, dealing with your lawyers and my lawyers and a private investigator digging through our affairs," Faye said quietly as she dropped back into her seat. "It's been awful. I'm nauseous all the time and my fingers are too fat to wear my rings."

"To be fair, I didn't hound you," I said quietly, trailing off when I realized no one was listening. The Wendells were focused on each other and their lawyers were focused on them.

"I am so sorry," said Steve. Instead of sitting, he pushed back his chair and walked around the table, reaching out to his wife. When she wouldn't take his hand, or even stand up, he dropped his hand to his side. "Can you ever forgive me?" he asked softly.

Faye crossed her arms and looked away. "Why should I when you're divorcing me?"

"I'll stop it. I'll stop all of it... if you want me to?" he asked hesitantly. Faye bit her lip and stared at the floor.

"Of course she wants you too," I chipped in. "Both of you told me, separately, you don't want to be divorced. Neither of you has done anything wrong except you both have very poor communication skills. Steve, you didn't listen. Faye, you should have started with the pregnancy. Those skills can be polished before the baby comes." I pushed the envelope into the middle of the table. "Inside is all the evidence you need that there was no financial wrongdoing on either part or any motivation to marry for money on either side. My agency has confirmed Faye's investment has made her a very rich woman. Additionally, there is some information about college funds that you might like to read. I've also included a list of marriage counselors who can help you communicate better."

"Good work," said Faye's lawyer, reaching for the envelope. He shot a death glare at Steve's lawyer, Marianne, as she reached for the envelope. "I'll make you a copy," he hissed.

"Don't stiff me with the whole bill," she hissed back.

"I would never!"

"You stiffed me with the breakfast bill," she whispered, entirely oblivious to my observing them with absolute fascination.

"You chose the restaurant."

"Only because you can't cook!"

I raised my eyebrows and glanced away from them, but not before noticing Faye had gotten to her feet and the Wendells now had their arms wrapped around each other, whispering things in each other's ears that I hoped wouldn't lead to another miscommunication. I couldn't help smiling. My work was done. I successfully saved a marriage and wrapped up a case all before lunch. Speaking of lunch... I glanced at my watch. Solomon would be waiting for me.

"Please don't hesitate to call if you need further assistance," I said, not that anyone was listening. Leaving one couple caressing and the lawyers bickering about their own relationship issues, I grabbed my purse and hightailed it out of the boardroom.

~

"How did it go?" asked Solomon when I slid into the booth twenty minutes later.

"Case is all wrapped up and the clients appeared satisfied," I told him. "I'm sure they will be happy to settle the bill as soon as you send it. This is nice. I'm glad we can meet for lunch."

"Since you spent the evening whining about your sore muscles, something I didn't quite understand about idiot former colleagues, and then ate three quarters of the Chinese food I picked up before falling asleep, I figured we could have a nice lunch."

"It wasn't the best evening," I agreed, "But the food was great." The takeout also eliminated the green smoothie aftertaste and I was sure I could justify the delicious food, thanks to the workout. I might not be any fitter but I certainly wasn't any worse off.

"I thought you were trying to eat healthier in the run-up to the wedding."

"I am but all that exercise meant I had to load up on food. I needed protein."

"Lean protein not crispy, battered protein in sauce."

"I had a healthy breakfast," I pointed out. "All that fruit."

"On pancakes."

"Made from eggs. They're healthy!"

"Maple syrup?"

"Organic. It said so on the bottle."

Solomon simply shook his head. "You look fine as you are. I don't know why you're worried, although I think your definition of worried and mine are two different things."

The server approached us and took our order: two chicken salads. It was healthy, tasty and I would feel thoroughly virtuous. The way I saw it was, I could eat whatever I damn well pleased, just so long as I didn't eat mountains of it. Unlike some of my friends and relatives over the years, I hadn't become obsessed with dieting although I was not foolish enough to pretend my metabolism was that of someone ten years younger. When it came to food consumption, I was just sensible. Four words I never thought I'd use to describe myself but that was maturity for you.

"So do you want this to be your last case before the wedding?" Solomon continued. "There are several final preparations to do and I can't help until the end of the week when I wrap up my current site visit." Solomon was working with a local private school to upgrade their security systems after a burglary resulted in the theft of all their IT equipment. The school was part of a wealthy consortium and he hoped the others in the group would also want to upgrade their security systems.

"Actually, I might have another case. A walk-in," I told him. I gave him the overview of the case and waited for his comment.

"What's your impression?"

I sucked air into my cheeks and blew it out again, pulling a puzzled face. "I don't know. There doesn't appear to be anything in it and yet... I keep thinking about it. I met Julia, the apparent victim, by chance at the gym, that's who the potential client is worried about, and there's definitely... something. I don't know what it is. I can't quite put my finger on it. Jas has a hunch. I have a gut feeling."

"I'm not giving you anymore cases so take a few days to explore it. See if there's anything in it that sets off any alarm bells. If you find something, come to me and I'll assign it to someone."

"Thanks," I said, feeling strangely relieved. A few days were all I needed to delve into some background research. Plus, there was the small matter of the tank that would be a trickier topic. "There's something else but it's highly confidential."

Solomon nodded. "Of course."

"I mean classified confidential."

That got Solomon's attention. "Classified as in... officially classified?" he asked.

We paused as the server delivered our food, then leaned in across the table to speak quietly in the busy diner. "It involves the Army only... they don't know about it."

"You lost me."

"Remember I told you about the time I joined the Army?" Solomon's lips quivered as he tried not to smile. "Yes, okay. It wasn't my finest hour. A couple of my Army buddies got in touch with me last night about a problem they need my help with. It doesn't sound huge, it just sounds... dumb." Might as well call it what it was. "They lost a tank."

Solomon's eyes widened. "How does someone lose a tank?"

I pulled a face. "They weren't absolutely clear on that."

"A tank?"

"Yep."

"An actual tank?"

"They showed me a picture and yes, it's a real tank. Not a little, diddly, toy one."

"A tank?" repeated Solomon.

"I think we've established that."

"I'm incredulous. I feel like I need to ask again."

"I will only keep saying yes."

"To every question?"

"Yes."

"Early night tonight?"

"I knew you would throw in a trick question but... yes." When Solomon raised his hand, I high-fived it. "So about that tank. They need help finding it."

"Shouldn't be too difficult. It will stand out. Not many tanks rolling around the state."

"That's what I said but they said they tried looking everywhere and they can't find it. It's missing and if they don't find it before some display thing they're putting on at Fort Charles, they're in big trouble. Hey, how much are tanks worth anyway?"

"You can pick up a Scorpion tank on eBay for forty thousand dollars."

"Wow! That's a lot of money."

"What kind of tank did they lose?"

I consulted the note I made on my phone. "An Abrams battle tank. Latest model."

Solomon swallowed.

"Is that so bad? Is it more than forty thousand dollars? Fifty? More? A hundred thousand? More? Seriously?" I paused and picked a big number. "A million?"

"More than eight million dollars."

"Holy crap! They lost eight million dollars of tank!" I squeaked.

"Do their superiors know?" Solomon asked.

"I don't think so. They're hoping no one noticed."

Solomon shook his head. "Amazing."

"This is an excellent chicken salad," I said, forking a piece of chicken into my mouth.

"Take the case," said Solomon. "Wait, are they paying clients, or is this a favor?"

"A favor although they did offer ten bucks, Army-issued boots in my size, a discount voucher for a pancake place near Fort Charles and a Butterfinger."

"Just one Butterfinger?"

"Apparently there were two but they shared the other one on the way over."

"Big incentives."

"I suppose I could hold out for a Three Musketeers."

"You could."

I stopped. "You're not telling me to *not* take the case."

"That's correct."

"So, you think I should? I really thought you'd tell me this is crazy and that I should stay a million miles away from a stolen tank."

Solomon smiled. "I think it's the perfect case to keep you occupied. It won't take you long to find a tank and how much trouble could you get into?"

"Eight million dollars of trouble. Someone went to a great deal of effort to steal a state-of-the-art tank. I have to wonder what kind of people want it." Now I said it, that sounded like a lot more trouble than I anticipated. A lost tank was one thing; a stolen tank was another altogether. I could only hope the person, or people, who stole the tank were only in it for a joyride and had no real idea of its true value.

"Now you've raised that, I'm already regretting my advice that you should take the case."

"And yet I am," I decided. "I can't not help them. They both helped me a bunch of times during boot camp." On one particular occasion, I recalled both of them launching me like a cannonball over a ten-foot wall on an assault course that didn't make me fitter but did make me want to assault the course designers. Being thrown over the enormous wall was the only time in my life I felt like I could fly like Superwoman. Right until I landed face first in the muddy pit on the other side. I was lucky to have survived! While I had no inclination to repeat that feat, I did appreciate the fact that without their help on numerous occasions, not to mention their unfailing good spirits, I would have flunked out of boot camp much earlier than I actually did; and then where would I have been? Home to Montgomery earlier and less emotionally equipped to get past the betrayal from my former fiancé that sent me on a ricochet course to the Army in the first place.

"Get Lucas to help you locate it. If you can narrow it down to where they last saw the tank, you can start there and follow the trail from a safe and remote distance. A tank that size should leave a sizable trail. Once you've located it, turn the information over to your buddies for retrieval." Solomon paused. "Please tell me they don't want you to retrieve it too?"

"Not so far as I know; plus, I don't know how to drive a tank anyway."

"Thank everything above," said Solomon.

"I hope that wasn't a critique on my driving skills."

"Your driving is excellent. Plus, your VW barely has a scratch on it to prove it. What are your plans for the rest of the day?"

"Wedding dress shopping. I'm down to three gowns, all of equal beauty. I have to make a decision today."

"Didn't you say exactly the same thing a month ago?"

"Yes, then I couldn't make a decision. Today is my last day to make a choice."

"I thought dresses needed weeks of fitting and alterations."

"Some do. These are all in my size and unless something catastrophic happens, they barely need altering." I wondered if the takeout counted as catastrophic, then decided not to worry about it.

"Let's not tempt fate," said Solomon.

"The bridesmaid dresses are all fitted and paid for," I told him, since that was positive news. "And I spoke to our wedding planner and she says everything is good to go. Did you get your suit?"

"Two weeks ago."

"Oh! I didn't know. Where is it? I didn't see a suit bag."

"Hanging in the closet at home." Solomon paused, then clarified, "The Chilton house."

For a brief moment, I felt like all the air had been sucked out of me. The Chilton house, Solomon's house, until very recently had been our home but that all changed the day Solomon was shot in the doorway. After being rushed to hospital for surgery and then in a coma for several days, leaving me uncertain about whether he would live or die, he woke up. With help from everyone we knew, the assailants were swiftly apprehended and the mystery about why Solomon was targeted was solved.

I'd barely been back to the house since that day. I couldn't return. Every time I closed my eyes, I could see him slumped in the doorway. Even when that image started to fade, every so often, it would pop into my head again, unbidden and unwelcome, leaving me nauseous and reeling. I couldn't face crossing that threshold every day, reliving the trauma multiple times a day, so we moved into the pretty, yellow bungalow I owned since I hadn't made a decision to either sell or rent it.

It was smaller than Solomon's house, and although it was in a nice area, much less well-heeled than the Chilton neighborhood. Yet, the security was top of the line because Solomon had installed it previously.

Crucially, for me, he'd never been shot in my doorway and I didn't have to visualize finding his slumped body there. I felt safe and comfortable in the yellow bungalow and no one could track Solomon to my house. No one could hurt him there. I wasn't sure Solomon felt the same, but as he'd said to me on the day we officially moved in, "I was unconscious and don't remember most of it. You're the one who had to see me like that so we'll move." It was a temporary thing but we'd been living there two months and neither of us ever mentioned moving back to the Chilton house.

"I didn't realize you'd been there recently," I said.

"I drop in every few days and check on the place. Occasionally, I need to pick something up."

"Oh." I wasn't sure what else to say.

"You don't have to come with me," he said.

"Hurrah." My voice was flat.

"It's just a house."

"I know."

"No bad guys."

"I know."

"We have to go back one day," he said.

I knew this was coming but I wasn't sure when. Part of me thought he was right: it was just a house, and although it had been the scene of an awful crime, that was in the past and every successive day took it a little further away. Eventually, I would rarely think about it at all.

Solomon laid his fork on his plate and reached for my hand, intertwining his fingers with mine, warm and comforting. "We don't have to go back there yet but at some point, we need to move on from what happened and just live. No fear of the past. No letting it decide our future. We own what we want to do."

"You should be a fridge magnet," I told him as I toyed with his fingers.

"We'll talk about this another time," said Solomon. "We need to decide where our marital home is going to be anyway."

"I thought we'd stay at my house."

"Forever? Sweetheart, we won't fit."

"We fit now."

"What about having a family? A dog?"

"You want a dog?"

"Maybe. Not one of those tiny ones. I can't walk a chihuahua or a dachshund."

"Why not? Is it because they're not manly?"

"The dog doesn't need to be manly. I am manly enough. I'm just not sure those little legs can keep up with me."

"You could get a stroller for it." I held back a smile at the image.

"I could make that look manly too. Anyway, the only time we're getting a stroller is when we have something with two legs to put in it."

"No maiming small dogs," I said and Solomon laughed.

"If I work hard at it, we could get a double stroller," he said.

The idea of pushing a double stroller with two junior Solomons in it, a big dog on a leash, and heading out to brunch somewhere was a very appealing fantasy. In my head, I added a very glamorous mommy outfit that did not involve wearing a gun, pedestrians that would coo at our delightful progeny, and absolutely nothing dangerous.

"You're smiling," said Solomon.

"A double stroller, huh?"

"My swimmers are like the Navy SEALS. They can penetrate anything. Ten bucks says triplets, first go."

This time, the air knocked out of me was for real. There was no way on earth was I letting that happen to me, unless it was a lot of fun.

CHAPTER SIX

"I love it!"

"Beautiful!"

"Gorgeous!"

"Stunning!" The compliments came quickly and enthusiastically.

Standing in front of the mirror, on top of a little podium that I guessed was supposed to make me feel like a princess—news flash, it did!—I checked my reflection. The dress was lovely. White, floor-length lace with a tiny train, a nipped-in waist and a sweetheart strapless bodice. It was everything a wedding dress should be: feminine, elegant and accentuating all the right assets without being too va va voom.

Yet, it wasn't quite perfect. Try as I might, I couldn't imagine walking down the aisle in it, or Solomon's face as he looked up and saw me.

It was exactly the same with the first dress I tried on. That gown was simpler than the other two I'd chosen for my final try-ons. A column of white satin with a fluted skirt, a fitted bodice and a crew neck. It made me feel long and slinky, like an old-fashioned movie star. Only something was missing.

"I think I want to try the other dress on," I said, echoing the same words I said ten minutes before... and ten minutes before that.

"Absolutely," grinned the perpetually happy-looking sales assistant dressed in black. A shiny, rectangular name plate on her chest read "Cherry" but I'd already renamed her "Cheery" in my head. "We are trying on the last dress," she announced to the small crowd assembled on the two velvet sofas that bookended the podium.

"Great choice!"

"It's an amazing dress!"

"Spoiled for choice!"

I half turned, smiling at my mom who held my sister Serena's daughter, Victoria, Lily with baby Poppy in her arms, and my sisters-in-law, Traci and Alice. They chose not to bring their daughters who would serve as my flower girls.

The only person missing from the group was Serena and being on her honeymoon, she was forgiven. Also, I was pleased to be spared her barbed comments. Although she had softened substantially since she met her husband—thanks to me—there were still frequent traces of her acerbic nature. Plus, she would have surely voiced her concern at anything that might outshine her own recent wedding. Not that she had to worry. Her wedding was intimate and chic with a lovely outdoor ceremony under an arch of cream and pink roses followed by one of the most delicious meals I'd ever eaten, all to the accompaniment of a string quartet. Since it was her second wedding, she deviated from tradition with a dress in the softest blush pink and wore tiny roses in her hair. Delgado complemented her in a gray suit and pink tie with a pink buttonhole. He spent the whole day with a huge smile plastered on his face. The entire thing was delightfully romantic.

"Do you prefer the first gown?" asked Mom. She bounced Victoria, made some cooing noises that had the little girl laughing and looked up.

"I don't know," I said hesitantly. Then I sighed. Who knew that buying gorgeous dresses would be such hard work?

"This is not supposed to be hard work," said Lily, apparently reading my mind.

"You could buy them both," suggested Alice. "I had two dresses. One for the ceremony and one for the reception."

I recalled the price tags. "I'm only buying one," I decided. "I just need to make sure it's the right one."

"If this were the right one, you wouldn't want to try the first one on again," pointed out Lily. "Go and get changed. We'll wait."

"Thank you," I said, hoping my appreciation seeped through. We'd already been here an hour while I pranced and preened in front of the mirror, turning this way and that. Cherry eagerly brought a steady stream of tiaras, veils and jeweled hair clips for me to try on. So far, the only thing I was dead certain about were my vertiginous high-heeled sandals in a deep sapphire blue. They would serve as "something blue" to peep out from under my gown and also for wearing long after the eventful day was over.

I gathered up the skirt and stepped down from the podium, hurrying to the changing room, which was the size of a small bedroom. Decorated in soft, shimmering white wallpaper, a series of large, glossy frames held photos of models in stunning gowns. An armoire offered an array of props, silk bouquets, lace parasols, imitation pearl and crystal jewelry, and everything a bride might need to give her a finished look. Obviously, I played with everything because if ever there was a time to indulge in dress-up, it was this day.

"I'll help you with the zip then just hang the dress on the hanger and holler when you're ready for me to help you with the buttons on the other dress," said Cherry as she closed the door behind us. I turned around and she pulled the long zip that ended at the base of my spine. "I think we're nearly there with a decision," she said cheerfully. "I can just feel it!"

"Great!" I chirped back, despite the sense of dread suddenly hitting my stomach. What if I couldn't make a decision? What if I made the wrong one and I looked back in twenty years and wondered what the hell I was thinking?

"Take your time," Cherry instructed with a quick movement before she was out the door, closing it silently behind her.

I shuffled out of the dress and hung it on the padded hanger. I hooked the hanger over one of the large, glittery hooks mounted on the wall and stepped back. The energy seemed to ebb out of me, my legs turned to jelly and I stumbled backwards, dropping into the big, pink wing chair in nothing but my white shorties and strapless bra. I slumped back, catching my breath and reminding myself not to panic. What was I so worried about anyway? It was just a dress. Just a wedding. My wedding, but just a day all the same even if it did involve a large wad of cash and a big party. I closed my eyes and saw Solomon there again, in the doorway of our home, blood seeping from his chest like a terrible inkblot.

"He didn't die," I muttered aloud. "He didn't die. He didn't leave me. I am okay." It was a mantra I'd repeated every day for weeks. That I had come so close to losing him was unthinkable. Yet it wasn't that past memory that terrified me. No, it was the knowledge that it could so easily happen again.

We lived lives that weren't designed to be safe. We crossed paths with people who didn't care if we were injured or even died. Criminals who didn't care if we bled out, alone, just so long as we got out of their way. Or, in Solomon's case, served a purpose as a warning. It wasn't even because of his actions that he'd been shot and yet, I delved deep into his life to find out if his attempted murder was some kind of payback. What if next time it was? The *what if* was exhausting me. Fear was hampering my every decision from where to live to buying a dress.

I leaned forwards, my elbows on my knees, my face in my hands and breathed deeply. In, one, two, three... out, one, two, three... until I felt calmer. I stood, checking how steady my legs felt and smiling to see they were okay. People were waiting for me outside; people who wanted me to be happy and to celebrate our marriage. I couldn't let them see how fear crippled me.

I reached for the other dress, spinning it around on the padded hanger before I let it drop to the floor so I could step into it and slide it up my body. This dress fell neatly between the two: strapless with a form-fitted body made of gentle folds of silk and a gathered skirt that swept around my ankles. The back had the pearl buttons I loved and even better, pockets! It was the wedding dress of my dreams.

When the knock sounded at the door, I jumped, startled, my breathing quickening again.

"Only me!" said Cherry as she ducked her head around the door. "You didn't holler and I figured you'd be ready now. Let's see... oh, isn't that a great dress? Turn around, I'll have those buttons fastened in a jiffy!"

I did as I was told, turning to face the long mirror encased in a baroque silver frame, looking myself over as she fastened the long column of pearl buttons at the back of the dress. Blood seeped from my middle. I blinked and the blood disappeared. I rolled my shoulders and stared at the ceiling until she was finished.

"Let's go see what your family thinks," said Cherry, still effortlessly perky. She pulled open the door and ushered me out along the corridor, giving me a nudge towards the podium.

"Amazing!"

"Adore it!"

"You look fabulous!"

I stood silently in front of the mirrors while my family chattered their opinions.

"You know, it needs something else," said Cherry. She hurried away, returning less than a couple of minutes later with a rhinestone sash in her hand. She wrapped it around my waist, tied it with a bow at the back and stepped back. "What do you think?" she asked.

I nodded. "This is the one," I said, nodding rapidly, sure now, and I smiled when my family burst into applause. The sound lifted my spirits and I forced myself to push away all the residual bad thoughts. I had to be realistic: what were the odds of something so terrible happening twice? It couldn't!

I sucked in a deep breath and smiled. Solomon and I were going to have a wonderful wedding and a lifetime of wedded bliss. All I had to do was enjoy it. "This is definitely the dress and the sash is perfect," I said again, investing all of my belief that everything would be okay into my words.

"Wonderful! I just knew it!" Cherry clapped her hands together. "I think it needs a little hemming on the skirt but otherwise, the fit is perfect. You're lucky that you happened to be the same size as the sample we had in stock. I can order you a new one of course, but I don't think that would fit your time scale..." She trailed off, waiting for me to confirm.

"I'll take the sample. Can we do the alterations today?"

"I'll call our seamstress and she can pin the hem into place, then leave it with us and you can pick it up next week."

Behind me, my mother began to sob.

"What's wrong, Mom?" I asked, half turning.

"I can't believe you're getting married!"

"I told you someone would marry her," said Lily.

"You did, honey, you did," sobbed Mom as she patted Lily's knee with one hand and squeezed Victoria with the other. "I just never really believed it. I thought I might have to pay someone!"

I pulled a face. "Mom, I can hear you!"

"And your father... he was so sure you would marry a police officer," Mom wailed but I wondered if she were relieved or disappointed.

"Solomon is so much more than that," said Lily. "He's probably got a uniform for everything. Does he, Lexi, does he?" Silence dropped over the room as all eyes turned to me. I was sure not a single person breathed as they considered all the uniform wearing options Solomon could possibly wear.

"He's wearing a suit to the wedding," I said to collective sighs of disappointment.

"Shame he isn't going in his commando suit," snickered Lily.

"What's a commando suit?" asked Mom. "Is that from his time in the Army?"

I sighed. I refused to explain that one. My mom might drop my niece and then Serena would be on my case for eternity.

"And how about a veil?" asked Cherry, mercifully stepping in. She skirted the podium, an array of frothy white veils in her arms and an assistant trailing behind her. "We have a lace trim, a cathedral-length though maybe not with this dress, there's a completely plain, two-tier..." she continued as I zoned out for a moment. "Lexi?"

I blinked. "Yes?"

"Do you want to try them all on?"

"The short one," I decided.

"The birdcage veil. Great choice. Very contemporary." Cherry tipped the veils into her assistant's arms and raised a small veil on a headband and slid it onto my head, playing and fluffing the net until she decided it was just right before she stepped back.

I blinked again. It was perfect. The dress, the rhinestone sash, the shoes, the tiny veil that swept down under my chin and allowed my hair to sweep freely down my back. I looked like a bride.

"Oh, Alexandra," breathed Mom. "You look stunning."

"I'll take the veil and the sash," I decided, not caring about the price tags. If I had to work every crappy case searching for missing pets, misplaced family members, and stolen goods for the next five years, I would do it without a single complaint. Well, without a single *audible* complaint. That is to say, I might complain a lot but I would still be grateful to wear these beautiful items.

"Wonderful! Here's the seamstress. She'll pin the hem and then you can take this all off and I will have the veil and sash wrapped and waiting for you to collect when the dress is ready. We can take care of everything else at the cash register before you go."

"Thank you, Cherry." I smiled at her, grateful for her patience.

"No, thank you," she said, squeezing my hand before she took off.

While the seamstress hemmed the dress and cooed at my blue heeled sandals, my family began to mill around, examining all the other dresses until one-by-one they began to leave. By the time the seamstress had finished, only my Mom, Lily and the two baby girls remained.

I told them I would be a few minutes, then hurried to get changed, slipping off the dress and hanging it on the padded satin hanger before pulling my own clothes back on. Except for that moment of panic, it was fun to try on my remaining three options of beautiful dresses and now that I knew my final choice was made, relief yielded to excitement. The dress was the final decision to make in the wedding plans. All I had left to do now was find a tank, and work out what was puzzling me about the strange case Jas Kapoor asked me to work on. Then Solomon and I could get married, party the night away and the next day, we could get on a jet and leave Montgomery behind us. Perhaps that was what I needed to close the past for good: a well-deserved vacation.

By the time I emerged from the changing room, I was in better spirits. "Mom? Lily?" I called as I returned to the salon but they weren't there. I turned around, following the corridor back to the front of the salon and found my mother at the cash register, handing over her card. "Mom? What are you doing?"

"Paying for your dress and the veil and the sash," said Mom as Cherry returned her card. "Your father and I agreed that when you got married, we would pay for your dress. You know that."

"You didn't have to pay for the extra things too!"

"We know, but we chipped in for your brothers' and sister's weddings and we want to do the same for you too. No arguments. Just a thank you will do."

"Thank you," I said graciously. Then I rushed over and hugged her.

"I'm so pleased you're marrying a man," breathed Mom.

I let her go gently. "I have no idea what to say to that," I said.

"We'll call you when your dress is ready," said Cherry. "Then you'll come in, and we'll do one last fitting before you take the dress home with you. I hope you'll send us a snap of the big day for our wall of fame," she added, nodding to the wall of framed photos of happy couples. Behind us, the door opened, causing the bell atop to jingle.

I glanced over my shoulder at the newcomer as Cherry began to wrap the veil and sash in a pristine white box.

"Lexi?" said Julia Atwater, frowning in surprise, then smiling. She carried a garment bag over one arm.

"Hi, Julia," I said, hoping that I concealed my astonishment in time. I didn't need to worry that she thought anything untoward about my reaction because she seemed preoccupied with the garment bag.

"It's so nice to bump into you. Are you here for a wedding dress?" she asked.

"That's right. Finally made a choice and my mom generously bought it for me. Is that a wedding dress?" I pointed to the bag.

"Oh, how lovely of your mom," smiled Julia. Then she shook her head. "No, this is my dress for the engagement party. Bryce thought I should get the hem altered to make it the right length."

"Here's your purchase," said Cherry, handing me the box. "I just love your choice."

"Thank you!"

The door bell jangled again and a tall man with a crop of dark hair stepped in and looked around. His face split into a gleaming white smile when he saw Julia. "Honey, did you drop off the dress?" he asked.

"Just doing it now," she said, smiling happily at him before she turned and draped the bag over the counter, unzipping it to reveal a flash of deep rosy pink. She turned back and said, "Lexi, this is my fiancé, Bryce. Bryce, this is the woman I told you I ran into at the gym. She's a friend of Jas and also a friend of the owner of Lily's Bar. Oh, and this is Lily. I'm sorry, I didn't see you there," she said when Lily moved.

"Hi," said Lily, grinning as she maneuvered Poppy in her arms. "I'm so happy to host your engagement party," she told Bryce.

"I recognize you! I've seen you at the bar. We can't thank you enough, especially after that disaster at the other place; it looked like we'd have to cancel. Am I a lucky guy to get to take this woman out or what?" he asked, flashing a smile at everyone in the salon. My mother beamed at him, Lily frowned a little but nodded. I took the moment to study him. Tall, in good shape beneath the tan chinos and white shirt, two buttons open casually at the neck. His watch was expensive, like his shoes, and his teeth had been given the Hollywood whiter-than-white treatment. His smile was big and his eyes dazzling. I could see why Julia fell for him: he was a terrific looking man. "Honey," he continued, his attention back on Julia, "I'm going to wait outside. We're on a parking meter so don't take forever. And remember, just two inches will make the dress perfect." He winked at us, then slipped out again.

Julia handed the dress over, repeated the alterations, paid and turned back to us. "Lily, I'll call you later to confirm the plans and then I guess we'll see you at the party?"

"Sounds perfect," agreed Lily.

"Bye, everyone!" Julia waved, smiling as she left the salon.

"Lucky girl," muttered my mom. "Did you see the way he looked at her? Like she was the only woman in the room. Oh, to be looked at like that!"

"Dad looks at you like that," I said.

"He looks at the Sunday roast like that," said Mom but she smiled. She was wrong. Well, partially. My dad did gaze at food with nothing but unbridled love in his eyes; but after more than four decades of marriage to my mom, it was clear he still loved her. That love was part of what made me and my siblings who we were.

We said our goodbyes to the sales assistants and stepped outside into the warmth of the sun. Victoria clapped her hands and reached for the sky as she bounced in my mom's arms. Poppy snuggled against Lily's shoulder and closed her eyes.

"I'm going to take this one to the car," said Mom. She kissed my cheek. "Call me later."

"Thanks again, Mom. I really appreciate you and Dad buying my dress."

"I know that guy," said Lily as my mom walked away.

"Who?" I asked,

"Julia's fiancé. Bryce. He comes into the bar occasionally with his buddies."

"Oh?"

"Well, obviously he's cute so he stands out."

I laughed. "What are your impressions of him?"

"He's great! Really nice guy. Friendly, chatty. Always the first one at the bar with his wallet out, getting the drinks in. The bar staff all love him, of course. He tips well and makes sure to ask everyone how they're doing and even remembers stuff they said; he never fails to ask them about it the next time he comes in. Oh, he got into it once with a guy who was harassing Ruby and told him to get lost or he'd make him get lost!"

"Really?"

"Yeah! I wasn't there but she told me the next day that he really stood up for her when that jerk tried to cop a feel. He was just sitting at the bar having a drink and he called out that guy. She said he got angry real quick and was right back to his usual self a few minutes later. I'm glad I can help them out with the party. I heard him talking about his new girlfriend occasionally so it's nice to put a face to her name too. I didn't realize the two were together when you introduced us at the gym."

"Does he talk about Julia regularly?" I asked.

"Yes, much to the heartbreak of every woman in my bar. He's always talking her up and telling everyone how wonderful she makes him feel and how she totally gets him. I think he's had issues with women in the past."

"How do you mean?"

"I think his ex was a hard case. Always on him about something. Playing games. Wanted money. The one before that was the same."

"Hmm."

"Hey, you're thinking about investigating Julia. Is it anything that will affect Bryce? I really hope not. He seems so happy and I would hate to think Julia is another crazy case. Bryce is a really great guy."

He did seem to be great from what Lily reported, but then why was Jas so sure he wasn't treating Julia well? And why was I worried that her hunch was right?

CHAPTER SEVEN

I spent the rest of the afternoon parked at my desk. Two files flanked either side of my laptop. One was the file Jas gave me to think about. The other was the file I just created for the missing tank. I still wasn't sure what to think about Julia and Bryce but I did note Lily's observations. I slid them into the file along with a memo to talk to Ruby about her impressions of Bryce to see if they matched Lily's.

Until I could speak to Ruby, I searched online for tanks. For most people, that would be an odd thing to search for on the internet, but for me, it didn't even make it into the top ten.

A few minutes later, I had a good idea of what a state-of-the-art military tank looked like and a reasonable idea of its size. What I had no idea about was where a person could hide one. Wherever it was, it would surely stand out.

Solomon's idea about looking into where it was last seen and working from there was a good idea. If I could find out how it was stolen, I could possibly ascertain a number of things. One, how it was stolen. Surely no one could simply drive a tank out of Fort Charles without being noticed? Two, there might be a camera image of the thieves and the possibility someone would recognize them. Three, it might be someone who was playing an elaborate hoax on my buddies who, no doubt, must have done something to deserve it.

I grabbed my phone and called. "Did you find it?" asked Captain Harris, his voice hushed.

"No," I said, "did it turn up?"

"Did it turn up?" he repeated in a skeptical tone. "No, it didn't! That's why you need to find it."

"Where did you last see it?"

"Parked in the hangar. Before you ask, I've checked every day and it's still not there."

"When did you last see it?"

"Three days ago."

"Okay. Morning? Afternoon? Evening?"

"Evening, around eight pm. I was making my final checks before I met the guys in the bar."

"The bar in Fort Charles?"

"Yeah. You know it?"

"I do." Solomon and I once worked a case there and we pretended to be married for our cover. It was funny that now we really were going to be married. No more pretend rings, this time, we'd be exchanging real ones. I still had the fake wedding ring. For some reason, I never wanted to get rid of it. I wondered if Solomon still had his. "Who were you there with?" I asked before I became too distracted.

"What? You think I had something to do with it?"

"I have to ask, Luke. Plus, if I know who you were with, it might rule out a few people."

"No one on base would do this!"

"Someone had to get on the base in the first place," I pointed out. "It's sensible to assume someone on the inside helped. So, who were you with?"

"Let's see. Kafsky was there before me. We sat together at the bar, then Willacy and DuPont came in. The four of us hung out until ten and then we turned in. Separately, before you ask, so I can't account for anyone after that time and no one can account for me."

"Okay. Did you notice anything unusual?"

"You mean like a tank rolling past? No."

"What about a large transport vehicle?"

"Several vehicles left the base late that night. I was off duty and enjoying a beer. I didn't pay much attention."

"Were any of the vehicles large enough to transport a tank?"

"Maybe. Yes, I think so."

"How did you get the tank to Fort Charles in the first place? I figure you didn't drive it from wherever it came from."

"You're right, I didn't. It wouldn't do the tracks any good; plus, there would be complaints about damaging the road surfaces. Besides, no one wants to make a cross country trip in one of those things. It would take forever. It came in on a tank transporter driven by a guy called

Simmons. The transporter looks like a heavy tractor and trailer unit."

"Where's the tractor and trailer now?" I asked.

Harris paused. "I don't know. I can go check. It should still be parked behind the hangar since it was supposed to take the tank back to its home base next week."

"Please check and get back to me," I told him. "When did you realize the tank was missing?"

"Eight the next morning."

That was a twelve-hour window. Not great but at least something to work with. "Any cameras in the hangar?" I asked.

"Yeah, there're two."

"I need to see that feed. Can you arrange that?"

"I guess, but it won't be easy. What am I supposed to say?"

"I'm sure you'll come up with something. Let me know when you get access and if you can get me a copy. I can come to the base if it makes it any easier."

"I will let you know. What will you do until then?" he asked.

"I'll work with my team here to find out which traffic cameras are closest to the base and see if we can pick up a tank transporter somewhere near Fort Charles between eight that night and eight the next morning." Something else occurred to me. "What if it never left the base?"

"It definitely left the base. Kafsky and I have looked everywhere."

"You're certain?"

"It's a tank, Lexi. Hiding a tank isn't easy."

And yet someone had managed to do it. "Call me when you have access to the security tapes," I added and after we said our goodbyes, I hung up and went upstairs to talk to Lucas.

Lucas was our resident tech geek although he didn't look it with his ruffled, blond surfer hair and relaxed jeans and t-shirt look. If I saw him on the street, I'd probably think he was a college dropout or a hipster in waiting, minus an enormous beard. Like me, he was the opposite of our other colleagues, most of whom I wouldn't want to bump into on a dark night; not if I didn't know them for the good guys they were. Unlike me, however, Lucas didn't go out in the field. Instead he worked behind a large bank of monitors, observing the world from the deep, dark corners of the internet.

"Hey," he said, looking up and grinning when I dragged an office chair over to his station and plonked down on it. "I heard you lost a tank."

"I didn't lose it," I pointed out, "and how do you know anyway?"

"I know everything," he said, flicking his eyebrows up and down.

"Do you know where the tank is?"

He frowned. "I know *almost* everything."

"Are you busy?"

"For you, no. For everyone else, yes."

"Awesome. I need to find the closest cameras to Fort Charles and access their security feeds between eight and eight three days ago."

"Okay. What are we looking for?"

"A tank, preferably but unlikely. A tank transporter most likely."

"Have you ever seen a tank transporter before?"

"Of course!" Five minutes ago on my laptop, but there was no need to tell Lucas that. It was better that he thought I knew everything too. Bluffing was one of my key life skills.

"Let me see." Lucas turned to the keyboard and began tapping the keys, writing something unintelligible on the screen. I read it anyway like I knew what I was looking at and crossed my fingers that there wouldn't be a pop quiz in coding later. "There are six cameras in the area but none within a mile, which makes sense since I'm sure Fort Charles has their own system and probably doesn't want to be closely observed by their neighbors. There are two traffic cameras on the major routes out of Fort Charles heading towards the highway. There's a gas station on one route, two stores on a strip mall just before the Chester town limits and what looks like a farm. All have security cameras."

"Can you access all of them?"

Lucas laughed. "Can I access them? she asks! Okay, the traffic cameras won't pose a problem but it will take me a little longer to bypass their firewall. I tapped into the feed from the gas station. They upload their feed to an off-site server that has questionable security. I downloaded the time frame you requested."

"That's great! What about the other route?"

"Give me a sec... Okay, one of the strip malls deletes their video history after forty-eight hours but the other has it on a drive on the same IP address. It doesn't look like I can lift a segment so I'll grab the lot."

"Will they notice?"

"Oh, please," scoffed Lucas. "I'll work on the other cameras. Is there anything else you need?"

"Are these definitely the only two routes out of Fort Charles?"

"I guess. I don't know the area. Did you check a map?"

"Did I check a map?" I scoffed. Then I pulled out my cell phone, called up the maps program and checked. I found Fort Charles, zoomed in and verified there were only two routes away from the base. The tank had to have been taken via one of them. "Yes, send me anything you have and I'll check back later. When I know which route the tank transporter took, I'm going to need you to follow the route until we find it."

"I've never wanted to take a sick day more."

"Glad you're looking forward to it," I said, ruffling his hair as I left. While the idea of searching through hours of footage in the hope of seeing a tank transporter pass by didn't exactly thrill me, at least it was a nice, safe job before the wedding.

When I got back to my desk, I punched the password into my laptop and downloaded the video Lucas sent me. The map program marked the gas station on the route heading out of town. The tank transporter—if there even was one—could have been taken out of town, in which case it would be hard to track, especially if it crossed state lines. I didn't relish passing that news onto my old buddies. Until that became a real possibility, I picked the easier option: the strip mall was on the way into the nearest town, Chester. If the tank went into the town, it was more than likely that it was stashed there.

I got up, made a coffee at the small coffee station across the room, then sat, my mug in hand, and opened the store's video, setting it to play from eight pm in double time. After fifteen minutes, I set it to four times faster. I was pretty sure I would see something as large as a tank transporter and I didn't need to see every little vehicle or tree branch waving in the breeze. At that zoomed-up speed, it took me an hour to watch four hours of tape and just as I became excessively bored, a very large vehicle lumbered past the screen.

Popping upright in my chair, I hit pause, then rewind, and reset the tape to play in normal time. The vehicle was a tractor in a dark color with a low loader trailer. The trailer was covered with a tarp but it was the size, shape and bulk of a tank. Yes, that was definitely a tank transporter and I would stake money on a tank being its cargo! I rewound and played the tape again, searching for any details but the footage was too grainy to make out the face of the person inside the tractor's cab.

"Lucas?" I said when he answered my call.

"Nearly there with the traffic cams," he replied.

"Forget them. I have footage of the tank going past the strip mall at midnight, heading towards Chester. Can you track it from there?"

"I can write a program to track it," he said. "It'll take a little time as I'll need to collate data from hundreds of cameras and you know, if it goes into a no camera zone, we'll lose it."

"Find me as much information as you can," I said.

"You got it."

I printed off a screenshot of the tank transporter and added the page to my file. Now that I knew the tank had definitely been taken off base, I had something to work with. I called Harris back and got his voicemail so I left a cryptic message about tracking his parcel from the depot just in case anyone else happened to listen in.

While I waited for Lucas to work his tracking magic, I printed off a map of Chester. Since the transporter was heading that way, it was possible the tank had been stashed nearby during the night when no one would notice its movements. There weren't many places a tank and a tank transporter could be hidden without attracting someone's attention. I knew that I could immediately rule out large swathes of open land. Any public parking lots and residential areas would all result in too much attention. Ditto anywhere outside. If a tank turned up somewhere public, people would have noticed and there would be some chatter in law enforcement. I hadn't heard a thing.

That meant the tank had to be hidden well. Within fifteen minutes, I highlighted several warehouses in neon pink, two business parks, and one disused industrial site.

My desk phone rang and I answered. "That was fast," I said.

"I got a hit already."

"Where?"

"Strangely enough, in Montgomery. Around an hour after you spotted the vehicle leaving the base."

"Here in Montgomery?" I frowned. I couldn't fathom why a tank would be transported here.

"Yes, this Montgomery, not the one in Alabama. I accidentally inputted the wrong search coordinates instead of those for Chester and it popped up."

"Where was the sighting?" I asked.

"On the west side of town. I'll need to check into the cameras around there to pick up the trail but I thought you'd want to know right away."

"I did, thank you."

"Do you want me to cancel the search around Chester?"

"No, keep going with that," I decided. "I'd like to build a trail of the tank's journey, but since we know where it was around one am, you can focus your search on that time and location."

"On it."

I pushed the map of Chester to one side and printed a new one for Montgomery; then I printed another that focused specifically on the west side and outskirts of town. I'd grown up in West Montgomery, a nice, safe, family-oriented neighborhood where my parents still lived. If a tank inexplicably appeared there, the whole neighborhood would know about it. Since my parents hadn't called to let me know that some idiot had parked a tank on their driveway, that meant I should focus my search on the outskirts where there were less nosy neighbors.

First, I checked the map for any roads that led out to the highway rather than through the West Montgomery neighborhood. There was one but it was narrow and winding; not the sort of road a tank transporter would find easy to navigate. That didn't mean it couldn't be done, only that it probably wasn't the first choice.

Several large buildings occupied this area but I remembered there were reports in the Montgomery Gazette about some kind of financial mismanagement of the land rents a few years back and the businesses had gradually moved out, leaving the warehouses empty. I stabbed my finger on the map. These would be perfect places to hide a tank: big, empty and away from prying eyes.

I checked my watch. I had plenty of time to drive out there and take a look before I headed home. Plus, it would be nice to get out in the fresh air. My mind made up, I locked my laptop in the drawer beneath my desk, grabbed my purse and keys and headed towards the underground parking lot.

Thirty minutes later, and after some loud singing along to the radio and several curse words later, I exited Century and its jammed-up traffic backlog. I pointed my inconspicuous VW west. I had zero plans to actually find the tank—and zero clues what to do with it even if I did —but some light reconnaissance would be interesting. All I had to do was drive around the industrial park, maybe park and peek in a few windows, perhaps ask a bored security guard if he'd seen anything suspicious recently and then head home.

The closer I got to the warehouses, the more spaced out the traffic became until there was only my car. I rolled past the first warehouse and pulled over to the side of the road, suddenly aware of how lonely the area was. There was no one around to hear me... no, I had no intention of screaming. I wasn't even going to fully finish that thought!

I pulled the printed map from my purse and spread it across the steering wheel. The buildings didn't follow a logical grid system. Instead, they seemed to have been dropped into place. Most were situated alongside the main road with a few more having narrow access roads leading to warehouses behind other warehouses. The map showed the warehouses were all different sizes, some small, some sprawling but now as I looked at the one opposite, I realized even the small one on the map was huge in reality.

Dropping the map on the passenger seat, I pulled back onto the road and drove at a steady pace around the area before heading towards the road that led out to the highway. Ten minutes later, I'd run the entire length of the road and pulled a U-turn before I was forced onto the highway. The road wasn't as narrow as the map appeared and the twists and turns were longer rather than jackknifing. I wasn't entirely sure of the space a tank transporter took up on a road, but at night and without a single other vehicle around, I couldn't see a reason why it couldn't easily take this route.

Starting my search at the nearest warehouse, I pulled into a small parking lot in front of a gray building. I got out and walked the perimeter, my phone in hand, just in case. A door around the side hung open so I pulled it open a little further, grateful the hinges were well oiled so they didn't scream with the movement, and stepped into the doorway. There was nothing but cavernous space. I shut the door and made a mental note to tell Solomon to submit a bid to manage the security here.

Climbing back into my car, I repeated the same actions on two more abandoned warehouses and marked a large "X" on the map over the four warehouses I couldn't get close to. Two had secure chain link fences, one had a security guard who said the site was unoccupied and didn't seem very chatty, and a fourth had a pair of rottweilers that looked like they intended to eat me. All but one could have concealed a tank.

My final warehouse was along a service route that led between two empty warehouses. I drove up, hopped out and started my perimeter walk but not before something red and blinking caught my eye. An active security camera. I froze, watching it for a moment but it didn't move. All the same, I got a feeling that I didn't like. Someone was watching, but whom?

Two dumpsters were pushed up against the front of the building, and above them were a row of grimy windows. I hoisted myself up, prepared to take one quick look and then get out of there. Thanks to Lily's commitment to exercising me, pulling myself up onto the dumpster lid was no problem. I climbed up, steadied my feet shoulder-width apart, and leaned against the building, my palms against the filthy glass as I squinted.

Somebody—no, several somebodies!—were moving around inside and I could see racks of shelving and tables full of open laptops.

Behind me I heard a click.

I turned, gulping as fear washed over me, and blinked at the man holding a gun on me. "Maddox?" I said, frowning. Then the dumpster shifted under me and I fell backwards, my arms flailing into the air.

CHAPTER EIGHT

You know how sometimes life doesn't turn out quite like you planned? This was one of those moments. There was no way I could have figured my current misfortune into the day's events. A moment ago, I was on the cusp of a big discovery; now I lay on my back atop a soft layer of who knew what? All I detected was how much it stank and it was getting worse by the minute. Then something ran over my foot.

"Unbelievable," I muttered as I stared upwards.

"Hi! Lexi?" Maddox's head appeared over the lip of the dumpster. He brushed back his short crop of dark brown hair, sniffed, pulled an appalled expression then disappeared.

Wait. *Something ran over my foot?!*

"Help!" I yelled as I began to flounder. What if the creature that ran over my foot wanted to eat me? "Help!" I yelled again, only louder this time. Grasping for the sides of the dumpster, I leveraged my body upright and something squelched under me. That lit a rocket under my ass. I grabbed the hand that appeared over the lid and launched my torso up and over the top, catapulting my body in a most ungainly fashion. I landed on the ground with a nasty thump and winced. Struggling upright, I leaned my back against the dumpster, my heart racing, and pulled my knees up to my chest.

"Hey," said Maddox, crouching next to me. He leaned forward and tucked a piece of hair behind my ear. Nope. He didn't do that. He actually just extracted what appeared to be a piece of lettuce from my hair. His nostrils flaring, he mashed his lips together to prevent the laughter from escaping as he flung it away. "Are you okay?"

"Don't laugh." I looked him over, noting his black suit pants and open collared blue shirt, the sleeves rolled up. I sniffed. He smelled great. Fresh. Whatever was emanating from me smelled like shit. I really hoped it wasn't.

"I'm not laughing," he said, his face contorting.

"I could have been eaten in there."

"By what?"

"I don't know. Check."

Maddox looked up. "No."

"Why not?"

"If there's something alive in there, I don't want to know what it is."

I rolled my eyes.

"Are you okay?" he asked again.

"I think so," I mumbled, still stunned. First from Maddox appearing out of nowhere, then from falling backwards into a stinking dumpster populated with something alive besides me. Then from Maddox pulling me out and landing unceremoniously on the ground. It was hard to know what stunned me the most.

"What are you doing here?" he asked.

All I could do was blink at him. Then I realized how much I hurt. "Ow," I muttered as I pushed onto my feet. I leaned over, brushing my jeans, and was glad my flat pumps managed to stay on my feet. Not that it helped with the strange stains around my knees. I didn't even want to think what they were. I checked my exposed lower arms and face. No cuts or scratches. Hurrah!

"How did you know about this place?" Maddox asked. He handed me a tissue and I wiped my hands before returning it to him. Unsurprisingly, he shook his head so I tossed it over my shoulder and into the dumpster. There was a squeak and some scrabbling as we stared at each other, wondering who would acknowledge it first. However, neither of us volunteered.

Then I remembered Maddox asked me a question. "What do you mean?" I asked.

"How did you know?" he asked again. He nodded to the camera above the door. "You looked directly at the camera."

"Of course I did! It's a security camera and the light was blinking so the feed was live!" I snapped angrily. What was he talking about? How did I know about this place?

"So... you don't know?"

"Know what?" Now I was getting annoyed. I was filthy. I stank. And Maddox was talking in riddles.

"Ahh." Maddox rocked back on his heels like everything had just become crystal clear to him. It was all right for some! "Listen," he said, taking my elbow and steering me towards my car. "Forget you came here. Forget you saw anything. You can't come back."

"Huh?" We came to a standstill at my car. I tugged my keys from my pocket, grateful they hadn't fallen out.

"You were lucky I saw you when I did. I just got off my break and was passing the security monitor when I saw you standing outside. I don't know how I'm going to explain this to my boss."

"Your boss?"

"If this is part of a case, I'll need to see your case file," he said.

"It's not," I told him, the stunned feeling gradually ebbing away. *What had I stumbled onto?* "That is, I was checking several buildings in the area."

"Yes, I heard a report that someone was driving around, snooping. That was you?"

I shrugged and something slimy dropped to the floor. "Must be. No one else is around except you and me and..." I stepped to one side, gazing at the building behind Maddox. "Is this a black site?" I asked, my eyes widening as he gulped. "It is, isn't it? What are you doing, Adam?"

"Nothing. Like I said, you didn't see anything. What were you looking for, if not for me?"

"A tank." It slipped out before I had a chance to engage my brain.

Maddox blinked. "A what now?"

"A tank." I started to mime driving a car, then honking a car horn before realizing I had no idea how people drove tanks or even if tanks had horns. "Never mind. Have you seen a tank around here?" I asked.

"No," he said decisively.

"Can you ask the people inside? The ones whom you want me to forget I saw?"

"Uh..." He sighed as he shook his head. "I'll ask."

"Thank you." I took another long look at him. "That's a very nice shirt. It brings out your eyes."

"You bought it."

"I have great taste."

"You can't sweet talk me into mobilizing the FBI to locate a tank for you."

I gave him an indignant look. "It was just a compliment. It *is* a nice color."

"That's why I wear it. Lexi, it's important you don't come back. If you need something, call me. You don't look injured. Are you injured?" His eyes roamed over me. Then a sliver of something slipped off my capped sleeve and onto the floor. Both of us had the good grace not to look it. Well, I only glanced from the side of my eye at what looked like green salami. That knowledge didn't fill me with joy.

"Only my pride," I decided.

"I don't imagine your insurance covers that anymore. I'll check in on you later, okay? But it's best you leave. Now." Maddox took my keys, beeped the car open and gave me a gentle push inside. He handed me the keys. "Nice seeing you," he said before shutting the door.

I waited for him to go back inside but he took a couple paces backwards and waited with his arms folded.

Something else occurred to me as I revved the engine. I rolled down the window and stuck my head out. "You pulled a gun on me!" I yelled at him.

"You're lucky I didn't shoot it!" he yelled back.

"You still pulled a gun on me! You said you knew it was me!"

He stepped closer, stooping down, and lowered his voice. "I didn't say I told anyone else it was you! Do not tell anyone what you saw here. Or even that you saw me here. Now go!"

"Fine," I snipped as I tore out of the parking lot, one eye on Maddox's reflection in the mirror. I didn't even bother rolling the window up. It made sense to keep it open all the way home. That way I wouldn't pass out from the clinging scent of Eau de Eww!

~

"Lexi?" Solomon's voice sounded up the stairs followed by a series of footsteps.

I pushed my toe at the faucet one last time and the water shut off. Sinking back into the bubbles, I closed my eyes. I was not prepared for whatever conversation was upcoming.

"Lexi?" This time, his voice came from the doorway. Solomon leaned against the architrave, his arms folded across his chest.

I opened one eye, smiled, and shut my eye again.

"What is that smell?" he asked.

"What smell?" I countered.

"I thought it was our neighbor's dog but I don't think so."

"Why would it be our neighbor's dog?"

"Because he's asleep at the foot of the stairs. The dog, not Aidan."

"Wha..." I gave up. There was no point in asking. My neighbor's dog was a service animal and supposed to be Aidan's ears since he was deaf. The dog was also a canine Houdini that had managed to break into my house several times. I hadn't been able to ascertain how and I was pretty sure the dog was too smart to leave an obvious trail. "Never mind. Neither of us know the answer to how he got in."

"One of these days, I'll find out, and then I'm going to stop that dog. It still doesn't explain the smell; but since the washing machine is running and you look a little wrinkled, I'm guessing that it has something to do with you."

My eyes shot open. "Did you just call me wrinkled?"

"Bath wrinkled."

I contemplated getting out, then decided against it. Solomon could still smell me. I could still smell me. "It might have something to do with me," I sighed as I closed my eyes again.

Solomon walked across the bathroom, perched on the edge of the tub and gently flicked water at me until I opened my eyes.

"Fine, it has everything to do with me," I admitted.

"What happened?"

"I was out looking for the tank and fell into a dumpster."

"You know a tank won't fit inside a dumpster."

"I was aware of that. I was standing on a closed dumpster, looking through a window when I got surprised and fell into the one next to it."

"What surprised you?"

"Maddox pulling a gun on me," I said without thinking. The air around me stilled and electricity charged the atmosphere. I glanced up at Solomon and noticed the tautness of his face, the hard steel of his eyes.

"He threatened you?" he said in a low, calm voice, the kind he usually reserved for someone he was really angry with when he didn't want to betray his annoyance.

"I think it was more of a show for whomever else was watching."

"Who else was watching?"

I should have seen that question coming. "I don't know," I said. "There was a security camera over the door. I thought the warehouses in that area were all abandoned."

"Where?"

"The industrial park out by West Montgomery. The one that had all the land rent issues a while back."

"I know the one. And Maddox was there?"

"I'm not supposed to tell anyone," I told him. "He asked me not to say anything but he didn't say 'promise' so technically, it's okay that I'm telling you."

"I'm not worried about the technicalities," said Solomon. "I'm glad you told me. Why didn't you call me?"

"I thought coming home and taking a bath was the best course of action. Next step is burning my car."

Solomon nodded thoughtfully but didn't disagree. "You know the tub at my house is bigger," he said, flicking some more water at me.

"Umm-hmm." I waited for more; Solomon would no doubt have many compelling arguments about why we should we return to his oversized, elegant house in Chilton. It was bigger, for one thing, with a stunningly designed eat-in kitchen and a tub that could easily fit two. There were more bedrooms than my little bungalow's two bedrooms. The yard was lushly landscaped. The exterior wasn't yellow but instead, a beautifully hued brick. The area was nicer. Yet, despite all those things, I couldn't get past the thought that he might have died there in the doorway of that house. No assassins tried to kill him here. Well, there was that one time when someone broke in and tried to kill me but that wasn't the point. I managed to deal with that fairly efficiently. Did it make a difference that I could protect myself then but I couldn't protect Solomon that day? That was something to think about.

"Just saying," he said, leaning over to kiss me on the lips. "Enjoy the bath. Take your time. I'll make dinner."

I smiled, partly relieved that he hadn't tried to convince me to move, and partly because I realized how hungry I was. "Thank you."

Once the water started to cool, I emptied the tub, turned on the shower attachment and washed my hair one more time. Then I got out, dressed in my current favorite elephant-printed pajamas and made my way downstairs. The dog had gone, thankfully, but then, so too apparently had Solomon. The kitchen was empty but for a bubbling pot on the stove. I lifted the lid and inhaled deeply. Chorizo and chickpeas formed the basis of a delicious smelling stew and there was a fresh baguette on the counter ready to slide into the oven.

"John?" I called out as I turned and walked out of the kitchen. Two minutes later, I scoured downstairs.

Solomon was nowhere to be seen. I looked through the living room windows and couldn't see his car.

My cell phone began to ring so I darted into the entryway, grabbing it from the console. It wasn't Solomon, it was Maddox.

"Hi," I said, narrowly avoiding calling him "jerk!"

"I'm sorry," said Maddox. "I shouldn't have pulled a gun on you but if I'd had any choice in the matter, I wouldn't have."

"That sounded like an apology but also not an apology."

"Please take it as an apology. I really am sorry for scaring you."

"You didn't scare me. You surprised me."

"I noticed."

"I needed three baths and two showers," I told him. "My car needs detailing."

"I will pay for it."

"So what's up at the black site that I don't know about?" I asked. I couldn't help it. Tell me that I'm not supposed to know something and the first thing I want to know is everything about it.

"There isn't any black site," said Maddox predictably.

"Huh," I snorted. "Are you torturing people?"

"No! The FBI doesn't do that!"

"You know I'll find out."

"There's nothing to find out. Really, Lexi. There's no story here."

"Yeah," I said skeptically, "I believe you."

"Okay, fine, it has to do with work. It's an operations and storage facility for the project I'm working on. That's as much as I'm telling you and I'm only telling you that because I don't want you digging in your heels and getting into more trouble, the kind I can't bail you out of. My boss isn't keen on nosy visitors. Can we leave it at that?"

"You would tell me if you were in trouble, wouldn't you?" I asked, growing worried now.

"Yes, but I'm a professional and I can get myself out of trouble. You know that."

"I do."

"And there's no way I'd put you in harm's way. I told Solomon that too."

I paused. "When did you see Solomon?"

"He left my place five minutes ago?"

I frowned hard. "What was he doing at your place?"

"He was waiting for me when I got home. Just sitting on my couch like he belonged there. He even opened a beer. Then he read me the riot act and left."

"Wow." I wasn't sure what to say. Solomon hadn't looked that pissed when he announced he was going to make dinner.

"I don't appreciate him breaking into my apartment but I think he understood you weren't in any danger."

"I will reiterate that to him," I said, not eager to determine the rights and wrongs of what Solomon had just done. Solomon and Maddox didn't have the easiest relationship, and a large part of that was owing to me, but usually, they had a grudging respect for each other.

"There's one more thing. I asked around about a tank and there was a very large vehicle that passed through the area in the early hours three days ago. It didn't stop at any warehouse in the industrial park that we're aware of. I hope that helps."

"Thanks," I said. "That does help."

"Talk soon," said Maddox and we hung up. I dropped the cell phone back on the console and returned to the kitchen to check on the stew Solomon left cooking while he undertook his mission to menace my ex. A few minutes later, my fiancé walked in the door and strode into the kitchen.

"You're dry," he said, approaching me from behind. He wrapped his arms around me, dropped a small bag onto the counter, and kissed my neck. "Are you hungry?"

"Where have you been?" I asked.

"We were out of butter," he said, pointing to the bag. "I wanted to turn that baguette into garlic bread."

"Did you break into Maddox's apartment and threaten him?" I asked, cutting directly to the question I wanted to ask.

"He was on the way to the grocery store so I thought I'd pay him a visit," he replied without missing a beat. He probably wasn't even surprised that I knew already.

"Maddox described it as breaking and entering."

"Such a tattletale," Solomon whispered against my neck.

"I appreciate the sentiment of protecting me but I don't believe Maddox would have shot me. He was putting on a show for his superiors. You know that as well as I do."

"All the same," said Solomon. He released me and went to work on the baguette, slicing it part way into sections and placing it on a baking pan. I handed him a couple cloves of garlic and he mashed it with the butter before rolling it into a sausage shape and then slicing discs to insert into the bread.

"You do remember I'm marrying you, don't you?" I asked.

Solomon smiled. "I do."

"And I can take care of myself?"

"I know... although... the elephant pajamas don't foster unequivocal faith." He tweaked my collar and I playfully swatted his hand away. "You didn't tell me if you found the tank."

"I didn't find it," I confessed. "Lucas got a sighting of it in that area but when I poked around, I saw no evidence of it ever being there. Maddox made inquiries too and he said a vehicle that could have been a tank transporter was seen passing through the area in the early hours of the morning but they weren't aware of it stopping."

"You're building a trail. That's good. Keep looking. It'll turn up."

"If it isn't already out of state."

"Strange route to choose if they wanted to take the tank across state lines."

"Good point," I agreed. "All signs currently point to the tank being hidden in the local area. Perhaps if I knew why it was stolen, I'd be able to calculate where it is, although I don't mind if where comes first."

"A task for tomorrow," said Solomon. He inserted the baking tray into the oven and closed the door. Then he lifted the lid of the pan and stirred gently while the delicious aroma filled the air. "Ten minutes," he said.

"What shall we do for ten minutes?" I wondered aloud.

Solomon smiled, circled his arms around my waist and tugged me closer. "I can think of one or two things."

"We only have time for one," I murmured against his lips.

"That's what you think," he said and winked.

CHAPTER NINE

By the time I woke up the next morning, Solomon had already left and my elephant pajamas were folded in a neat pile next to the bed. On top of them was a note that read "Love you." Smiling, I tucked the note away in my nightstand, went about my morning routine and headed to work.

I spent a large part of the day at my desk wading my way through the digital data Lucas collected from multiple sources. When I wasn't viewing footage of empty streets at night, I was bent over several maps, attempting to identify where the tank might be. There was no evidence to suggest the tank had left Montgomery but so far, I had no indication of where it could be. It seemed like—poof!—it literally disappeared.

Finally, I picked up the phone and placed a call. "Any sign of it?" Harris asked.

"There was a sighting but I hit a dead end," I told him. "Any chatter on your end?"

I heard the sound of a chair scraping, footsteps, then a door closing. "None, and so far, no one else has noticed it's gone but I don't know how long until someone finds out," said Harris when he came back on the line. "Shit's gonna get real when someone notices and then I'm a dead man."

"Literally?"

"Metaphorically. Kafsky isn't thrilled either but I'm the captain so I'll have to suck it up. Most likely, I'll get court-martialed, imprisoned, or dishonorably discharged. I don't like any of those options."

"That's understandable." A thought occurred to me. "Has the tank transporter turned up?"

"Yes. It's parked behind the hangar like usual."

"And it's the same one?"

"We don't exactly have a fleet of them. But yeah, the license plate is the same. I already checked."

"So someone returned it after stealing the tank," I mused. "Is there a regular driver?"

"Yeah, but he only blew into Fort Charles with the tank. He's based somewhere west. I think I told you his name is Simmons but I'll need to make sure of it."

"Can you find out if he was driving it the night the tank disappeared? Perhaps he got an order to move it and doesn't realize he was participating in a theft?"

"You mean someone treated him like a stooge? I guess that could happen. I'll look deeper into it," Harris agreed.

"Be careful. If Simmons was the driver that night, then he definitely knows the tank is gone. If he's not in on it, he might inadvertently reveal that fact. If he is in on it, he might drop you into it if things get hot."

"So, I'm still in trouble either way?"

"'Fraid so."

"I'll proceed with caution. Do you have any good news?"

"Yes. I'm pretty sure the *you know what* came through Chester and into Montgomery. I have the sighting coming into town, but nothing with regard to leaving. It's here somewhere."

"Why would they stick it in your town? Why not load it up on an aircraft or transport it out of state?"

"I wondered that too," I told him. "Perhaps the sale hasn't been negotiated yet or the thief is waiting for any alerts to die down before they move it."

"No one knows it's missing yet. There is no heat."

"Good point. Call me back when you speak to Simmons. Be discreet."

"Of course. I'm not going to stroll up to him and shout 'yo, where's my tank?!'"

I suspected that was exactly the sort of thing Harris would say, which was why I suggested he be discreet.

"Hey, why don't you speak to Simmons? A group of us are off base later today and heading into Montgomery. I could make sure he comes along and you can interview him?"

"Why can't you?" I asked.

"He's more likely to spill to a pretty girl than he is to me. Plus, it can't come back on me if I'm not the one asking the questions."

"Yet another good point."

"Plus, I'm paying you."

"That's where your good points end. You paid me ten bucks," I reminded him.

"And a Butterfinger," Harris reminded me. "And a bunch of other good stuff too."

"Fine. I'm working at my friend's bar tonight. I'll reserve you a table and you can bring your buddies."

"Is it a good bar?"

"It's very popular."

"I mean..."

I rolled my eyes. "Yes, there are ladies."

"Reputable?"

"The tank, Harris. You're married," I said sternly. "Keep your mind on the tank."

"Gotcha. And the ladies aren't for me. They're to entice the guys into heading off base. Send me the address of the bar and I'll make sure we're there."

As soon as we hung up, I called Lily at the bar and asked her to reserve a table. "Your infamous Army buddies," she breathed when I explained, her excitement almost lost in the awe. "I cannot wait."

"You can't tell anyone I went to boot camp with some of them. I'm undercover."

"Well, damn. I have a list of questions to ask them about your time in service."

"How can you have a list? I only just told you they would be there." Already, I regretted it. Why did I pick Lily's bar? Why didn't I say I would meet them somewhere else later?

"I started compiling an inventory from when you enlisted. I have a lot of questions."

"I can answer whatever questions you have?"

"Okay. What was the craziest thing you did when in boot camp?"

I thought about it, winced and decided that was a story I'd never tell. "Nothing. I was a model cadet," I lied.

Lily made a rude noise. "Okay. How about this? Did you get up to any inappropriate behavior while in training?"

"None whatsoever." Also a story—no, *stories*—that I would never tell. Not even to my best friend.

"If I offer free drinks, will I hear anything that will shock me?"

I thought about that for a whole second. "Do not, under any circumstances, offer free drinks."

"I knew it," she said. "Tell them the first pitcher of beer is on the house. Don't be late. You need to get into your uniform before the engagement party starts. If you're going undercover, you have to look the part."

"What uni... Lily? Lily!" Lily had already hung up. "Terrific," I muttered. The uniform couldn't be that bad. I'd been in Lily's many times, and helped out on occasions too, but she never made me wear anything awful before. One time, however, I made her wear the butt end of a plush pony costume so there was always a chance she was secretly waiting to get me back for that.

Julia and her fiancé, Bryce, didn't seem the type to ask for any party theme that would be considered truly horrific so Lily was probably just messing with me. Or was she? Once or twice I suspected Lily was an evil genius and this could have been one of those times since I was now in a worried state.

With only an hour to go until I was due at the bar, I didn't have anymore time for fruitless searching for the magical disappearing tank. Admitting defeat, for the day anyway, I packed my work things away and headed for my freshly detailed car.

There was a small area reserved for parking behind Lily's bar and I managed to squeeze my car in between Lily's car and a rust bucket that I was pretty sure belonged to Ruby, our friend and Lily's most trusted employee. I entered through the back door and could already hear soft music drifting from the bar and the noisy buzz of the arriving post-work crowd.

"Great! You're here!" said Lily. She stuck her head out of her office and grinned.

"You told me not to be late."

"I didn't think you'd take me seriously. You can't wear that," she said, waving a hand over my jeans and blouse. "This bar is sexy chic, not..." She wrinkled her nose, her brain clearly ticking over as she searched for a word.

I looked down. Yes, the blouse was the wrong color for Lily's employees and so were the jeans. Ruby was wearing black jeans so that was promising. "What's wrong with what I'm wearing?"

"It's not going to increase your tips."

"I'm not working for big tips. I'm working strictly for information."

"Can I have her tips?" asked Ruby as she walked past and disappeared into the stock room. A moment later, she emerged with a bucket of lemons.

"How good are the tips likely to be?" I asked, growing curious.

"Zero if you're dressed in that. Pretty good if you wear our new cocktail waitress uniform," said Lily.

"That's sexist."

"It's not that bad," said Lily. "You get to wear a bra."

"I've seen the outfits you wore in those weird bars you used to work at. Your baseline for 'not that bad' is different to everyone else's."

"True, but all the same, you need to fit in." Lily motioned for me to follow her. I stepped into the room as she reached for a hanger, which she offered to me.

"Oh, that's okay," I said, looking at the black short-sleeved t-shirt with Lily's Bar emblazoned across the front, and smart shorts with a cute, little, turned-up cuff on the leg.

"Heels," said Lily, handing me a pair of high black heels.

"These are mine," I said.

"I know. Good thing I hung onto them. They'll look great with the uniform. You can change in here or in the bathroom. I have to run out and make sure the private room is ready for the party." With that, she was gone, leaving me alone. I nudged the door shut and wriggled out of my jeans and blouse before pulling on the uniform. It was a little snug and clung to all the right places and not too badly in the wrong ones. Thankfully, my body image was perfectly fine and I didn't care if someone else thought I had the "wrong" bits so long as I thought I was the bomb. Also, in my years of temping, I learned to perfect the death stare, which I reserved for any givers of inappropriate comments.

Fortunately, I was wearing trainer socks so I didn't have any elastic impressions to rub off my ankles as I slid on the heels. I folded my clothes onto the chair in the corner, brushed my hair and added a fresh swipe of lipstick. Tips might not be the main objective, but if they came along with the information, I was sure I could put the cash to good use.

"All good with the party room?" I asked when Lily returned with a camera in hand.

"It looks very chic. I had to take a few photos for the events page of the website. The more people see stuff like this, the more they'll want to book parties here too," she beamed. "Bryce came by earlier with all the decorations and helped us set up. He said he wanted it to look perfect for Julia and their guests and it does!"

"That was nice of him."

"I thought so too. Often the client just shoves a box of stuff at us and leaves us to it. And you know what else? He brought a drill with him and fixed those wobbly shelves," she said pointing to the shelves behind her desk, "and he fixed my desk chair so the arm stops falling off. I was so pleased."

"That is nice," I agreed.

"I hope this investigation you're doing turns out okay. So far, he's been a really nice guy. I would hate to think there's any issues for him with Julia."

"I'm sure I'll find out tonight. Did Bryce say who was coming?"

"He gave me a copy of the guest list and it looks like everyone they invited can still come even though the venue change was on short notice. There's his family, her family, a bunch of their friends and some co-workers. We'll be at full capacity in the private room. Then a bunch of the booths and tables in the main bar are reserved for other groups too. I know you're here primarily to investigate but we're going to be busy serving tonight."

"I can handle it. This is not my first bar job." It wasn't even my tenth but if we went into that, Lily might remind me how many bars had fired me. "Hey, have you heard anything weird lately?"

She raised an eyebrow. "I'm a bartender. Sixty percent of what I hear is weird."

"Does it involve tanks?"

"Is that a sex thing?"

I frowned. "No. Is it?"

"I hope not!"

"I mean an actual tank. The kind the Army uses."

"Then, no, I haven't heard anything about a tank. If you want to hear a story about a chipmunk, a family-sized bottle of ketchup, and a naked guy, I have one of those stories."

I thought about it, seriously considered it, then replied, "No, thanks."

"What about the one with three socks, an eggplant and a bunch of frat guys?"

I blinked. "Nooo."

"What about..."

"No!"

"Then no," said Lily, shaking her head. "I have no stories for you."

That was a relief, although there was the strong possibility I would want to know all about those stories later. Sometimes, curiosity got the best of me and made me hear things I couldn't unhear but by then it was too late. I'm filled with unwanted knowledge. "Where do you want me?" I asked. "I can help with the set-up."

"Can you grab snacks from the stockroom and put them on the tables in the private room? I'm going to put out the ice buckets and glasses for the champagne toasts."

"Fancy!"

"Bryce said to me that he didn't want to spare any expense for the engagement party of a lifetime but I talked him into wine and cocktails rather than free-flowing champagne all night. Plus, I'm throwing the snacks in for free, given how much booze they're buying and they bringing their own cake. You should see it. Bryce showed me a photo. It's three tiers of sugar roses. So romantic!"

"It does sound romantic. It sounds like it will be a great party."

"I hope so and good for business too if they tell all their friends." The phone on Lily's desk began to ring so I left her to answer it and went into the stockroom to collect the snacks she set out. I began emptying tubs of chips and nuts into little dishes and when I had a tray full of dishes, I carried them all through to the private room.

"Hey, let me get that for you," said a man as I tried to wedge the door open with my elbow while balancing the tray.

"Thanks!" I chirped, steadying the tray as he grabbed the door and pushed it open.

"I thought you were going to topple over," he said. I looked up, smiling, and my breath caught. It was Bryce Maynard. "We've met before, haven't we?" he asked, looking down at me.

"Yes, at the bridal boutique," I said. "This is your party tonight? I remember Julia mentioning something about it."

"It is. I thought I'd get here early and check over a few things before our guests arrive."

"Is your fiancée here already?"

"No, Julia will be here in a half hour. She's not great on the little details so she's finishing her makeup."

"We girls have to look great if we're going to be the center of attention," I said, preening slightly. The more vacuous he thought I was, the better for gleaning information.

Bryce gave me a long look from head to toe and back again. "I bet you're the center of attention a lot," he said.

I gulped back mild discomfort at the flattery. Instead, I winked and said, "You know it."

"Do you need a hand with this stuff?" He waved his hand over the tray.

I set it down on the nearest table and shook my head. "I've got it, thanks. Let me know if I can help you with anything else?" As I busied myself setting out the snack bowls, arranging them neatly beside the pretty floral centerpieces that were already on the tables, I kept an eye on Bryce. He walked around the room, seemingly oblivious to me, and checked out the table set-ups while contemplating the position of the bar. A balloon arch was set up against one wall and he examined the props that were arranged for the purpose of photography. It was a cute idea that I thought the guests would enjoy. Once or twice, I thought I saw him watching me but he didn't say anything. As I was putting out the last of the dishes, Bryce got a phone call, left, then returned a few minutes later with a large cake box.

"Where should I put this?" he asked. "It's the cake."

"I think Lily put a table out for it next to the bar."

"Can you give me a hand with it?" he asked. "I'm afraid of dropping it and I'm not the kind of person that's great at putting a cake in its proper place. I must have missed that class in school!" He laughed at his own joke.

"Sure." I walked across the room, aware Bryce's eyes were on me the whole time. I couldn't shake the feeling there was something not quite right about the way he looked at me. Not unfriendly, perhaps a little too friendly, but with something else too. Greed, I realized, and entitlement. I didn't like it.

Then he turned to unpack the cake and the uncomfortable moment was gone. With the sides of the cake box down, I could see Lily was right. The cake was beautiful and very much like a wedding cake with delicate sugar roses cascading down every side.

"This is beautiful," I breathed.

"Julia loved it but it wasn't her first choice for wedding cake so I thought I'd surprise her with it for an engagement cake instead."

"That's very thoughtful."

"I know most guys would go for something humorous but I think there's a time and place for that and this party isn't it."

"I'm sure she won't mind you having a groom's cake at the wedding."

"I will tell her you said that! Are you working the party tonight?"

"Yes, Lily says it will be busy so I'll be serving at the bar here and helping your guests with whatever they need."

"Make sure to take a break. Those heels cannot be comfortable all night," he said, taking a long look at my legs.

"I will be sure to do that," I said.

Bryce leaned in and said in a conspiratorial voice, "Just in case I need to take a break from all the fun, where can I hide?"

"There's a small smoking area out the back for patrons but it's not exactly a hiding area," I told him.

He laughed. "No, I guess not. I'll find somewhere. There, I think the cake looks good. No tasting," he teased, nudging me with his elbow. "Hey, guys!" he called out as someone behind us squealed his name. He walked towards them, reaching out his arms, all wide smiles and compliments.

I grabbed the empty cake box and dodged out of the room just as Lily arrived carrying the ice buckets, with Ruby on her heels bearing a tray of cocktails for the first guests. By the time I returned to tend bar, Julia, in her rosy pink dress, and twenty more guests arrived, ensuring I was busy serving, pouring glasses of wine and cocktails, smiling and thanking guests for all the bills they added to the tip jar.

At first, I didn't have chance to do anything but serve but I did get to see all the guests, taking extra care to ask their names and how they knew the newly engaged couple. Most people were happy for any small talk, describing how they knew the couple and how excited they were for the party and the eventual wedding. In between serving, I kept an eye on Bryce but he barely looked my way except to raise his glass once, when he smiled and nodded before turning back to his conversation. He buzzed around the different groups, charming and laughing, clinking glasses, slapping backs of guys and cheek-kissing ladies, always gravitating back to Julia. Out of the two, she was definitely the quieter but they looked at each other with such sweetness, it was hard to remind myself why I was there.

"What do you think?" said Jas. She stood next to the bar, half turned to me, half watching the crowd. I didn't see her come in.

"It's a great party."

"It is. And him?" She nodded towards Bryce.

I recalled the way he looked at me earlier, like I was a body for the taking. I brushed the thought away. What person didn't look at the opposite sex? It wasn't like he made any lascivious comments, plus, I could have been mistaken. "He's very attentive," I said. "And he's put a lot of thought into the party."

"You say *thought*, I say controlling. Everything always has to be perfect for him."

"It is an engagement party," I pointed out. My engagement party was held in the same room and it was perfect too but I didn't need to mention that.

"Hey," said Ruby, sliding behind the bar. "Lexi, it's your break. You have been running off your feet."

"I've hardly left the bar," I admitted.

"Lily said I should take over and after you've taken your break, you can circulate."

"Perfect. I'll be right back," I told Jas. "I need to take off my shoes for a few minutes."

She nodded, then plastered a bright smile on her face and waved to the giggling group of women a few paces away. "We'll talk later," she said. "I almost don't want you to find anything. I prefer to be wrong about him."

"What's that about?" asked Ruby.

"I'm investigating the groom," I told her as softly as I could while no one approached the bar. "She's a friend of the bride and she has a bad feeling about him."

"About Bryce? He's great!"

"Lily mentioned he helped you out."

"He did. What does Julia's friend think he's done?"

"Not sure yet," I said. "But keep your ears open. I'm going to take that break."

I was glad Jas was in that mind set of wanting to be proven wrong because unless I did hear something soon, it was likely I would have to tell her I refused to investigate any further. I excused myself from the bar as a couple approached and left Ruby to serve them. I escaped from the room, quickly ducked my head into the main bar—no sign of my Army buddies yet—and then hurried to Lily's office before anyone else saw me. Inside, I shut the door and tugged off my heels, dropping into the chair. It wasn't exactly the employee break room, but at least I had a chance to think quietly and... words drifted through the open window along with the acrid scent of cigarette smoke.

"Bryce is too good for Julia, you know," said a female voice. "I don't know what he sees in her. I mean... He's hot and she's... not. She's like a timid, little mouse. *Yes, Bryce; no, Bryce.*"

"You mean, you don't know why he isn't marrying you," said the second woman.

"Bitch!" The pair giggled.

I eased off the chair and tiptoed to the open window above my head. The lights were off and they must have assumed the room was empty.

"Does she know you and I and he used to..." There was more laughter.

"No! Apparently, Julia saw some text messages once but he dismissed it and told her not to think anymore of it. They were old messages anyway."

"She was snooping on his phone? Lame!"

"I don't know. I didn't ask. Anyway, it's not like she could ever get rid of me. Bryce and I have been friends since high school."

"And screwing every few years in between his relationships and yours."

My eyes widened. I pushed up as far as I could go, holding onto the shelf for support.

"Yeah... well... and sometimes during." They laughed again. "All I can say is he was mine first and if she doesn't hold onto him, we both know he'll waltz right back to me. It wouldn't be the first time. He can't keep his hands off me."

"Oh! Did you and he..."

I gripped the shelf, alarmed at what I heard. Two fat books tumbled off the shelf and crashed to the floor. Outside, the voices stopped, then there was some whispering and a door opened and closed, the hinges squeaking. Any moment now, they would walk past the office on their way to the bar. I edged over to the door, easing it open as two sets of footsteps hurried past. I pulled the door open but all I had time to see was a flash of blond hair and black cocktail dresses, which narrowed down the women to at least thirty percent of the guests. I couldn't deny what I'd heard. Both of them knew Bryce was a cheater but was he cheating on Julia now?

CHAPTER TEN

"Hey, are you okay?" asked Ruby when I returned. Instead of immediately grabbing a tray and circulating among the guests, I slipped behind the bar alongside her. She poured the last of the champagne into a glass and tossed the bottle into the trashcan hidden behind the bar, then reached for another. "We need to circulate with these because there's going to be a toast soon. I know Lily said you wanted to talk to the guests and I don't mind handing out the drinks if you need to be hands-free."

"I'm fine."

"You look a little pale."

"You know when you hear something you're not supposed to hear and it surprises you?"

"Ahh. All the time." She nodded knowingly.

"Hey, do you remember when Bryce helped you out with a creepy customer?" I said, moving my eyes from

Ruby to his direction. She discreetly followed my glance.

"Sure, he's a regular."

"What do you think of him?"

Ruby beamed. "He's the sweetest! He comes in with three of his buddies, those two guys in the corner with the blue shirts," she added, nodding towards two men of slightly shorter heights but similar builds to Bryce. "I haven't seen the other guy they hang out with but I think I heard he's going through something with his wife and couldn't make it."

"What are Bryce and his buddies like when they're here? Have you ever seen him with another woman?"

"He talks to women and he's a good tipper so all the bartenders like serving him. I don't think I've ever seen him hitting on anyone though, if that's what you mean."

That was exactly what I meant. "Never?"

"No. His dark-haired buddy however—the one on the left—now he's got no problem chatting up the ladies. Bryce and the other guys just let him get on with it or act as his wingmen occasionally. You know, we were all really pleased when Bryce and his fiancée got together."

"Why's that?"

"He had such a rough relationship before. I overheard him talking with the guys once when they were sitting at the bar and he was discussing his ex. They'd been together two years or something and she just threw him out of the house one day. No warning or anything! He was telling his friends that he never really noticed how she was getting crazier and crazier about even the littlest things so he should have seen that kind of behavior coming, but he loved her so much, he just hoped she would seek help for her problems instead of blaming them on him."

"You remember all of that?" I asked, wondering exactly how long she listened in.

"Well, sure. It was a quiet night, they were seated at the bar, and he seemed so upset."

"Do you remember who the girl was?"

Ruby wrinkled her nose. "Jessica something, or Jessie, maybe. I don't remember her at all so I doubt I ever met her."

"Do you know if she could be here tonight?" I asked, thinking about the conversation I overheard. Was one of the women in black dresses Jessica or Jessie? Or was the woman who so casually detailed her flings with Bryce someone else?

"No, I don't think so. I don't think I'd recognize her anyway. Like I said, I don't recall her ever coming into the bar with him. Anyway, who would invite the crazy ex?"

"Did he tell you anything else?"

"Well, he wasn't exactly telling me, but I could hear so... he said she started accusing him of stuff and it was like she believed all the crap she made up. Then one of his buddies—I don't remember which one—said he noticed she was getting cold and had stopped bothering with them all; he said it was disappointing but Bryce was better off not dealing with that shit. I agreed with him."

"Did you tell him that?" I asked.

"Oh, yeah. I said he should move on and not dwell on the past. What was done was done and he needed to make himself happy. It was the first time he cracked a smile that night. A month or so later, he met Julia."

"Only a month later?"

"Yeah. I told him that I knew there was someone decent around the corner for him and he should move on and never look back. Now look at them!" Ruby grinned as Bryce leaned in and kissed Julia on the lips to a smattering of applause. "I'm really pleased for him. He deserves some happiness after all the crap his ex put him through."

I watched the couple pull apart and beam at each other. Then Bryce lifted his glass and said he thought it was time for a proper toast and where was the champagne? he added, shooting a look toward the bar.

"That's us," said Ruby. "Grab a tray and start circulating while I put glasses on the bar."

I took the tray and weaved my way through the closest guests, making pleasantries and encouraging them to take a glass. After the speech was over, I planned on circulating again, but this time, I would have some subtle questions for the guests. So far, I had conflicting reports of Bryce. Jas thought he wasn't treating Julia properly; Lily and Ruby thought he was great. And me? The looks I got from him made me uncomfortable and I couldn't deny what I overheard.

Every time I returned to the bar, Ruby had a new tray ready for me and Lily eventually joined us, ensuring everyone had a glass in their hands within minutes and all the empties had disappeared.

Taking up my position behind the bar again, I waited for Bryce to finish raising and waving his arms, encouraging his guests to quiet down. "I just want to start by thanking Lily for graciously offering us this room for our engagement party... yes, thank you, thank you!" He laughed to the whistles and smattering of applause. "Lily, thank you again for saving our party. We don't know where we would be without you and we really appreciate it. As soon as I knew this room was free, I had to book it."

Lily smiled and waved while the guests applauded.

"I'm sure all of you know our story by now," Bryce continued. "This beautiful woman walked into my life and changed it in an instant. I got up that day, thinking it would be just another ordinary day at work. Nothing would happen. I would eat lunch at my desk. Go home, the usual stuff. Instead, when I was getting a sandwich from the cart outside my office, who should turn around and throw her smoothie down my shirt than this wonderful person?" He tucked his arm around Julia's shoulder and pulled her in while she blushed.

"I could have gotten mad but instead, I took one look at her and knew I had to ask her out to a dinner where they served the drinks in sippy cups. I'm kidding. I'm kidding! But I did ask her out to dinner and we laughed at her klutzy moment. I changed my shirt, of course, and she's never admitted that she threw that smoothie deliberately over me, but I think we both knew it was fate." Bryce paused, looking down at Julia with such reverence and love that it was like everyone else faded away around them. If I hadn't overheard that conversation only minutes before, I would have probably looked as thrilled as everyone else. Well, almost everyone else. The older gentleman in the corner with his arms crossed didn't look overly thrilled either.

"Who's that?" I asked Ruby.

"Who?"

"Arms crossed in the corner. Gray hair."

"The bride's dad. He got here while you were on break."

"I'm going to take him a drink," I said, noticing his empty hands.

"Okay, I'll be here sobbing at the speech." Ruby raised a tissue to her eye and dabbed carefully. I suppressed the urge to eye roll and grabbed a glass of champagne, placing it on a tray and maneuvering my way around the bar before walking over to the man.

"Can I offer you a drink, Mr. Atwater?" I asked, showing him the tray.

He glanced at me and shook his head. "No, thanks."

"Moving speech," I said, nodding to the couple. Bryce smoothly segued into a tale about their first date, which had the small crowd laughing.

"Umm-hmmm," said the man.

"I suppose he's not good enough for your little girl," I said, smiling to show I was teasing. Except I wasn't. Julia's father looked like he'd rather have been anywhere else but here.

This time, he looked directly at me and reached for a glass. "Damn right he's not."

"He seems to think a lot of your daughter." I moved to stand shoulder-to-shoulder with him, so we could both observe the couple.

"He's full of hot air. All talk, no substance. You notice how the story is really about him?" Mr. Atwater tipped his glass towards them. "He's not said one nice thing about her. Oh, I know it sounds funny and romantic but it's all in relation to him. She's beautiful but *he* got her. She spilled her drink but *he* didn't get mad.

He's not holding it against her but reminds her all the time she's a klutz. She's not, by the way. And if you ask me, what about this sudden need to get married after only a few months? Why so fast?" He looked directly at me, his forehead furrowed with worry lines before he seemed to remember himself. "I'm sorry. I didn't mean to say all that. Just forget it."

"Sir, I don't want to step out of line here, but have you spoken to your daughter about your concerns?"

Mr. Atwater sighed. "Yes, but she says I don't know what I'm talking about. Kids these days. They don't seem to realize even us old folks were young and romantic once!" He glanced across at me, a wry smile on his lips. "We couldn't admit our mistakes either."

"Is that what you think this is? A mistake?" I asked softly.

"I think if she marries him, it will be the biggest mistake of my daughter's life. Excuse me. I see my brother and his wife." He pulled his wallet from his pocket and dropped a twenty-dollar bill on the tray. "For your trouble," he said before walking away.

I palmed the bill and added it to the tip jar on the bar while I assessed the crowd. Bryce had just stopped talking and was receiving congratulations while insisting everyone take a look at the engagement ring flashing on Julia's hand. Plenty of backs were patted and air kisses exchanged before someone called for cake.

"Yes, cake," agreed Bryce loudly. He grabbed Julia's hand and raised it above their heads in a victory salute. "Honey, let's cut the cake. It'll be great practice for the wedding," he added to a roar of cheers. They moved their way through the guests, stopping at the cake table. I produced the knife Lily left under the bar for the cake cutting and handed it to Bryce's outreached hand before I turned away. I began looking for the cake plates and dessert forks Lily had to have left somewhere. The shelves under the bar were empty.

"Where are the plates?" I asked Ruby.

"Lily said to leave them in the stockroom. The plan is for them to make the first cut here and then we'll take the cake to the stockroom for proper slicing. There's an extra sheet cake for easier cutting too and we'll bring the plates back here."

"Makes sense," I agreed. Cutting the cake and distributing plates would be an unwieldy exercise given the lack of space on the bar. "Are the napkins in there..." I whipped around at the sound of a scream and a loud curse just in time to see the cake tumble from the table onto the floor where it smashed into the tastiest looking mess I'd ever seen.

"I don't know what happened," gasped Julia as she stared down at it and then at the frosting-covered knife in her hand. "I just cut it and there was a splintering sound..."

"It's all fine," said Bryce through gritted teeth. He took the knife from Julia and handed it to me. I looked at it and handed it to Ruby, which spared me from having to work out what to do with it that didn't involve licking it. "We can rescue this. Honey, some of the frosting is on your skirt. Why don't you go clean up?" He turned her around and gave her a gentle push towards the door. "See what I mean?" he laughed, shaking his head. "Such a klutz! No, it's okay, I've got this and we have another cake behind the scenes. Hold fast, people!" He smiled, laughed at something the man next to him said, and patted his shoulder. The tension seemed to diffuse quickly as Julia hurried from the room.

I grabbed a roll of paper towels and stooped down. "Don't worry about it," Bryce said, scooping up the two bottom layers from the smashed top layer, now upside down. "I'll handle it."

"Why don't you take that piece to the stockroom and I'll clear this up?" I replied. "You don't have to clean up. That's what we're here for."

"No, really. I should. My future wife made this mess."

"And she's probably very upset. Like you said, there's another cake in the back so don't worry about it."

Bryce hesitated. "If you're sure?"

"I'm sure," I said, waving him away as I began to clean up the cake mess.

"Thanks," he said gratefully. He balanced the cake and scooted from the room, holding it like it was the most precious cargo.

"Yikes," said Ruby as she dropped to her knees and reached for the paper towels. "Oh, look, the leg splintered," she said, pointing to the broken table leg peeking out from under the cloth. "I thought it was a bit wobbly earlier."

"We should take the table out and tell Lily. She might have to refund the cake since it's the table's fault."

"I feel really bad. I should have examined the table beforehand while we were setting up. Do you think I should go check on the rest of them?"

"No, just make sure everyone has plenty of drinks and forgets all about this. I'll go check on the couple and then I'll bring back as much sliced cake as I can carry. The sooner everyone starts eating and moves on from this, the better."

"What do I tell Lily?" wondered Ruby.

"The truth. It was a simple accident. It could have happened to anyone. There. I think the floor is clean." I grabbed the used towels and hurried out of the room, dropping them into the trashcan in the stockroom. Bryce had already left the cake in there but he was nowhere to be seen. I needed to wash my hands before I cut the cake so I walked over to the washroom. Just as I reached for the door, my hand on the knob, I heard voices inside.

"You stupid bitch. You couldn't even get that right!"

"I'm sorry, Bryce. I just pushed the knife and the cake collapsed. I don't know what happened!" Sobs sounded through the crack in the door.

"You must have pushed too hard! Now everyone is laughing at you," he snapped.

"They are?"

"I made a joke about it to try and defuse the situation but everyone knows you do stupid stuff like this all the time. Why do you think they don't want you around?"

"They... they don't?" Julia sniffed.

"I make excuses for you all the time. I tell them you're stressed or tired and you don't mean it but everyone can see through them. I keep thinking maybe if I pay you more attention or help you more often, things will improve but in reality what you need is a kick in the right direction. You're a grownup now, Julia. You need to act like it."

"I'm trying. You're right. I must have pushed too hard. I'm sorry, Bryce."

"And now you have cake down your dress. You're such a mess."

"I can clean it off with some water and a paper towel."

"My ex never did stuff like this. Why do you? Do you deliberately want to embarrass me? In front of our family and friends?"

"No, of course I don't!"

I jumped when a slap sound emanated from the room and my heart thumped. "Now look what you've done! I'm mad enough to hit the wall!" he growled.

"Please don't do that. You'll hurt yourself. Please don't be so mad at me! I really am sorry!"

"If you weren't such a clumsy shit, none of this would have happened. I spent a lot of time planning the perfect party for you. I do everything to make you happy and you can't even make an effort this one time."

"I'm so sorry. I really am. I'll try harder I promise."

"Clean yourself up and fix your makeup. I'm sure no one will mention the huge stain on your dress. People are polite like that," huffed Bryce.

"And you had the foresight to order the extra sheet cake. I think we should be careful about the drinks though. It's a lot of money to spend and we're supposed to be careful."

"Now you want to talk about money? I've told you, I'll pay you back but you're never satisfied," he sighed.

"I'm really sorry. Okay, Bryce? It won't happen again. I promise. And don't worry about the money. I'll pay for the party."

"I know you'll try harder, honey," he said, softly this time. "I just want everything to be perfect for us. You clean up. I'll go check on the cake." Footsteps started towards me and I darted back, letting go of the door. The closest room was the stockroom so I jogged into it and grabbed some more paper towels to clean my hands before I grabbed a knife and bent over the cake, like I'd been there the whole time. Plus, it gave me chance to cover my shocked face at the disgusting way Bryce addressed his fiancée.

"Oh, hi," Bryce said when he stepped inside. "Lexi, right? I didn't realize you were here. Julia is just using the employee washroom. I hope that's okay. She didn't want to walk through the bar to the restrooms."

"Sure!" I plastered a smile on my face. "That's no problem. I just started to cut the cake and I'll bring it through in a few minutes if you want to rejoin your guests. I can handle it from here!" I was probably too perky but he didn't seem to notice as he leaned against the doorframe.

"I bet you've never dropped a cake in your life," Bryce said, smiling now, his personality a contradiction to his shocking comments only moments before. "The way you carry all those glasses. It's a true skill."

"Thank you," I said, not sure if he was offering a compliment.

"And in heels too. How long have you worked here?"

"I just help out from time to time."

"What do you do for a regular job?"

"I'm a temp," I lied quickly. "I do office work."

Bryce pulled a card from his pocket and laid it on the table next to me. "We hire temps in the office all the time. If you ever need a job, give me a call. I'm sure I can set you up. Can you type? Answer the phones?" He flashed a broad smile full of white teeth. Where he had once looked friendly, he now looked like a crocodile, ready to snap my head off.

"Sure!"

"Then you're already a mile ahead of most our temps. I'll leave you to it, okay?"

"Great!" I hesitated, then added, "We checked the table the cake was standing on and the leg was splintered. I think that's why the cake fell. I'm sure Lily will cover the cost." If not, I would, but I couldn't let him think the smashed cake was Julia's fault. He'd been so angry and she apologized too many times for something that wasn't even her fault.

"That so? No harm done," he said, surprising me. "Don't mention it to Julia. She's upset enough. I'll take care of everything. Let's get that cake out to the guests as fast as we can though, okay?" He winked and stepped back out of the door, disappearing from view.

I set to work slicing cake and filling the plates as quickly as I could. After a couple of minutes, Julia dashed past the doorway. When I returned to the party room with my laden tray so Ruby and Lily could hand the plates out, the atmosphere had returned to the same jovial one it was before the cake incident.

After two more trips, all the cake was served and I took the moment to rest and observe the party from the bar. Bryce and Julia were hand-in-hand, smiling and chatting like nothing ever happened. Julia looked strained and her smile a little false, but Bryce seemed not to have a care in the world. Everyone was eating cake and the cake table had disappeared.

"Can I get another glass of wine?" asked Jas, approaching me with an empty glass in her hand.

"White or red?" I replied, taking the glass and replacing it with a fresh one.

"White. What do you think of the party?"

"Most everyone seems supportive," I said, thinking of the unidentified pair of women and Julia's father.

"Hmmm, yes." She leaned in, "and your impression of Bryce now?"

I paused for a moment, thinking. Alarm bells buzzed in my head all night. The way he spoke to his fiancée in private and her desperate apologies jarred with his public persona of Mr. Nice Guy. Was everyone taken in by him? Was it all just an act? "I'm taking the case," I said. "I've heard a few things tonight and I didn't like what I heard."

CHAPTER ELEVEN

After Jas returned to talk to her friends, I busied myself serving drinks and eavesdropping conversations but I didn't hear anything else that set off alarm bells. Mr. Atwater stood with other people so I couldn't pull him aside and ask for more information and there was no way to identify the two women I'd overheard. Too many female guests wore black dresses.

With time running out until the party ended, I called Lily and Ruby back to the bar. "Has either of you overheard anything about the couple this evening?" I asked. "Anything negative?"

They glanced at each other and shook their heads, then Ruby said, "I suppose I did hear this one thing about the bride-to-be."

"What was it?" I asked.

"It was nothing, really. I just overheard one of the guys saying Bryce always manages to pick the crazy girls. Then he said Julia was okay but she's always acted like a nervous wreck," said Ruby. "She is jumpy."

"I think she felt bad about the cake," said Lily. "I'll talk to them in a moment about that. It wasn't her fault that the table leg broke. I noticed it wobbled earlier but in the rush to get the room ready, I forget to swap the table out for another one."

"Can you both ask a few subtle questions?" I inquired.

Lily and Ruby both nodded. "Like what?" replied Lily.

"Just try to get people to talk about the couple, how they treat each other, when did they meet, do they know anything about the wedding, that sort of thing. Be extra subtle."

"Why are you investigating them?" Lily asked. "It's not really about Julia, is it?"

"There are some concerns about how Bryce treats her," I said.

Lily sighed. "I hoped you wouldn't say that. He seems so nice."

"He really does," agreed Ruby. "I can usually spot the jerks a mile away."

"He might be a special kind of jerk," I told them quickly while no one was in earshot. "Great in public and terrible in private. Julia's friend saw an unexplained bruise and there was another injury." Both of my friends turned to look at Bryce. He was busy telling another story to a small group. Julia stood slightly behind him, smiling but every chance she tried to say something, Bryce interrupted her.

"I'll see what I can find out," said Lily. "Let's mingle."

Lily went left and I went right, both of us moving between the guests, relieving them of empty glasses and plates, offering fresh beverages and making polite small talk about the couple. I didn't garner too much. Most of the guests seemed more connected to Bryce than to Julia, and of Julia's friends, their main focus was on all the lovely things Bryce did for her as they faux-grumbled about their own partners not living up to him. Bryce's parents were a little more forthcoming.

"She's a lovely person but so mousey," said Bryce's mom, a tall, curvy woman squeezed into a dark purple sheath dress. "Always so quiet at our gatherings but we never fail to invite her to everything."

"Perhaps she needs to come out of her shell," I suggested.

"Hmph," snorted Bryce's dad. "She was chatty enough when we first met but now she hardly says a thing. If I didn't know better, I would say she didn't like us at all."

"She just wants to make our boy happy," cut in Bryce's mom. "She always checks with him before she says anything and he's always so sweet to accompany her everywhere."

"There's your sister, late again," said Bryce's dad. "Thank you for the drinks, young lady," he said to me before they stepped around me. I took their empty glasses to the bar where Lily waited for me.

"Anything?" I asked.

"All I hear is they're always together," said Lily. "Not exactly gripping stuff."

"I heard the same thing. He never leaves her alone. Don't you think that's weird?"

Lily wrinkled her nose. "Kinda."

"Solomon and I don't do everything together. Neither do you and Jord."

"Perhaps one of them is super needy," said Ruby. "Co-dependency is a real thing."

"Maybe," I said, but I didn't like it. Why would a smart, capable woman like Julia Atwater need to check with Bryce before she said anything? My impression was a classy woman who was friendly and polite. That wasn't something that needed to be curtailed. If anything, she was a great guest.

"Twenty minutes and the party is over," said Lily. She checked her watch. "People are already leaving. Please encourage people to take a flyer and tell them we're available for more bookings. I need to head over to the main bar and help with serving."

"There's someone asking for Lexi at the main bar," said Ruby, nudging me. "Looked like an Army type. Big, muscle-bound, starved of female companionship."

That sounded promising. "Great. I don't think I need to observe anymore here so I'm going to head out there. Can you handle everything for now?" I asked, not wanting to leave Ruby single-handedly serving the last of the party guests.

"Go. I've got it. I think more people are going to leave soon anyway."

I glanced at the small crowd. The cake we served had disappeared and the conversation still looked strong but I noticed a couple of people checking their wristwatches. Bryce still held court across the room and Julia was talking quietly with a smattering of her friends. As I watched, Bryce shot a hand out, caught her by the elbow and maneuvered her next to him, not even checking to see if she wanted to leave her conversation. It was both entitled and rude and my initial good impressions of him were rapidly dissolving the longer I observed him.

"Thanks." I nodded to Ruby as I ducked out of the room. I deposited the tray of empty glasses in the stockroom, then hurried through to the main bar. When I first arrived it was fairly quiet; now most of the booths and tables were filled and the talking on top of the music bursting through the sound system made for a lively atmosphere. It wasn't hard to see why Lily's Bar was rapidly becoming the hot place to go in Montgomery.

I slipped behind the bar and moved over to Lily. She finished making the pitcher of cocktails and handed it to one of the waitresses. "Did you get what you needed?" she asked during a lull in the patrons.

"I think so. There's something strange going on there," I told her.

She gave me a sad smile. "That's a shame. He seems so nice."

"He ripped into Julia about the cake incident."

"Really?" Lily's eyebrows rose. "I offered to refund him a percentage and he declined. He said it didn't matter."

"It definitely mattered to him when he was yelling at Julia in the restroom. Then he just switched over and was all smiles and laughter again."

"It couldn't have been a moment of stress?"

"I don't think so. Plus, I believe Julia is paying for the whole party. He started to get mad at her for being careful about their budget for the alcohol."

"Julia paid the deposit," Lily confirmed. "But the rest of the balance isn't due until I total up what they spent. Your friends arrived. I reserved them a booth at the back. Why don't you take them the cocktail menu? Not that they look like cocktail guys but you never know what a pretty woman can persuade them into buying."

"You're so cynical," I said as I grabbed a menu.

"Thank you."

I paused. "Do I actually need to do anything else?"

Lily laughed. "No, we're covered. You can work that table exclusively and I'll just get another waitress to handle anything else that comes in."

That was good news because my feet were already aching from standing so long in my heels. I rounded the bar, menu in hand, and quickly spotted the table where my buddies were seated. Five men were wedged into the booth, beer glasses in front of them. Their uniforms were gone, replaced by jeans and shirts or t-shirts but the buzz cuts and tough, square jaws, gave them away immediately. There was a time when Kafsky suggested I get a buzz cut too, a thought that still filled me with dread. Instead I dyed my hair blond on the way home and kept it that way for years until an unfortunate encounter with two hitmen ensured I needed a new look.

"Hey, guys," I said, my smile reaching from ear-to-ear in what I hoped was a vacant but welcoming smile. "I'm Lexi; I'm your waitress for this evening. You don't look like regulars? Let me guess." I paused, placing a finger on my lips, like I was thinking. "You must be from Fort Charles," I said, grinning again like I was pleased with my own cleverness. "Am I right?"

"Yes, ma'am," said the man in the middle. "These boys are stationed there and I'm visiting for a few days."

"That so?" I peered at him, wondering if he was Simmons, the transporter driver. "Like vacation?"

"No." He shook his head. "I'm a driver. I made a delivery and in a few days, I'll head back to my own base."

"We're showing him the local nightlife before he heads home," said Harris without giving away that he knew me. "What do you recommend?"

"Depends what you're looking for but I can tell you, you're in the best bar in town and it's a pleasure to meet you all." I stuck out my hand, leaving them no option but to politely shake mine and introduce themselves. I was right, the man in the middle was Simmons, but the other two, Dan Willacy, and Frank DuPont, weren't familiar.

"I see you already got some beers but can I get you anything else? We have a great cocktail menu and I can bring you some tasty snacks too." I placed the menu on the table and waited, the vacant smile still on my face. In my previous bar jobs, vacuous worked well. Usually, I just hoped that the customer became uncomfortable enough to order something if only so I would go away. This time, I simply wanted to stay but be assumed to be so dim that they could say anything in front of me. It wasn't a smart ruse, but one that would probably work.

"We'll take another round of beers and a round of shots," said Kafsky, without looking at the menu.

"Coming right up." I grinned again and scooted away to collect their drinks. Since they didn't specify which kind of shots, I scrutinized the bottles lined up behind the bar for the most potent alcohol. I didn't have all night to spend standing up in these heels so the sooner Simmons' lips loosened, the better.

I hurried back in time to hear the tail end of the conversation, something about a friendly baseball match that turned less than friendly a few days before, then they all laughed.

"You seem like you're all having a good time. Have you been at the base for long?" I asked.

My two buddies and the other two guys flanking Simmons all nodded. "Willacy here has been stationed there the longest," said Harris. "Kafsky and I are only there for a couple months. It's a nice place."

"How about you?" I asked Simmons. "Are you enjoying your visit?"

"I am. It was a long drive and I'm glad to have some down time before I head back."

"Do you drive one of those Jeep-type vehicles?" I asked.

"A tank transporter," he said, looking proud.

"Oh, wow. Don't see many of those around." I placed a finger on my lips thoughtfully. "In fact, I don't think I've ever seen one. How do you park it?"

"Very carefully," said Simmons and they all laughed.

"Oh, you." I swatted a playful hand at him. "But really. Where do you park something like that?"

"Behind one of the hangars. It's not something a person drives around as a rule and it won't fit inside a regular parking lot."

"I imagine not. Is it a silly question to ask if you were actually transporting a tank?"

"Yes, I was. The boys here need one for their big show so I brought it in and I'll take it back home after the show."

"Just the one show?" I asked.

"Yes, ma'am."

"I would love to see that!"

"I'm sure we can get you a pass."

"That would be so exciting! So, does the tank stay on the back of the tank thingy? What do you do with it otherwise?" I pressed.

"The tank gets parked in a hangar," explained Simmons. "I just unload it, leave it there, and load it when it needs to go somewhere else."

"You don't take it anywhere else while you're here?"

"Nope."

"Now that I think about it, I'm sure I saw a real big vehicle in Montgomery just a couple nights ago. It looked like it had a tank on it. Maybe another one came in?"

"Just the one I brought in, so far as I know," said Simmons, with a shrug.

"Huh. It definitely looked like one. Tuesday, I think it was, or maybe Wednesday. Are you sure you weren't taking it somewhere else? I'm sure I wouldn't mistake something like that."

"Tuesday or Wednesday, you say? Definitely not! I got food poisoning Tuesday night. Spent the night praying to God, if you know what I mean." Simmons pulled a face.

"Food poisoning? Uh-oh! How'd you get that?"

"No idea. I was having something to eat in the mess hall and it hit me. Might have been a bug because no one else was ill. Just me. I feel fine now," he said and smiled.

"Well, you look fine now," I agreed and in the dim light, Simmons blushed.

"Don't forget your shots," I said as I unloaded them and nudged them in front of each man. "Plenty more where they came from. Shall I get another round?"

"Yes!" yelled Harris as he downed his shot and slammed it on the table. The rest followed suit and the volume level at the table amped up again.

"Coming up!" I darted away before anyone had the sense to decline and returned quickly, encouraging them to drink and then darting away for another round.

"Hey, Lexi."

Turning, I found Harris following me, stopping on the patron side of the bar, and leaning towards me. "When are you going to ask the big questions?" he asked.

"Like what?"

"Like if Simmons stole the tank."

I raised my eyebrows. "Not exactly being subtle, Harris."

"Neither is stealing a tank."

"What do you know about the food poisoning thing?" I asked.

Harris frowned. "I remember Simmons taking ill. I think someone called the doctor for him."

"You think? Or you know?"

"I think but I can check up on it."

"Kind of strange for only him to get ill that night, don't you agree?" I asked.

Harris moved his head from side-to-side. "Now you say it, yeah, it is a little convenient."

"Could be that someone wanted him out of the way so they could grab his keys and make off with the vehicle."

"The keys are kept in the office inside the hangar."

"Then maybe they just wanted him out of the way."

"You don't think he's involved?"

"Doesn't seem that way, unless he was faking being ill. But if the doctor did attend to him, then he has an alibi and couldn't have left the base. Did he come to Fort Charles with anyone else?"

"Yeah, there was another guy. Sergeant Todd McTavett."

"Do you recall seeing him the same night the tank disappeared?"

Harris shook his head. "No, not that I recall."

"Then we need to find him. I have to return to your table with these drinks and ask a few more questions. You'd better head back," I told him as I turned around and assembled the glasses. When I looked up, Bryce and Julia walked past the bar, hand-in-hand. They stopped and Bryce leaned over. "Hey, Lexi," he called over the noise.

"Hi, guys. Leaving already?"

"Yes, and we just wanted to say thanks again for helping set this whole thing up. It was a great engagement party. A perfect precursor to the wedding." Bryce flashed a smile at Julia and tucked his arm around her shoulders. She gave me a weak smile and looked down.

"Have you set a date yet?" I asked.

"A month from now," he replied. "Why wait?"

"Great!" I grinned. "Hope to see you more frequently, and sorry about the cake table. We'll make sure that never happens again in the future."

Bryce shrugged and stepped back, waving before both of them were lost in the rising crowd within seconds. I grabbed my tray and weaved my way back to the table.

"What else are you planning on doing tonight?" I asked the soldiers conversationally.

"We might barhop," said DuPont. "So long as we're back by curfew, we're gold."

"You are all too manly to have a curfew," I laughed, then threw a wink in Simmons' direction. A little flirting didn't hurt to get the job done and apparently, I nailed it. Simmons immediately dropped his eyes to his glass, then snuck another look at me when he thought I was busy serving.

"Hi there!" I looked up after serving the last glass and winced at the sight of Lily appearing next to me. "I'm Lily. Are you having a good night? Is Lexi getting you everything you need?" she asked.

"She's been great," said Kafsky. A chorus of yeses and nods emphasized that.

"I have you all pegged as Army," continued Lily. "You know, my girlfriend from high school once joined the Army. Do you have any girls at your base?"

"A few," said Harris, "but we don't call them girls because that's politically incorrect."

"I bet you've had a few girly girls join up though, am I right?" Lily teased. "Can you think of any?"

I glared at her and thought about elbowing her into the crowd but I remembered Lily did me a big favor by letting me eavesdrop and observe tonight. That said, she probably wasn't paying me and I was providing her with extra cocktail waitress labor. All the same, I kept my elbows to myself as I tried to remember what embarrassing incidents I might have buried in my past which I preferred remain concealed. If Harris and Kafsky still wanted my help, hopefully they wouldn't suddenly remember anything.

"There was this one chick," said Harris. "Do you remember her from boot camp, Kafsky?"

"Oh, yeah." Kafsky leaned back in the booth and laughed. Neither of my old friends looked at me. "She was... not particularly suited for the job."

"How's that?" asked Simmons.

"Yes, tell me everything," encouraged Lily, grinning at them.

"She rolled off the bus that first day with her makeup all just so and announced she was ready to serve our country but she had to fix her nails first and asked where was the nearest manicurist?" said Kafsky, his face creasing at the memory.

"Nails are very important," I said, rolling my eyes. "The Army encourages clean nails."

"Just not long, pink ones," countered Harris. "Or with little, glittery tips."

"Amazing," said Lily. "Tell me more."

"She didn't like the uniform, remember?" said Kafsky. He nudged Harris and they both laughed as the other guys leaned in, eager to hear more.

"That's right. She cropped the standard issue camouflage pants and gave her t-shirt little turn-ups on the sleeves." He pretended to roll up his t-shirt sleeves and flexed his bicep.

"She asked if the boots came with a peep toe."

"She wanted to wear her hair long and flowing."

"She asked if there was Army-issued lipstick or should she could bring her own."

"She wanted to know if it was true if there were dancing classes to disarm the enemy."

"To be fair," laughed Harris. "I made that one up and told her."

"She sounds very creative," I interjected as Lily bit back a laugh. "And anyone would fall for dancing countermeasures classes."

"Is this for real?" asked Simmons. "Does this woman exist?"

"So real," said Harris. "She was a great gal, just not a great soldier."

"Did she ever actually *try* to be a soldier?" Lily wondered.

"She took part in everything," said Kafsky.

"Do you call the morning runs taking part? She wasn't exactly enthusiastic," chipped in Harris.

"She did petition for sleep-ins three times a week."

"And she asked for a boot camp mixer on Saturday nights."

"That sounds lovely," I said. "A great way to meet new people, and who doesn't appreciate a sleep-in?"

"She asked the cooks if the food was organic."

"She told our drill sergeant he would be cute if he smiled once in a while."

"Ooh," cooed Lily. "What happened when she said that?"

"I think she made out with him the following Saturday night," said Kafsky.

Heat rose to my cheeks. No one was supposed to know about that!

"Remember when she got everyone punished and we had to spend all night marching in the rain?"

"Not as well as I remember cutting the lawn outside the main office with nail scissors."

"She sounds a nightmare," said Lily. "Did you make her suffer?"

"Never," said Harris. "She was too damn nice."

"Nice? Really?" asked Lily. She darted a disappointed glance at me. I shrugged.

"Very nice. Sweet, actually. She kept us all motivated and she stuck up for her fellow cadets. She probably would have been a good soldier if she'd stayed around," said Kafsky.

"Yeah, she still holds the record for fastest assault course completion for a cadet," said Harris. "I suppose throwing her over that wall helped." Harris and Kafsky high-fived each other.

"I do? I mean, she does?" I asked, surprised and also, a little touched by their kind remarks.

"She sure had guts," added Kafsky.

"Pink, glittery guts with bows on," said Harris.

"Like her boots. She tied them with the neatest bows."

"And she got us out of that sticky situation when we went night venturing and Kafsky fell in the ditch and broke his arm in two places. She splinted it for him."

"And that final exercise we did to capture the flag from the other team..."

"Couldn't have done it without her," agreed Harris.

"So what you're saying is... this female cadet was actually pretty good?" asked Lily.

Harris looked up at me and fixed me with a long look. "She was the best."

"We miss her," said Kafsky.

"But we don't miss the time where she wanted to jazz up the jackets with appliques. That was just wrong." Then they all laughed again and I stepped back, radiant warmth filling me. I had no idea they thought so fondly of me. More than ever, I wanted to repay them for their friendship and kindness in those dark days by finding their tank in the coming days.

"Next round is on me," I said and they all cheered.

CHAPTER TWELVE

"Hey, Garrett," I chirped, sounding brighter than I felt. I got home around one am, climbed into bed beside a sleeping Solomon and arose at eight, after he'd gone. Now it was mid morning, I had a strong black coffee in front of me on my desk and a half eaten cherry muffin.

"Hi, sis," said Garrett, sounding as distracted as usual. "I'm taking Traci away for the weekend without the kids. There's the choice between New York with a Broadway show and galleries and fancy stuff. Or a bed and breakfast place called the Blackberry Inn in some sleepy little town in the middle of nowhere called Calendar. That involves antiquing, country walks, and romantic dining. Or I could take her to Lake Pierce and get a cabin. What do you think?"

"You can go to Lake Pierce any time. You've been to New York a bunch of times so I say go for the romantic bed and breakfast."

"Good choice. It looks pretty. She will love it."

"She will love being with you." My brother and his wife were among the happiest married people I'd ever known and given that they'd been together forever, and produced three children, that was high praise indeed.

"What can I do for you? I'm sure you didn't call to help me book a break for my wife."

"I need a couple of background checks," I said.

"Go on?"

"Bryce Maynard. His online presence is easy to find but I'm interested in knowing if he's had any convictions, even minor ones."

"That I can do. Stay on the line."

"You're being remarkably helpful." I was instantly suspicious.

"I think I used up all my favors with you," admitted Garrett. "I need to stockpile some more."

"No babysitting before the wedding," I replied.

"Agreed. What's this guy's birthdate?"

I ran my finger across the paperwork Jas supplied and gave it to him.

"Yeah, he's in the system. Couple o' minor things. He was arrested for drunk conduct. Not a DUI, more like disturbing the peace a couple years back, and there was a driving violation five years ago. Let me see... Yeah, here it is. He got pulled over for a busted taillight and he gave the officer so much mouth that the officer arrested him."

"Really?" I scribbled my notes and waited for Garrett to confirm the dates.

"Yeah. Wait; there's one more. He punched a guy in a parking lot in spring of last year. A cop happened to be driving past at the same time."

"Was there a reason?"

"According to the report, the victim looked at your guy's girlfriend the wrong way. There's no record of it ever going to court. Looks like he paid his fines on everything and kept his nose clean since then."

"Thanks for checking."

"Anything else I can do for you?"

"Have you heard anything about a tank turning up?"

"A tank?" Garrett paused. "Not a word. Should I be worried?"

I had no idea how to answer that so I went with, "Nope."

"Good to know. I'll see you at dinner at Mom and Dad's tonight?"

"I'll be there." I hung up and looked over my notes. Three arrests in five years wasn't good news. I'd already seen Bryce's short temper in action and now there was official confirmation, I couldn't consider it a single incident that could have been blamed on tiredness, annoyance or any other excuse.

I tapped my pen against the final charge. The victim got punched for apparently looking at Bryce's girlfriend the wrong way but that couldn't have been Julia. They weren't together last spring. So who was the woman? I called Garrett back and asked him.

"It didn't say. She didn't give a statement," he said. "I have to go. A call just came in about a body."

"Anything come in about a tank?"

"It wasn't run over by one if that's what you're asking. What is it with you and tanks?"

"Nothing," I muttered as I hung up before he could extract the story from me. I was pretty sure the last thing my Army buddies needed was police involvement that could escalate quickly and land them in the kind of hot water they specifically hired me to avoid.

I called Jas next but she didn't answer so I left her a short message to call me back.

Over the next few minutes, I thought back to the things I heard about Bryce the night before. There had apparently been a "crazy" ex in the past. Ruby and Lily both mentioned a woman that he complained about. Was it the same woman who witnessed the assault in the parking lot? I wanted to know who that woman was.

I called up an internet browser on my laptop and plugged in the addresses for Bryce's social media accounts. Apparently, I'd missed another Instagram account in his name on my first search and now I found one busily populated. Thankfully, he was the kind of guy who liked to broadcast his life and there were a lot of artfully shot images showing him leading his "#bestlife." There were plenty with Julia too. Nice photos of them on day trips, and a vacation at a pretty inn somewhere along the coast, leaning in and smiling, arms around each other, kissing in the sunset, and the ubiquitous brunch shots. There were plenty of Bryce alone or with his guy buddies too, the images interspersed with random things he'd seen and shared.

I had to scroll a long way back before I found the month that corresponded to the assault. From that point, I scrolled slower, not wanting to miss a thing. Finally, I found what I was looking for but it wasn't even a photo of the mystery ex, instead it featured a sunset over dunes that could have been anywhere, with just a caption reading "Jessica and I at the beach. Amazing day!" Other than that one single caption, it was like Jessica never existed. There wasn't a single other photo or reference to her. Bryce went to great pains to remove any traces of her.

Noting her name on a slip of paper with a large question mark, I relaxed back in my chair to think. There had to be a bunch of Jessicas in Montgomery and there was no way to narrow her down from a first name alone. If she lived further afield, I couldn't imagine ever finding her. Plus, there wasn't even a photo of her that I could show around. So far, apart from her first name, the Jessica lead was a bust. The only way I was going to find her would be through interviewing Bryce's close friends and family. It would be difficult to do that without someone tipping him off.

While I waited for Jas to return my call, I closed the file and opened the one on the tank, pleased that I had something else to focus on.

Since last night, I was sure I could rule out Simmons as the tank thief. If his story about being treated for food poisoning was true, he couldn't have been the culprit. Unfortunately, that left a whole base of people it could have been. I needed to watch the security footage to see who was in the area near the tank in the time window I narrowed down for the theft.

Something else still puzzled me. What was the motive? If the tank was intended for illegal sale, it would be hotter than hot and bizarrely audacious for anyone to steal from the government. They wouldn't stop looking for it, that was for sure, and who wanted a hot tank? It could hardly have its identification numbers shaved off or be chopped up for parts.

No, someone wanted it for something. But what?

The more I thought about how hard it would be to sell, the more I wondered if there was ever any intention to make a profit on the stolen tank. Could it be that money wasn't the motive?

"What if they intended to give it back?" I asked out loud. "What if they want something in return for it?"

"Return for what?" asked a voice behind me as I jumped. I spun around and grinned.

"Delgado?"

"In the flesh."

"How was your honeymoon?"

"Beautiful. Wonderful. Everything I wanted." He smiled broadly. "I just came in to pick up a couple things before I head home. I'm officially still on vacation until the end of the week."

"Then hurry up and go," I told him. He had moved into my sister's house permanently just before the wedding and I knew neither of them had time to unpack his boxes yet.

"And miss you talking to yourself?"

"You can talk to yourself too," I told him. "It's a free country."

"I'll see you at the family dinner tonight?"

"Absolutely."

"Great." Delgado busied himself at his desk and a few minutes later, he was ready to go. "Hey," he said as he slipped his backpack over his shoulder. "Did you hear about those guys from Fort Charles?"

I frowned. How did he know I was working with them? "Did Solomon tell you?" I asked.

Delgado shook his head. "No, I heard it from an old buddy. The audacity of stealing the goat mascot from

Camp Callihan. I swear, the rivalry between those bases is going to blow up in someone's face one day."

I spun in my chair at this new information. "Someone stole a goat? An actual goat? Or a pretend goat?"

"A real live goat. Camp Callihan likes to roll it out as a good luck mascot."

"Does stuff like that happen often?"

"Stealing goats?" asked Delgado.

"No, the rivalry between the two bases?"

"All the time."

"Huh."

"See you later," said Delgado and he was gone before I could ask him anymore questions. I turned back to my desk and added "goat" under motivations. Would someone really steal a tank as revenge for stealing a goat? Even as I thought that, I knew it could happen.

Sighing, I picked up my phone and called Harris. "Do you have a goat in your possession?" I asked.

"I think I misheard you."

"A goat. Like a sheep but not." I thought about trying to describe it further before I realized I wasn't too sure. Goats were never on my radar.

"Yeah, I know what a goat is. No, I don't have one. What's this got to do with the other thing?"

"I just got intel that Camp Callihan's mascot was stolen and I wondered if it had anything to do with you."

There was a pause and a cough that sounded like it could have been a laugh. "I might have heard something but I swear it wasn't me."

"Was it Kafsky?"

"No!"

"Can you repatriate the goat?" I asked.

"Maybe. I'll make a call."

"Is there any chance someone stole your—"

"Don't say it out loud!" warned Harris.

"Did someone steal the *you-know-what* because someone at Fort Charles stole a goat?" I asked.

"No, that's absurd! Plus, I have it on good authority that the goat was liberated because someone got their face Sharpie'd on a very drunken night out in Chester. Anyway, enough about those idiots. I got those security files. I can't take them off base but can you come down and have a look? I think there's something you might want to see."

I checked my watch. There was plenty of time between now and the family dinner so long as I didn't dawdle. "I can make it. I'll be there in under an hour."

"Great. I'll meet you at the gate."

I was on the road within minutes, Jennifer Lopez on the radio, the volume turned up, and my best sing-along voice, which was a good distraction from thinking about goats. Part of me hoped that it was a simple, childish spat between people who really should have had better things to do. However, I was sure Harris would have admitted it if that were the case. Instead, he intrigued me by wanting to show me whatever footage he'd found.

As promised, he was waiting for me at the gate, this time in uniform, and I was waved through as soon as I produced my ID. I pulled over and he hopped into the passenger side. "Go directly ahead," he told me, pointing in case I got confused about which way "directly ahead" was. To be fair, back in boot camp, I demonstrated poor directional skills on several occasions.

"How's your head today?" I asked.

"A little sore. How many shots did I do?"

"Six, that I counted."

"Yeah, that sounds right." He adjusted his sunglasses. "Simmons is smitten with you. He talked about getting a transfer."

"Did you mention I'm happily engaged?"

"I did point out the rock on your finger but he was too far gone with the booze. I doubt he'll remember much."

I laughed. "Tell me about the footage from the security feed. What did you find?"

"It's better if I show you. I'm not sure what it is but I think it's something. Pull over here." He pointed to a small empty parking lot. I pulled in and hopped out, following him into the nearby hangar. There wasn't a lot of activity going on. Six guys were playing cards on a makeshift table in the corner. Two other guys were talking quietly and a Jeep rolled past us. Harris guided me to a set of metal stairs. I hurried after him and we stepped into a drafty, enclosed office set up with several monitors.

"I swapped shifts with a guy whose wife just had a baby," explained Harris. "It gave me chance to look through the footage from when the tank disappeared. I can't copy it onto a disk because I don't know the password and I don't want to break any laws."

"That's fine. Show me what you have."

"Okay, here it is." Harris tapped a key and the monitor in front of me came to life. For a couple of minutes, nothing happened, then a figure strolled into the building and walked over to the corner and reached for something. "That's the key box," explained Harris. "I don't know if he had a key to it or it was open already, but I figure that's how he got the key to the transporter."

"Your sure this is the guy?"

"Yes." The man turned and walked towards the camera, keeping his head down. Harris tapped the keyboard and the camera zoomed in until we could read the name tag on the uniform.

"That says Simmons," I said, pointing to the screen.

"I know, right? But that *isn't* Simmons. I looked into his story about food poisoning and it checked out. He was in the infirmary all night and well into the next day."

"Maybe he had an accomplice? He's not a regular on base so the doctor wouldn't know who he was. All a person would have to do is give a name and no one would question it."

"That's what I thought, so I took another look at this guy. Wait a moment." The figure started moving again and as he got to the hangar doors, he raised his arm. Harris hit pause. "See that tattoo on his forearm? Simmons doesn't have one. That's proof it isn't him."

"He took Simmons' uniform while he was incapacitated, being careful to get his name on camera while keeping his face shielded but forgot about the tattoo." I sat back in the chair. "Someone tried to frame Simmons. Any idea who it could be?"

"I don't recognize him or the tattoo but I don't know everyone here. Kafsky and I talked about it and he doesn't know either."

"Where is Kafsky?"

"He's talking to the boss about the show the tank is supposed to be the star of. Someone's gonna want to see it real soon, Lexi. Whoever stole it left a Jeep under a tarp and somehow no one noticed but me and Kaf that the tank was gone."

"Zoom in on the tattoo," I told him and when he did, I snapped a photo of the grainy image with my camera phone. "Where does he go next?"

"He leaves the hangar and a few minutes later, the other camera picks him up walking around the outside to the tank transporter. He parks that outside the hangar and then this camera picks him up again getting into the tank and boarding it."

"Play it all for me so I can note all the timings."

Harris did as I asked and I made careful notes of all the mystery man's movements, asking him to pause it every time I thought there might be a glimpse of his face. Unfortunately, he was smart enough to keep his face covered but his one failing was allowing the forearm tattoo to be visible. That was lucky for Simmons. If this all went bad and he was implicated, he could easily prove he wasn't the man in the video, despite the man wearing his uniform.

When the transporter drove away out of the shot, Harris paused the video.

"How tall would you say Simmons is?" I asked.

"Six foot."

"And I'm guessing he weighs one-ninety?" I waited for Harris to nod. "The uniform doesn't look tight. We're looking for a Caucasian male who's similar in stature to Simmons."

"That's sixty percent of the base."

"But not many of them will have a tattoo on one arm and the ability to drive a tank transporter or a tank. Who do you know who can drive either or both?"

"I can't think of anyone. We don't usually have that kind of vehicle here so anyone who's interested in taking that route would be in another unit. There's only Simmons and his partner who can drive both, to my knowledge."

"Simmons' partner? Who's that?"

"I think I told you about him already. McTavett. He came in with Simmons."

"Could he pass for Simmons? Height and weight?"

Harris frowned. "I guess."

"Do you know where he was the night the tank was stolen?"

"He took off to his room after dinner. Said he was tired and wanted to get some sleep."

"Can anyone account for him?"

"I don't remember seeing him until breakfast the next day. But why would he want to steal a tank and set up his partner? It doesn't make sense."

"It might not be him," I pointed out. "But we have to rule him out too. Is there any footage of the tank transporter returning? We know it came back."

"I didn't check that far ahead. Give me a few minutes and I'll find it." Harris pulled up a chair and set to work edging the footage forwards. Finally, the tank transporter appeared on camera, minus the tank, and a few minutes later, the same figure jogged into the hangar and deposited the keys in the key box. Not once did he look up at the camera. All the same, I made a note for my records.

"Let's go find this guy," I said, pointing at the monitor.

CHAPTER THIRTEEN

We walked all over the base and Harris ducked into a few places that I couldn't go into but there was no sign of Sergeant McTavett. After an hour, I had to concede defeat.

"Maybe he's keeping a low profile," suggested Harris.

I shrugged. "Could be but if he is the thief, he doesn't know anyone is onto him yet. As far as he knows, no one has even noticed the tank is missing. That worries me, you know."

"Why?"

"If you can misplace a tank, what else can you misplace that no one's noticed?"

"When you put it like that..." Harris grimaced. "What do you want me to do now? Like I said, someone is going to notice it's gone soon. Kafsky can only head them off so long and then the shit's gonna hit the fan."

We stopped by my car. "As soon as you locate this guy, McTavett, try and take a look at his forearm. No tattoo, no problem. If he does have one, get a photo of it to compare to the one on the video."

"What if he's wearing long sleeves?"

"Get him to take them off."

Harris gave me a piercing look. "I've never asked a man to take his clothes off before."

I was way ahead of him there but I couldn't see any of my usual techniques working. "Throw a glass of water over him," I said. "Call me when you have something."

"I forgot to ask, any news on the tank's location?"

"Not yet but I'm sure it's still in Montgomery." I got into the car and waved goodbye. Harris didn't look happy as he watched me leave but there wasn't much I could do about that at the time. As I cleared the base and headed back to Montgomery, I placed a call to the one person I could think of who might know something about a missing tank.

"Hi, Lexi," said Maddox, answering on the second ring.

"Hello. Are you still at your top-secret hideout?" I asked.

"If I told you, it wouldn't be top secret."

"I'll take that as a yes."

"Is this call for business or pleasure?"

"Business. I'm still searching for the tank. I wondered if you heard anything since we last spoke."

"Oh, yeah. All kinds of people have told me about that."

I perked up. "Really?"

Maddox laughed. "No."

"Damn! I hoped you might have come across some intel about a stolen tank. Something on the deep web."

"Dark web."

"Whatever."

"Just out of curiosity, and I already regret asking, what sort of intel would I look out for?"

"Maybe something to do with the sale of a top-of-the-line American tank. I can't imagine who would want it specifically so I'm thinking foreign countries with suspicious motives, despots, home-grown crazies, and people with a lot of money and nothing better to spend it on. Maybe even some kind of blackmail."

"Not a short list."

"Could you help me narrow it down?"

"Sure. I have nothing better to do."

I was sure that was Maddox's brand of sarcasm but I was happy to ignore it. "There's another thing. I think the tank is still in Montgomery but I doubt it'll stay here for long. Whatever or whoever it's been stolen for, I guess it will be shipped out soon before someone notices it's gone."

"Wait... no one noticed their tank was stolen?"

"My clients noticed but their superiors are, as of yet, unaware. They need to get it back before their superiors get the wiser."

Maddox sighed. "The things you get yourself into. This doesn't sound safe at all."

"I don't think it's roaming the streets. The general public are safe."

"I meant you. Assuming you track it down, is there any point telling you not to try and retrieve it?"

I blew a raspberry into the phone, lightly and not particularly adult-like. "I'm not going to try and retrieve it. I can't drive a tank."

"Good. You see it, you call your clients to come get it and then you avoid the area until they're done. Anyone who went to the trouble of stealing a tank must intend to do their best to keep it."

"Good point." Maddox was right. The tank had to be under armed guard in case of any unforeseen events, like, say, the Army coming to retrieve it. That just added to the difficulties of identifying the location and then setting a plan into place to repatriate it. Thankfully, I hadn't been paid a pitiful sum to actually return it. "There's another case I'm working on," I told him, changing the subject quickly before he started making more pertinent points about the last time I had a run-in with rogue soldiers. "I've got a local background check on this guy but I wonder if there's anything nationwide you can tap into."

"Give me the name and I'll look into it."

"Bryce Maynard. His fiancé is Julia Atwater. Maybe background check her too?"

"What did she do?"

"Nothing, it seems, but a check into her history won't hurt. Maybe see if the name Jessica comes up in connection to Bryce too. It's him that I'm concerned about. He's got a temper, verbally and physically, but there's nothing to suggest he's a serial abuser. Concerns have been raised that he is an abuser and not just a jerk. I'm trying to find out if there's anything concrete that suggests he is bad news."

Someone in the background on Maddox's end yelled his name. "I have to go. Text me their birthdates and any other personal details and I'll get back to you soon."

"Thanks so much. Oh, one last thing." I gulped. I didn't want to ask but I had to. "You didn't RSVP."

"To?"

"My wedding."

There was a long pause, then Maddox exhaled. "I'm not sure I can make it."

I knew that might be the answer but it was still disappointing to hear. "I understand," I said, gulping again. If the situation were reversed, I wasn't sure I'd want to attend his wedding either. I didn't even want to talk to any of my other exes but there was something about Maddox. He was too good a guy to evict from my life; and our breakup was too complicated to completely blame anyone for it. Truthfully, it wasn't anyone's fault. It was just sad.

"Talk soon," he said before he hung up.

I tossed the phone on the seat and turned up the radio, forcing myself to concentrate on the lyrics so I didn't have to think about the past.

~

When I pulled up outside my parents' house in West Montgomery, I could see I was almost certainly the last to arrive. Solomon's car was already there, parked behind Serena and Delgado's. Jord's car was there too so Lily was probably with him. Garrett was parked down the street. I couldn't see Daniel and Alice's car but they might have walked.

I hopped out and walked up the driveway. My parents had recently painted the exterior but the motif remained the same. White with yellow trim. Like a daisy, said my mom. Like an egg, said everyone else. My parents bought the house early in their marriage and raised five children in it, which kindly imbued it with a lovely feeling of coming home. Although these days it felt a lot more crowded, even that was nice.

Opening the front door, I smiled. The older kids, an assortment of nieces and nephews produced by my siblings, were playing a game that involved a lot of giggling and I could hear sports on the television. Most of the adult-sounding noise came from the kitchen so that's where I headed.

"Oh, you're here. Finally," snipped Serena as she stepped into the kitchen. She glanced at her watch and rolled her eyes. "You're late."

"By ten minutes!"

"We managed to catch our flight, get home, unpack, grocery shop, and still get here on time." Serena turned away.

"Blah blah blah," I mouthed at her back. So much for chilled-out vacation Serena! She was just as uptight as usual.

"It's very rude to be late," continued Serena as I slid past her. She persisted in talking at me while I moved out of earshot and walked over to Solomon. He stood with Jord, who held baby Poppy in his arms. She had both hands pressed against Solomon's cheeks while he alternated between discussing the state of burglary in Montgomery with Jord, who was a detective in the burglary division, and blowing kisses at her.

"He's ready for babies," came a whisper in my ear.

I jumped. "Thanks for the advice, Mom."

"I can just tell. No man willingly interacts with a baby unless he's trying to stimulate his partner's ovaries."

"My ovaries are not stimulated." They were a little bit at the sight but there was no point in telling my mother that. She would be at my door with an ovulation test kit every day if she even suspected it. "What do you know about stimulating ovaries anyway?" I asked before immediately regretting it.

"I read an article in a magazine at the dentist."

"About ovaries?"

"About men's subtle clues that they're ready for fatherhood." Mom paused as Solomon handed Poppy to Jord. She reached for Solomon and wrapped her fingers around one of his and grinned gummily. "See how he's acknowledging the father? He's saying 'I could be a father too'."

"No, he isn't."

"He was holding her for ten minutes."

"And I wasn't even in the room," I pointed out.

"He couldn't possibly know when you would arrive. He was just being ready."

"I don't think he's noticed I've arrived yet." Solomon looked over and winked. Mom nudged me. "He just likes Poppy. He's going to be her uncle very soon," I added.

"I'm going to give him some pamphlets about healthy sperm."

I paled. "Please don't."

"Why not? What if his little swimmers aren't healthy? Have you checked? You could use that microscope kit your father and I bought you when you were nine."

The blood drained from me. I contemplated pretending to faint but I wasn't sure if my mother would take that as a definitive sign of pregnancy. "No, Mom. I'm waiting until marriage."

My mother did a double take so fast, she might have gotten whiplash. "You should always try the candy before you buy the candy."

"There's candy?" asked my nephew, Sam, appearing at my side. He belonged to Garrett and Traci and was either destined for great things or becoming brilliant, but evil. Possibly both.

"There's no candy," said Mom.

"You just said there was candy!"

"When you're a grownup and have a good job," replied Mom, turning him by the shoulders and nudging him towards his cousins.

"So confusing," muttered Sam as he scooted away. I heard him tell his siblings and cousins, "There's candy somewhere here but Grandma says we can't have it until we're grownups and have jobs." The children sighed collectively. "We can ask my dad," said Sam. "I bet he's got candy."

"Not lately," muttered Garrett as he walked past.

"How's the dead body?" I asked.

My brother shrugged. "Still dead."

"That's good."

"Is it?"

"Well, if it's been declared dead and it's not, someone is going to have a terrible day in the morgue," I said.

Garrett shuddered.

"Come and help me with serving dinner," said Mom.

"Do I have to listen to anymore advice?"

"No," said Mom, gazing at Solomon. "Is he a briefs or boxers man?"

"Mom!"

"Apparently there's a correlation between tight underwear, too much heat and low sperm counts."

"Oh, God." What I really wanted to say was, someone shoot me. Someone in the room had to be armed.

"Oh! What if you get a honeymoon baby?" said Mom. "You could call it Honey. Or Moon. Or give it the name of the location."

"I will note that down." I wouldn't.

Mom beamed. "So you are thinking about names. That's wonderful. I'm so happy. The last of my babies is having babies."

"There is no baby in the singular, never mind the plural. I'll take that," I said and I swiftly grabbed the dish of potato salad from the side. "Where are we eating?"

"Outside. It's too nice a summer night to sit inside and it's getting too crowded around the table. It will only get worse when Victoria and Poppy need highchairs. And you." She patted my stomach, then paused, and prodded cautiously.

I sucked it in. "I had a baguette for lunch," I explained. Also, maybe I would throw this blouse out. Clearly, it wasn't flattering.

Mom's face fell. "Take the napkins too. Garrett! Daniel!" she called. "Come help with the food."

I grabbed the napkins and took the food outside, pausing to kiss Solomon on my way.

"What do you need help with?" he asked.

"Pick a dish and bring it and don't answer any of my mother's questions," I said. "She's on a strictly need-to-know basis for the rest of her life."

Solomon frowned but didn't question why since he'd been here often enough to know my mother had achieved a level of invasive questioning that she wasn't even embarrassed about. My dad may have been a detective during his long career with MPD but it was my mom who knew everything about everyone.

I laid the potato salad dish on the garden table and dropped the napkins next to it, then returned to the kitchen, passing a neat line of other food carriers. By the time I deposited a platter of roast chicken, hewn into chunks, the garden table heaved with food and my family members were all attacking it. I grabbed a plate and joined in, then sat in a yard chair.

Daniel moved around with bottles of wine, filling glasses, while Jord handed out juice boxes to the kids and Dad announced he'd already chilled beers in an ice cooler. Patrick, the oldest of my nephews, produced a speaker that synced to his phone and the garden filled with the latest pop music.

Solomon pulled over a yard chair and sat next to me. "That is a lot of food," I said looking at his plate.

"I'm a big man. This is only starters."

"I'm both astounded and intrigued about where you put it."

Solomon laughed. "Francesca White called an hour ago to ask about a few wedding details," he said, changing the topic. "We need to have a meeting tomorrow. I said we would go at ten. Does that work?"

"It does. Did she say what it's about?"

"Finalizing some arrangements. Nothing serious."

"Can you believe it's really happening?" I asked.

"It was always going to happen."

"In a couple of weeks, you will be officially part of this." I waved my hand holding the wine toward my family.

"Don't scare him," said Jord, leaning in to pass Solomon a beer. "You'll be okay, man," he said to Solomon.

"I like being a part of this."

"When does Anastasia get here?" I asked. Solomon's sister stayed for a few days after Solomon got home from the hospital before heading back to her life in New York. We remained in touch, of course, and I was looking forward to seeing her again. Plus, she would be the only representative of Solomon's family to attend. His brother was still concealed in witness protection pending the trial he had to testify in so it was quite unlikely he could attend. I wasn't sure either Solomon or I would want him to come even if he could. Some actions were very hard to forget.

"Your face went dark for a moment. Are you okay?" asked Solomon.

I reached for him and squeezed his hand. "All okay."

"I also got a call from the restaurant regarding the rehearsal dinner to confirm the numbers and Francesca says she'll finalize the seating plan with us tomorrow. Apparently, there's a small issue with the florist but she doesn't think it's anything to worry about."

"I feel bad that you've been handling all this stuff."

"Don't be. A few minutes of phone calls, nothing more. So long as we're both at the meeting tomorrow, I think everything will be signed off. Did you get your dress?" he asked.

"Not yet but they will call as soon as it's ready."

"So you made a decision," said Solomon, looking pleased. "Will I like it?"

It was my turn to smile and say nothing.

"Are you talking about the wedding?" asked Mom. She pulled a chair over and sat next to me, leaning in so she could talk to Solomon too. "I bet you two are so excited."

"We were really excited for our wedding," chipped in Serena from a few meters away. How she'd overheard our quiet conversation, I didn't know.

"Of course you were, darling," said Mom. "And now Lexi is excited about hers. Have you written your vows?"

I darted a panicked glance at Solomon. "Am I supposed to?"

"You can be traditional if you prefer. Traditional is fine," said Mom quickly.

"Can you imagine Lexi offering to obey anyone?" snickered Jord and my siblings joined in.

"That won't be happening," I told them. "But I like the rest of it."

"Just don't write poetry. Your cousins' wedding had poetry for vows. Everything rhymed. It was very strange," said Mom.

"Strange wasn't the word," muttered Dad.

"Grandma O'Shaughnessy took back her gift," said Mom. "She didn't like the vows." At the mention of my maternal grandmother, the air stilled.

"Such a shame she can't make it," I said, doing my best to sound sad. It was hard work, and I didn't think I pulled it off, but the thought was there. Unlike Grandma O'Shaughnessy who rarely had a nice thought and even less nice things to say to anyone. Fortunately, she was somewhere in rural Ireland. As soon as my mother turned eighteen, my Irish grandmother packed for the airport and refused to return to the States for anything longer than a brief vacation to see her children and their children. "We'll send a photo."

"No need," said Mom. "She called earlier and said she's going to come after all. She's looking forward to seeing you, Lexi."

"Is she?" I frowned hard. Grandma never expressed that before. Her Christmas cards were invariably full of admonishments and promises to pray for me every day even though she "wasn't sure I deserved it, being a heathen and all."

"She didn't come to my wedding," pouted Serena.

"She went to the first one," said Dad. "Count your blessings she didn't make it two."

"She sent a nice card," said Delgado. "It had a picture of Jesus on it and a nice message inside."

"Did it?" asked Dad incredulously.

"Well, she asked what was the world coming to and said being married twice was better than being divorced once," said Delgado. "And at least I was a man."

"That is nice for Grandma," snorted Garrett. "She's still cross we only have three children and thinks it's some kind of divine intervention rather than actual family planning."

"Three is quite enough," said Traci.

"Is she still mad at me?" asked Daniel.

"Of course she is," said his wife, Alice, with a roll of her eyes. "She doesn't even acknowledge me on her Christmas cards simply because you remarried and she thinks it's sacrilegious."

"The woman's a hypocrite," said Dad.

"That's my mother!" said Mom.

Dad sighed. "The *dear* woman is a hypocrite."

"She stopped adding my ex-wife to the card," pointed out Daniel. "I think the old dinosaur is mellowing."

"Or she's forgotten," said Dad. "No one remind her."

"This is my mother you're all gossiping about," said Mom. "Lexi, you should be pleased she's making the effort to see you get married. It's a long way for an old lady."

"Which is why I will be very understanding if she can't make it," I said. "And if she does come, she will be sitting with you."

"Oh, God," said Dad. He swallowed the rest of his beer and reached for another bottle.

"Where is she staying?" asked Garrett.

"Um..." said Mom, her eyes suddenly going shifty.

"Oh, no," sighed Dad.

"Thankfully, I have my new skills from my family conflict resolution class to help pave the way to a serene and happy home life," said Mom.

"You were kicked out of the class for being too enthusiastic," said Dad.

"I don't want to talk about it," said Mom. "The instructor wasn't very nice but the reading material was excellent."

"I booked the bridal party into the hotel after the rehearsal dinner," said Solomon, thankfully changing the topic although the idea of my mother being kicked out of a class was gripping stuff. "Should I amend the booking to include your grandmother?"

"No!" I yelled. Then quieter, I added, "No, don't go to any trouble. Grandma doesn't like hotels."

"Wait, are you leaving me alone with her?" asked Dad.

"It's only one night," said Mom. "John, darling, that's very kind of you to book us rooms. What a luxurious way to spend the night before your wedding, Lexi."

"The booking covers Lexi, you, my sister and Lily as the bridesmaids," added Solomon. "I thought the little girls would prefer to be with their parents for the night before and then you ladies can get ready together in the morning. There's a spa with a pool too. They're awaiting your call." He produced pamphlets from his jacket pocket and handed them over. "I already arranged for the car service to collect you the next day to bring you to the ceremony."

"You thought of everything," cooed my mother.

"You really have," I agreed. "Where are you staying the night before?"

"At home. Delgado will collect me in the morning."

"This is nothing to do with you keeping me somewhere safe for the night? Somewhere I can't get into any kind of trouble?" I wondered.

Solomon smiled. "Why would you think that?"

CHAPTER FOURTEEN

Solomon and I drove to the wedding planner's salon together. It made sense since we both intended to go to the office afterwards. Solomon had a day with the risk assessment team to look forward to. I had some exciting background probing into Bryce. I'd already checked in with Harris but he'd yet to track down Simmons' partner and until he did, I had no plans to leave the office. It seemed to me that the best way to track down the tank was to track down the man who might have stolen it.

We walked hand-in-hand to the wedding planner's office and just as Solomon reached for the door, it flew open and a man hurried out, pulling his partner behind him. While looking over his shoulder at her and saying something, he collided with Solomon.

"Hey, watch it!" he snapped, his head whipping around to scowl.

Solomon stopped and raised his eyebrows.

"Lexi, hi!" Julia said, her face suddenly lighting up as she tugged Bryce's hand. "Honey, it's Lexi from my gym who helped us get Lily's Bar."

Bryce's face lightened, leaving no impression of his annoyance from a moment ago. "Oh, yeah, sure. How are you doing?"

"Good, thank you."

"Are you going inside?" asked Julia. "We just had our first meeting with the wedding planner."

"It might be the first and last," laughed Bryce, shaking his head.

"Oh, honey! Francesca was lovely."

Bryce laughed but it sounded hollow. "I'm kidding. We had a constructive discussion and I think this might be the planner we go with. Lexi, you didn't say you were getting married."

I held up my left hand and waggled my fingers so he could see the ring. "Never take it off," I said, not that he'd noticed clearly since I was sure he'd spent a lot of time looking at my other attributes.

"It's so pretty," said Julia, reaching for my hand and smiling.

"We have to run but let's catch up some time," said Bryce. He pulled Julia after him, leaving her to teeter in her heels, half-turning to wave an apologetic goodbye, half-hurrying to catch up with him.

"What was that all about?" asked Solomon.

"That's the couple I'm looking into," I explained.

"Kind of a jackass. Him not her."

"That's the current consensus."

"You can tell me more about it later," Solomon said as he pushed the door open.

"Good morning!" Francesca looked up from behind her desk when we entered. She smiled broadly. "How are you both?"

"Great," replied Solomon.

"Happy to hear that. I know this was short notice for a meeting and you're both busy so shall we get down to a business?" Francesca stood and rounded the desk, grabbing the only folder lying on top and gestured towards the rear salon. I walked into the small room first, Solomon close on my heels and Francesca shut the door behind her. "It's just a few formalities and some box checking," she explained. "Then you're all set for a happy, drama-free wedding day. The big day is getting close, huh? Just a week away!"

She placed the file on the table and opened it, flicking through the pages. "If I could get your signatures here, here and here, then a check for the venue, that would be great. Also, the venue would like to know if you preferred the cream or the white for the linens."

"White," I said.

"That's what I thought. Here's the seating plan. Can you double check it?" She pushed a simple graphic towards us with round tables and numbered squares around it. Each number corresponded to a name listed down the side of the page. "Of course this will look a lot prettier when I send it to the printers."

"We need to add my grandma," I told her. "She needs to sit with my mom because no one else can tolerate her."

"Okay," said Francesca without any sign of concern. "Let me see who we can bump from that table."

Ten minutes later, it was agreed that instead of moving a person, we would simply squeeze in another chair. We confirmed the numbers and Solomon and I both initialed the document.

"I checked with your dressmaker and the dress will be ready in the next couple of days," she said next. "You will need to make time for one final fitting but they don't expect any further alterations to be made. The last item is the florist. They're having trouble sourcing the roses you asked for and have sent over a selection for you to choose from." She pulled several photo prints from her file and arranged them next to each other.

"They all look identical," said Solomon.

"I agree but the florist insists there are subtle differences in color and size. They can still make them up in the same arrangements with the other flowers you liked so whatever you choose should be fine."

"Up to you," said Solomon.

I pressed my finger against one of the photos. "This one."

"Excellent choice. I will let them know today," she said, marking an "x" on the rose I'd chosen. "Where are we delivering the bridal bouquet, the bridesmaids' bouquets, and the groom's and groomsmen's buttonholes?"

"I'm staying at a hotel the night before, so there," I said.

"And the men's buttonholes can be delivered to our home," said Solomon. "We can take the flower girls' bouquets too."

"I won't be able to make your rehearsal dinner but my assistant, Keira, will. Is that okay?"

"Not a problem," I said. I knew Keira. She was both smart and efficient.

Francesca smiled. "In that case, all we have to do is settle the invoice and I won't see you again until your wedding day. Of course, I'm here to help in any way, and I will be at the ceremony venue an hour before your first guests arrive to oversee all the setting up. Keira will take over as soon as your vows are made and I will go straight to the reception to ensure your guests are greeted properly. You will not have to worry about a thing."

"That is good to hear," said Solomon.

"Is there anything else I can help you with?" asked Francesca.

"Actually, there is but it isn't wedding-related," I said. "That is, not our wedding."

"Oh?"

"The couple that were here before us. Bryce and Julia. Did they book your services?"

"No, it was just an initial meeting but I have a good feeling they will. Are they friends of yours? Did you refer them?"

"Not exactly. I wondered what you thought of them?"

"They were very nice," said Francesca. "He looks like he'll be a very involved groom if you get what I mean."

I shook my head. "I'm not sure I do."

"Some of our grooms don't get hugely involved in planning their weddings. Quite often it's the bride's vision that drives forward the planning. Of course, it's changing. Our couples are realizing they both want to enjoy their day so they both participate in the planning, just like you two."

"Bryce is different?" I asked.

"Very. I think he's more eager than his fiancée, which is rare. He had it all thought out from the ceremony to the color scheme. He even had some suggestions for the bridal gown."

"Did Julia agree with him?"

"I think she was a little surprised but I could tell she was delighted that he thought about it so much. He obviously wants it to be the perfect day. I'm sure they will tell you all about it. Oh, look at the time! My next appointment is due. I don't want to hurry you but if there's anything else, just call me or drop in anytime."

"Thanks," I said. When we left, I asked Solomon, "What did you make of that?"

"The bill?"

"No. Bryce's attitude towards his wedding."

"Francesca described him as very involved. Is that a bad thing?"

"He even knew what dress he wanted Julia to wear. Since when does a groom pick that?"

"Maybe she talked about it already?"

"Could be. It just seems a little strange. Dominating, even."

"Did anything come up about him in your research?"

"He has a temper that's gotten him into trouble and I overheard a woman saying something unpleasant about him."

"An ex?"

"Of sorts. A special friend, apparently."

Solomon frowned. "Special friend?"

"Special *special* friend."

"Ahh."

"Apart from him behaving like an ass a couple times, I'm not sure I can prove he's a bad guy. Julia hasn't said anything to anyone about him so far as I know but my gut senses something is wrong. I need to get closer to him."

"Given the temper you mentioned, be careful. He looked like he wanted to punch me when he walked into me at the salon."

"I will," I promised and I meant it. I didn't even cross my fingers which only showed how serious I was. Something popped into my head. "Bryce gave me his business card and said he could set me up with a job. I'm going to see if he's serious."

"You want to go undercover?"

"No, but it would be a good way to get some time with him without making him suspicious."

"Call me if you need backup."

"For a potential temping job?"

"You were temping when we first met," Solomon reminded me. "You definitely needed backup then."

"I solved that case," I replied smartly, "but I'm glad you still have my back."

"Always," said Solomon. "Where can I drop you?"

"The office as planned. I want to do some research first; then I'll try and get a meeting with Bryce."

Once at the office, we went our separate ways, Solomon disappearing upstairs to address a pressing issue with the risk management team, who looked after threats behind the general private investigations, and me to my desk.

I wanted to look into both Bryce and Julia so I set about accessing databases and plugging in the information I already knew. While I waited for the results to return, I poured a coffee and relaxed in my chair to think about the tank.

I hoped Harris and Kafsky would track down Sergeant McTavett soon; otherwise I would have to go back to my task of scouting out locations where a tank could be hidden. Realistically there wasn't enough time or manpower to conduct a stakeout of one location; never mind several but I wanted to help. They had been terrific to me during our boot camp days and even kinder when Lily pressed for information. They were my friends and they were in serious trouble. If I couldn't find the missing tank, Harris would be forced to tell his superiors what had happened and then they would all be on the hook.

So far it looked like Simmons was being set up but I couldn't rule out him loaning his uniform to someone while feigning sick for an alibi. He could lose his job either way and so could my buddies. I had no idea how far punishment would go but given the millions of dollars at stake, I could only imagine it would be bad.

My laptop pinged and I sat up straighter to look at the data returned. Bryce had a reasonable balance at his bank account although the only housing payment was rent rather than a mortgage, which seemed unusual for someone of his age with his salary. Of course it was possible he didn't believe in servicing a debt like that but as I dug through his finances, I found there was no record of any assets at all. However, there was a great deal of restaurants, bars, trips and shopping. His savings were low and there were two credit cards almost maxed out and a loan payment to a car company. Bryce was a man who liked to live the good life.

Julia's financial records showed a different state of affairs. She had a mortgage on an apartment that she bought several years ago. Her savings account was healthy, she had a very small balance on her credit card, and she stuck to a budget for her entertainment spending. Nothing wild or splashy when it came to eating out, clothes, or daily spending although there had been an upwards curve in spending on restaurants and bars in the last six months. There were a couple of purchases towards the wedding, including the cake for the engagement party and the bill to Lily's bar, but no big ticket items yet. There were also no deposits into her account from Bryce towards the party costs but I had to concede he could have given her cash or she could have paid without expectation of his contribution.

I turned back to Bryce's finances, combing through them carefully but I couldn't find anything that said cash withdrawals or alluded to weddings. It took me a while to find the line for the purchase of Julia's flashy engagement ring but it was there, albeit less than I expected.

When comparing the two, their financial styles were drastically different. Bryce drew the higher salary but blew most of it while Julia lived well within her means and siphoned off a portion for savings as soon as she was paid. To me, that said Bryce had little or no thought for the future whereas Julia did.

That pushed another very cynical question into my head. How was Bryce going to pay for the wedding when he lived paycheck to paycheck, and how attractive were Julia's assets to a man who had none? He didn't have to put anything into the marriage to leave with half of her carefully saved assets and dump her with half his accrued debt. That didn't seem fair to me.

I took another look through their finances but there weren't any lawyer payments, which suggested there wasn't a pre-nup in effect. Nor was there anything to suggest any family members were helping with funds towards the wedding.

When my cell phone rang, I dragged my gaze away from the laptop screen. "Hi, Lily."

"I have some very important news," said Lily.

"Really?"

"It could be. That guy you're investigating? Bryce? His buddies just came into the bar for lunch. They haven't ordered yet but if you hurry, you can get here and be their waitress."

"Do I have to wear a uniform again?"

"Just the Lily's Bar t-shirt. We don't wear shorts during the day or in winter. I have plenty of spare t-shirts here which is a good thing because you never return the ones I loan you."

"I'll be right there," I told her. Interrogating Bryce's friends, albeit subtly, would give me some more information and since they would probably recognize me from the engagement party, they would continue to think I was a genuine employee.

I called a cab and it was waiting outside by the time I was ready. A few minutes later, it deposited me at the front of the bar. I paid cash and hurried through the bar to the offices at the back.

"That was quick," said Lily.

"I didn't want to miss them."

"They're in the booth at the rear of the bar. The same one your Army buddies sat in," She reached into a box next to her desk and pulled out a t-shirt and tossed it to me. "I told Ruby you would be coming in to serve."

"Thank you!"

I changed my t-shirt then stashed my belongings in Lily's office. I waved to Ruby who was serving at the bar and grabbed a menu from the stack, then sauntered over to the booth. I recognized the men from the party, all dressed in nice suits and dress shirts, just like at the party, which made me wonder what professions they held.

"Sorry to keep you waiting," I said when I approached them. "Hey, I know you guys. You were at the engagement party for your friends, Bryce and Julia."

"And you're the cute waitress," said the stockier of the pair. "Wait. Am I allowed to say that anymore? Is that harassment? Shoot, I have just taken a class at work about harassment and I need to consult my notes." They both laughed like it was an inside joke.

"Cute is fine by me," I said, playing along. "Are you all excited about the wedding?"

"I guess," said the other guy. "Depends on who the bridesmaids are." They guffawed again.

"You're engaged," said the first guy. He glanced up at me and winked. "I am single and ready to mingle."

Oh, please. "Oh, you!" I squealed and giggled like he was the funniest man on the planet and not rolling out a tired, old line. "But seriously, a wedding is so exciting. Are you all close?"

"The groom and us have been buddies for years," said the first guy. "Since school."

"You must have been through everything together..." I trailed off smiling vacuously, hoping they took the hint to fill in the blanks.

"You name it. College. Graduations. Family drama. Trips. Girlfriends, crazy ex-girlfriends." Stocky raised his eyebrows and they both laughed.

"All three of you have crazy exes?" I asked. "Wow. That must be something."

"Not us, Bryce. He really does attract the loonies."

"Not Julia though. She's a sweetheart."

"Yes, she is. Kind of too quiet for me but a nice girl."

"What was so bad about the others?" I asked.

"Bryce was always telling us about the screaming and the crying and how that last chick actually threw a glass at his head! Remember that, Vincent? And she was always in a mood when we got together or called him up. It got to the point where he didn't even want to have us over to their house since she was psycho."

"He really tried," nodded Vincent. "He did everything he could."

"Oh?" I asked.

"He was always buying her flowers or candy, or taking her away for the weekend, and trying to smooth things over between Jessica and his family."

"Same with Lana. And Angie." Stocky shrugged.

"Jessica and Bryce's family didn't get on?"

"They didn't like her much. I'm not sure why but maybe it was the crazy." Stocky twirled a finger around his ear and temple, signifying crazy.

"I never really saw the crazy," said Dan, frowning now. "She must have kept that well hidden but those boardroom types can I guess."

"Boardroom types?"

"She's a lawyer. Lot of money. Put her career before him," replied Vincent.

"Where does she work?" I asked.

Vincent shrugged. "Somewhere downtown."

"Why did they break up?"

"She cheated," said Stocky.

"Oh, wow. How did he find out?" I asked.

"He said he saw messages on her phone and she wouldn't talk about it. He tried and tried and in the end it didn't matter, so he left. She even threatened him with the police but we told him, man, do not go back to that."

"Sounds terrible."

They both nodded. "We're so happy he met Julia. Getting married is exactly what he wanted."

"She'll probably perk up after the wedding," said Vincent. "I heard it's stressful planning a wedding. I'm glad my future wife is happy to get on with the planning. I just have to show up, wear a tux, and take her on a honeymoon."

Stocky glanced at his watch, then at me. "Are those the menus? We're just going to get hoagies and maybe some fries," he said.

"Oh, sure." I handed the menus over since their conversation had turned to food and less to gossiping about their friend's relationships. "If you know what you want, I can take your order right now." I pulled a pad and pen from my pocket and wrote down their order. "Your friend gave me his business card at the party and said there might be some temp work at his office. Do you know if that's true?"

"I work there and yes, there's some temp work available. I don't think it's anything exciting, just answering phones and filing. Did you want to come by and talk to someone?" asked Vincent.

"I'd love that. I don't get enough shifts at the bar," I lied. "It would be nice to work in an office environment. I've done some temping before."

"Drop by this afternoon," said Vincent giving me a friendly smile. "Bryce always tries to help and our temps never last long."

"Great. I'll do that." I flashed them a smile as I turned away and hurried the order over to the bar. I had a way in to talk to Bryce. Now I just needed to work out how to play it.

CHAPTER FIFTEEN

I left the bar a few minutes after Bryce's friends; I had to change out of the bar t-shirt and into my own clothes.

The information they provided wasn't anything wildly exciting but they did drop a couple of names that I needed to check out: Lana and Angie. Who were they? And just how likely was it that Bryce had dated three "crazy" women, one after the other?

That reminded me of a conversation I once had with Lily, right after I caught my ex-fiancé cheating. He unsuccessfully tried to put it all on me that I was "crazy" even after I'd seen the exact nature of the cheating with my own eyes. He wasn't the first guy to pull the crazy card. I'd heard it before when refusing dates, or during breakups, and just about every guy I ever dated—with the exception of Solomon and Maddox—called their exes *crazy*. "Men," Lily had said over cocktails one night, "always call women crazy when we don't do what they want. We should beware of any man who calls his ex crazy especially if she's not actually doing anything crazy like slashing his tires or stalking him. Crazy is probably him."

The problem for me now was how could I track down Lana and Angie? The names weren't uncommon but except for their link to Bryce I had no other information about them. However, his buddies dropped a useful piece of information regarding Jessica. She was a lawyer and according to them, at the boardroom level so she had to hold a senior position. Downtown narrowed the location of her firm a little but not by much. There were plenty of legal firms in the downtown area.

Before I continued my investigations, I ducked into a coffee shop and ordered an iced latte, taking it over to the bar at the window and hopping onto a tall stool. I called up a browser on my phone, thanked everything I knew that I wasn't a PI thirty years ago when the internet didn't exist, and searched for "Jessica + lawyer + Montgomery." The search results listed ten Jessicas; two were partners in local law firms, six were senior lawyers, and two were junior. Even if I discounted the two junior lawyers, I couldn't charge around town interrogating the remaining eight and asking if they knew Bryce. I needed more information to narrow down which Jessica she was.

I called Jas and after I filled her in on what I'd found out, I asked her.

"Yeah, I remember the name," said Jas. "Julia mentioned a Jessica a few times when they first started dating. She told me Bryce was worried about Jessica's behavior and that she should be careful."

"He told Julia to be careful? Why?"

"He said Jessica was nuts and he was afraid she would try to attack Julia because she would be jealous of her and how happy they were together. He said she made up stuff all the time and that's partly why he had to leave her. He also said he was afraid she would say something to Julia and upset her."

"Did Julia believe that?"

"Yes. Bryce showed her some texts and emails from Jessica and Julia said they were full of accusations and horrible stuff."

"Do you remember what kind of accusations?"

"No, I don't think Julia said what they were exactly, but she was definitely worried about it. She was pretty stressed for a while but said Bryce was very reassuring. Eventually, no more texts or messages came and Julia hasn't mentioned her in a few months. Why? Did you find out something?"

"Only the same story you just told me. That the ex, Jessica, is crazy."

"Well, if she is, he probably made her that way," said Jas. "I did tell Julia that he might not be telling her the whole truth but she was adamant that she trusted him. Plus, he had all that evidence to show her."

"I'm trying to track Jessica down. I've been told she's a lawyer downtown but I'm not sure which firm. Do you know?"

"I'm sorry I don't. I don't know her surname either or where she lives. My friend was my only concern."

"Is there any way you could ask Julia?"

Jas sighed. "I don't think she's talking to me right now."

"Why not?"

"I'm not really sure but I think Bryce said something to her after the party. I sent her a few texts but she hasn't replied. I haven't seen her in our building either. I hope she's okay."

"I saw her earlier at my wedding planner's office," I told her. "She's okay."

"Good. I'm glad."

"I'll call when I know some more," I told her and we hung up. Sipping my iced latte, I contemplated the people walking past the window. They all seemed busy and purposeful, with places to go, although there were a few people who strolled by like they had no timely commitments. Most of all, I fashion-watched, my idea of a very good time.

By the time I slurped the last of the iced coffee, my phone trilled. I picked it up, hoping it was Jas with a surname for the mysterious Jessica, but it was Maddox.

"I ran those checks you asked me to do," he said.

"And?" I waited hopefully.

"Sorry to disappoint you, but there aren't any federal warrants out on this guy. No outstanding complaints, none registered in the system anyway. No convictions. He's not even a suspect in anything."

"Nothing related to domestic abuse at all? Maybe the names Lana or Angie came up?"

"Not a thing related to abuse or either of those names. He's squeaky clean."

"I guess everyone has to start somewhere," I said, thinking about Bryce's local rap sheet. Maybe he didn't like to travel to get in trouble or maybe he'd gotten smarter about where he directed his anger.

"I know it's not what you're hoping for but I'm glad you're not investigating a verified lunatic."

"I guess everyone has to start somewhere," I repeated.

Maddox sighed. "Just terrific," he muttered.

"Did the name Jessica come up in relation to anything with him?" I asked.

"Nope. Nothing came up in relation to him."

"Thanks for checking."

"Anytime." Maddox hung up.

I took one last slurp, looking around to see if anyone noticed said slurp, then hopped off the tall stool and deposited the plastic cup in the trash. My clothing was presentable enough for a semi-formal interview but I didn't have a resume with me. It didn't seem worth running back to the office to print up a fake one, although if it were needed, I could do that later and email it from my personal email account.

Bryce's office was six blocks away, which was walkable and would definitely count as pre-wedding exercise and not nearly as embarrassing as Lily's pole dancing class. I took my time walking there since I didn't want to appear suspiciously eager, although something in the way Bryce looked at me in my Lily's Bar tight t-shirt and shorts suggested eager wouldn't go amiss with him.

The firm where Bryce worked was situated in a big glass building with a shiny logo and some snappy corporate message that could have meant anything. The firm was "asset management" but there was no clue as to what those assets were or what the management of them required. There were, however, some shiny brochures with smiling people in business suits shaking hands and a lot of corporate baloney.

I approached the reception desk and asked the headset-wearing young man for Bryce.

"Do you have an appointment?" he replied.

"No, but he asked me to drop by," I said.

"Your name, please."

"Lexi Graves."

"Fabulous." He held up one finger and tapped something behind the desk with his other hand. "Lexi Graves for you," he said. "Shall I send her up? You can go up now."

I continued looking at the brochure until the receptionist snapped his fingers and dropped a visitor's pass on the desk. "Hello! You can go up. Fifth floor. Mr. Maynard will meet you at the elevator."

"Thank you," I said but the young man was already on the phone again. I grabbed the pass and clipped it to my blouse pocket then moved around the desk to the elevators. I traveled up alone to the fifth floor and when I stepped out, Bryce was waiting for me.

"Lexi, it's great to see you again," Bryce said, shaking my hand warmly. "I'm glad you took me up on visiting Fitzgerald and Partners Asset Management. I'm sure we can find a slot here for you. I'll show you around and you can let me know what you think of the firm. I'm sure you'll love it. Hi, Joe," he added to the guy who walked past us. Joe grinned and held up the document he carried.

"We have the whole fifth floor," Bryce explained, taking us from the lobby, through frosted glass doors and into an open plan office. "This is Jean, our receptionist.

Jean knows everything about everyone and we all love her." He said this with a wink to Jean who simpered and giggled in response. "And over there is Natalie, our office manager. She takes care of all the temps so I'll introduce you two soon. Here's the application form," he added, taking a slip of paper from a tray on the desk near by and handing it to me.

"How many temps do you have?" I asked.

"I don't know for sure but currently around five, I think. It can vary; depends on how busy we are. There are interns too but I don't think they will interest you."

"Why's that?"

"They're unpaid, for one thing," explained Bryce. "Every summer we take on six interns who are seeking a career in finance and they get an intensive, hands-on education. It's priceless."

"Finance?"

"Asset management. That's what we do here."

"Ah."

"It's cute that you didn't know. Don't be embarrassed. We don't expect the temps to understand. The brainy stuff is for us big boys," he said without a trace of shame.

I held back from rolling my eyes but he didn't notice since he was greeting two other guys walking past. They made finger gun signs at each other and laughed.

"It's a great atmosphere here," Bryce continued as he indicated we should leave the open plan area and take the corridor. "Every Friday the firm puts on a luncheon buffet and opens the in-house bar at five. Temps and interns are always welcome to attend. The big bosses like everyone to mingle and it's a good opportunity to meet everyone on a different plane. Hey, you should mention your bartending skills on your application. It might give you that edge. This is the kitchen. The coffee cart and fruit bowl are for everyone. Can I get you anything? Cappuccino? Espresso? An apple?"

"No, thanks. This is a very nice kitchen," I said, looking around the bright, open space. Cabinets covered one stretch of wall and two refrigerators were situated under the counter. The coffee cart had a professional looking machine and stacks of cups with the firm's logo printed on the side. A long table flanked by benches took up the other wall and the fruit bowl in the middle was overflowing with apples, pears, oranges and grapes. There was even a pineapple and I wondered if anyone ever bothered to carve one.

"You'll have to fetch coffee occasionally but mostly everyone is encouraged to get their own. It's that kind of environment but offering to fetch drinks won't go amiss."

"Noted," I said.

"What you're wearing is fine," said Bryce. "Us guys like to wear suits because we're client-facing but the ladies in the office don't need to worry about that. A nice skirt or pants and a blouse is fine. Heels are more professional than flats and we expect good grooming, of course."

"Are there any female asset managers?" I asked.

"Sure. Oh, you mean here? Yes, we have two. One is kind of a ball-busting man-hater if you know what I mean."

"Not really."

"Never got married or had kids. Obviously hates men. I'll show you where the hot desks for the temps are," Bryce said before I could point out how sexist his comments were. "There's no assigned space but all the computers are linked to the firm's network so it really doesn't matter where you sit. How's your typing speed?"

"It's good."

"Great. Letters, documents, all that?"

"Not a problem."

"Perfect. Hi, ladies!" Bryce broke into a smile as we stepped into the room. The four women inside all looked up and smiled. "This is Lexi. She might apply to temp with us so I'm showing her around. Do you all love working here?"

The ladies nodded and smiled. "See?" said Bryce. "You'll love it here too. Debbie there is marrying one of the partners next month." He waved to her before we left. "It's not encouraged but the occasional office romance does pop up. Debbie was lucky to get noticed. I expect we'll be looking for another new temp once she's wed."

"She isn't staying on?"

Bryce frowned. "I can't see why she would once she has a husband."

"Does your fiancée work?" I asked.

"She does now but I know she wants to be at home. We're planning on starting a family as soon as possible and she can't do that and work," he said like I asked the most ridiculous question. "She knows I'll provide for her."

"That's so great," I said weakly, wondering if Julia had any choice in that decision.

"Come this way. The view over downtown Montgomery is great. We have a rooftop space that we share with the other firms in the building but you'll see that some other time. Here are the bathrooms and over there is the staircase emergency exit. Do you have any questions about the position?"

"Um, yes." I plundered my brain for some questions that related to my previous life as a career temp. "Are there any benefits?"

"Health and dental are standard and vacation, which is based on how many hours you work. It's better than most temps are offered. Your hours will probably vary according to the work demands. Natalie will take you through that when you apply."

"Aside from typing and filing, is there much else I need to do?"

"General office duties. You might be assigned to someone for the day if they require assistance or you might have to research, say, maybe an office party or a formal gathering. Sometimes, one of the partners will need help with corporate gifting or you might have to take notes at a meeting. It varies. Does any of that sound like a problem?"

"No, it all sounds fine."

"Great. How does your boyfriend feel about you working here?"

"He's very supportive of the idea," I said.

"You'll be home in time to make dinner so don't worry about that."

I opened my mouth, then shut it, which was probably the right reaction. Bryce wasn't interested in my opinion unless it was to tell him how fast I could type or did he want cream in his coffee? Be home to make my man's dinner? Thankfully, Solomon and I both knew he was a better cook than me, and also what was this, the 1950s?

"The partners all occupy offices on that corridor," Bryce continued obliviously. "My office is this way. What do you think so far?"

"It looks and sounds like a great place to work."

"Come into my office and I'll help you with the application."

"That's really kind of you." It would also be the perfect opportunity to grill him for information.

"So you're busy with the wedding plans, huh?" Bryce said as he directed us to another corridor. "When are you getting hitched?"

"In a week."

"Last few days of freedom," he said and laughed. "I bet your husband hates letting you out of his sight."

"He understands that I'm independent."

"Maybe we can get you some extra work after the big day. This is my office." Bryce reached for the door handle and opened it, ushering me inside. The office wasn't huge but it was neat and tidy with a desk and chair occupying the central area and a bookcase against the wall. The window overlooked the parking lot which meant the partners' offices on the other side of the building had the prime spots overlooking the street. A signed baseball in a glass case occupied the desk along with a laptop. Several framed certificates were displayed on the wall. "Take a seat and use the desk when you fill out the form."

I sat on the visitor side of the desk and laid the application form out. It looked easy enough. Name, address, social security number and some space to list my skills and references. "You must be looking forward to getting married too," I said as I reached for a pen. "Your fiancée seems like a nice person."

"Julia's the sweetest," he said as he took the chair opposite.

"Have you ever been engaged before?" I asked. It wouldn't take long to fill in the application form and I didn't have a lot of time to question him or find out who Jessica was.

"No. I wanted to wait for the right person who would support me in my career and the things I want to do in life."

"Oh?" I glanced up and gave him a friendly smile. "You've never had that before?"

"I've dated, of course, and met a lot of women but never the right one. Too many career women don't understand the importance of family or sacrifice or making time for the most special person in your life."

"That's why I'm not a lawyer," I said. "I couldn't imagine working hours like that. You must come across plenty of women who appreciate your perspective."

"A few," he said, not taking the bait. Instead he rocked back in his chair and reached for a stress ball that he tossed from one hand to the other. "Just fill in your details and hand it to Natalie on your way out. I'll add my own recommendation too."

"That's really kind of you." Bryce might be a sexist ass but at least he seemed genuine about helping me get a job, not that I planned on taking him up.

"How badly do you want this job?" he asked. "We get a lot of applications since it's a great firm to work for."

"Badly," I lied. "The money will really help out."

"What will you do to outshine the rest?"

I filled in my name and paused. "I have a college degree and a lot of experience and..."

"What will you do *for me?*" asked Bryce. He dropped the stress ball and stood up before skirting the desk, and coming to a stop in front of me, barely inches away. He reached for my chin, turning my face to look up at him.

"Um, I..." I frowned.

Bryce popped the button on his pants and reached for his fly. "If you're very good, I can give you an excellent recommendation," he said softly. "Are you going to be a good girl?"

I blinked twice, utterly stunned, then recovered enough to scoot back my chair, the legs making a soft scraping sound on the carpet. "No, I don't think so," I said, my voice strong and defiant as I rose steadily.

Bryce grabbed me by the waist as I stood up. "Don't play coy, Lexi. I know chicks like you. You pretend to be so chaste and sweet and the next minute, you're on your knees begging for it. I saw the way you looked at me in the bar."

"I think you're very much mistaken," I gasped, appalled. I stepped out of his grasp but with the chair pressed into the backs of my knees, there wasn't anywhere to go.

"I like women who play hard to get but I don't have all day. If you want this job, you know what you need to do."

"Yes, I do," I said, more than angry now.

Bryce's mouth curled into an unpleasant smile and he reached for me again, wrapping one hand around my waist. "You be nice to me and I'll be very nice to you," he said. "No one else needs to know about it and if you're very good, who knows? Maybe you can keep up the good work after hours." He winked.

"No, thank you," I said smartly. "There is no job in this world I want that much."

Bryce's smile dropped and he grabbed me with his other hand, tugging me towards him as he bent his head. I raised my knee swiftly, and sharply kneed him in the balls. I knew I connected the moment his face crumpled. "You little bitch," he groaned as he dropped to his knees. "You can forget the job."

"You can shove the job," I told him as I stepped over him and reached for the door handle.

"Tell anyone and I'll make your life hell, you crazy bitch," he groaned.

"I'd like to see you try," I spat as I tugged the door open and darted out. I ran for the exit, stumbling through the corridors before Bryce could chase after me. I didn't stop running until I was in the elevator, frantically punching the door close button. Inside the car, I slumped against the wall, shocked and disgusted, my breathing hard. The moment the doors opened, I ran out of the building, knowing I would never return.

CHAPTER SIXTEEN

The music was thumping, the lights were flashing and the air was hot and still. I couldn't remember the last time we danced like this, or on a table, or had drinks quite as potent as the ones in our hands. "I love this song," I yelled.

Lily swayed, her hands rising high above her head as she made a "What?" face at me.

"This song! I love it!" I yelled. Then I gesticulated wildly and swayed harder, my whole body reacting to the rhythm. Lily smiled and gave me the thumbs-up.

I sipped my cocktail, something raspberry red, and the glass rim was frosted with sugar. Delicious. Lily was right. After my afternoon with the sex pest, Bryce, I needed a wild night to forget about it. The track finished and another started, the bassline just as thumping as the last one. Lily's head bobbed along to the music and we both swayed and drank, glad to be alive and unmolested.

Then I was falling backwards in a moment of déjà vu, except instead of landing in a dumpster, strong arms were wrapped around my waist. No, not falling. Someone was lifting me and as I looked up with inebriated eyes, I smiled.

"I love you," I yelled as the room began to spin.

Solomon said something but I shook my head and jabbed a finger at my ears.

Solomon peeled my headphones off. "What are you doing?" he asked.

"Lily and I are dancing. We made cocktails! Do you want one?" I slurred as I held up my glass. He sniffed, pulled a face, and shook his head.

"I can see you're dancing. I meant why are you dancing on the coffee table in the living room?"

"Because we couldn't get a sitter for Poppy. She's asleep in the guest bedroom and we're clubbing in here!"

"Where did the disco ball come from?"

"The closet."

"The volume of your headphones could render you deaf."

"What did he say?" yelled Lily.

"He said we'll go deaf," I yelled back.

"Fine, just one more," said Lily, handing me her glass.

"Are you having a good time?" he asked, still holding me.

"Fabulous. I feel like I'm floating!"

"That's because I'm carrying you."

I looked down then at my legs and gave them a waggle. I couldn't feel my toes but that was probably owing to the alcohol. "Oh, yeah."

"Did you eat anything?" he asked.

"There was a raspberry in my drink."

"I will order some food," said Solomon. "I think it's a carb day. Pizza?"

"You're the best," I hiccupped as I linked my arms around his neck. "The best boyfriend ever. The best fiancé. I am so glad you're not dead."

"Me too. Do you want me to put you back on the table?"

"Yes, please."

Solomon adjusted my headphones over my ears and tipped me back onto the table. Lily grabbed my hand and twirled me around, then wobbled uncertainly. "I think I'm drunk," she yelled.

"Maybe we should stop," I yelled back.

"We should stop," yelled Lily. She slipped off her headphones and shook out her blond curls before stepping down and offering me her hand. I took it and stepped unsteadily onto the floor. "This was a good night!"

"Solomon's ordering pizza," I said, remembering his offer before I gulped.

"Great!"

"No, he's ordering pizza." The thought was sobering.

Lily wrinkled her nose. "Still great!"

"Last time he ordered pizza, someone shot him."

"It wasn't the pizza delivery guy," she pointed out.

"It was still pizza," I slurred. "We don't order pizza anymore."

"I'll get the door," said Lily, hugging me.

"You can't. You're my bridesmaid. You can't get shot!"

"Sit," ordered Lily, maneuvering me over to the couch. "Deep breaths."

"I'm not panicking!" I panicked.

"Close your eyes for a moment. Deep breaths, Lexi. Count with me. One... two... three..."

I was asleep by four.

~

I awoke and stretched, then wriggled. This wasn't my bed. Also, why wasn't I wearing my pajamas? And from where was the scent of fresh coffee emanating?

"Good morning, sleepyhead," said Solomon. He walked into the living room, wearing the black, hip-hugging jeans I liked best on him and a dark ink-blue shirt with the sleeves rolled up. He placed a large cup of coffee on the small table next to the couch.

I pushed the blanket covering me down and shuffled into a sitting position. My head throbbed, my mouth was dry and why did I smell like raspberries? "Did I fall asleep on the couch?" I asked.

"I trained you well. Your powers of deduction are second to none."

"Hah-hah," I said flatly.

"Yes, you passed out."

"I didn't have that much to drink!" My head, however, told me otherwise.

"Lily said you had a rough day."

"Oh." The memory of Bryce trying to coerce sexual favors from me filled my brain quickly and unpleasantly. I could hardly wait to have that conversation with Jas. She would be just as appalled as I was but how badly would it damage her friendship with Julia? What if Julia didn't believe her? No one wants to believe their fiancé was that kind of man!

"Lily filled me in on what happened. I'm not going to lecture you on why didn't you come to me, or why you were there alone in the first place. It seems like you dealt with everything to the best of your ability."

I shrugged and reached for the cup.

"Would you like to go to the police department and file charges?" asked Solomon.

"I have no proof."

"You think Montgomery's finest won't take you seriously?" Solomon raised his eyebrows.

"I think it will become a 'he said, she said' firing match and I have no proof to offer."

"Lily said you told her you ran out of the office. Someone will have seen that and they can be forced to testify."

"And risk losing their job? John, nothing happened. I'm fine. Bryce is an asshole who tried to get away with it and I'll make sure he goes down some other way but I don't think this is it."

Solomon took the cup from me and placed it on the table, then took my hands in his. "Lexi, did he try to force himself on you?"

"No, not exactly. He grabbed me. He made highly suggestive remarks about what he expected from me in order to get a job at his firm and he unbuttoned his pants. I kneed him in the balls and while he was temporarily incapacitated, I ran."

"Are you sure that's all?"

I looked Solomon squarely in the eyes. "If he sexually assaulted me, I would tell you. I wouldn't keep quiet about it. It wouldn't be my shame to bear. It would be his."

"That's right," said Solomon. He squeezed my hands. "I'm glad you're okay and I'm glad Lily made sure you had a good night even if you did turn the living room into a nightclub. You left a very suspicious looking stain that smells heavily of alcohol on the rug."

"Oh, no," I groaned. I sniffed the air. "Hey, did you order pizza?"

"Yes. You feel asleep before it got here."

"Is there any left?" I asked.

"Two slices."

"Great! Breakfast!"

"That is *not* breakfast."

"It is when you're an adult and can do anything you want. I might have ice cream too."

"Fine," said Solomon. "But not on the same plate."

I pulled him closer and kissed him on the lips. "Thank you," I said.

"What for?"

"Being one of the good guys."

"You shouldn't need to thank me for that. Being a good guy should be the default setting."

"Are you two making out?" asked Jord, now walking past us in socked feet.

"What's he doing here?" I asked.

"He came over after his shift and since Lily and Poppy were sleeping over, he did too. We have a fairly full house."

"That's nice." I tested my feet on the floor. I wondered if walking would hurt my hangover anymore than it hurt right now.

"We'd have more space if we moved back to the other house," said Solomon.

"Mmm-hmm," I murmured. I knew that. I also knew I panicked last night about the pizza delivery guy but that memory was hazy and indistinct. Solomon seemed perfectly healthy. The delivery guy clearly hadn't been a maniac in disguise.

"No hurry."

"I'll get therapy," I decided. "I think I need it."

"I'll come too if you like."

I looked up a touch too quickly for my thumping head. "Really?"

"In sickness and in health. That goes for our minds too."

"Lexi has a sick mind," said Lily, walking past with Poppy in her arms. Poppy waved and blew a raspberry.

"It's not true," I said. "My mind is delightful."

Solomon raised his eyebrows again. "We've been through a trauma and we'll get through it together. Drink your coffee," he said. "I'll warm your grown-up pizza breakfast."

An hour later, I was showered, my hair washed and blown silky straight, and dressed in jeans and a striped shirt with the cutest little floral embroidery on the pointed collar. My pizza breakfast was devoured along with another coffee, but the ice cream was placed on hold, which just went to show how grown up I really was.

Jord, Lily and Poppy stayed for breakfast, then the three of them left as one happy, little family. For a moment, I was jealous of how easy life was for them and then so pleased that they all chose to spend the night to make sure I was okay. Now just Solomon and I were in the kitchen.

"Let's take it easy tonight," said Solomon. "I will be home early. We could go for a walk in the park or to the movies?"

"Both."

"Both?"

"I feel indecisive, so both." My cell phone began to ring. Unfortunately, I had no idea where I left it. Even Solomon looked around, a confused expression on his face.

"It sounds like it's in the kitchen but I can't see it," he said.

The phone stopped ringing and a moment later, it started again. I got up, moving around until the dim ringing became louder. I opened the refrigerator door and there it was, next to the juice.

"Why is your phone in the fridge?" asked Solomon.

I shrugged as I answered.

"Lexi? We've got McTavett," said Kafsky.

"What do you mean 'you've got him'?" I asked. The image of McTavett tied up in some dark basement while Harris and Kafsky interrogated him flashed through my mind. It wouldn't be the first time they'd done it, but possibly the first time someone deserved it.

"We haven't *got* got him but we have our eyes fastened on him."

"Who's we?"

"Me and Harris. We saw him leave base this morning so we hopped in a car and followed him."

"An Army vehicle?"

"What do we look like? Stupid? Don't answer that. No, we're in my car. It's inconspicuous."

"Okay, good. Where is he?"

"He's sitting in a booth at that pancake place in Chester, the one on Underhill Road. He's looking at the menu and appears miserable but I don't think that's got anything to do with the menu. I'm getting the maple syrup and bacon and Harris is getting the French toast."

"I don't need to know your breakfast order."

"It smells damn good in here. Like what dreams are made of."

There was some muttering, then Harris came on the line. "Kafsky has gone cross-eyed with sugar," he said. "What shall we do with McTavett? Nab him after we've eaten?"

"No, I don't think that's a good idea."

"But following him was."

"I can't believe these guys defend our country," I mouthed to Solomon.

"What's that? I can't hear you," said Harris.

"Keep an eye on him," I told them. "I'm on my way. Order me the French toast and a juice."

"I have to go," I said to Solomon.

"Do you want company?"

I thought about it for a moment. A menacing man like Solomon could be very useful. Also, I didn't want to drive. "Yes," I decided. "But look mad."

"Not a problem. You only ordered French toast for one. I'm already mad."

"You had fruit for breakfast."

"And?"

"You're healthy!"

"Healthier than you at this moment in time. You're partially fueled by alcohol so I'll drive."

"Then you can eat half my French toast. I am being careful to fit into my wedding dress."

"Pizza and French toast for breakfast sound very careful," said Solomon.

"Sure they are. There're tomatoes on the pizza and that's a fruit and I'm getting a juice with the toast. That's more fruit! And you're eating half of my French toast."

"Oh, sweetheart," said Solomon as he kissed me properly.

Solomon stepped on the gas all the way to Chester and then navigated smoothly to the pancake place. "You've been here before," I said. "You've been stepping out on me."

"It's a guilty pleasure."

"I thought I knew all your guilty pleasures."

"I'm an endless path of discovery."

"That's my guilty pleasure."

Solomon winked and for a moment, I had a very warm feeling inside. I shook it off. I couldn't interrogate a man if I was thinking wild thoughts about my favorite man, sugary breakfasts and guilty pleasures.

Harris and Kafsky sat in a booth opposite the doors but slightly out of McTavett's sight. If they ducked to one side, they could observe him, but mostly they were hidden from view. From this vantage point, he couldn't leave without them noticing, and nobody else could enter without a visual check from them.

"What's he been doing?" I asked as Solomon and I slid into the booth.

"He ordered pancakes with whipped cream but he's been stabbing them and moving them around the plate more than actually eating them," said Kafsky.

"Has he spoken to anyone?" I asked.

"No. He looks glum."

"Has he used the phone?" I could see McTavett holding a cell phone. He didn't have earphones plugged in so he wasn't listening to music or a phone call, and his fingers weren't moving so he wasn't tapping out a text message. Perhaps he was reading emails or the news.

"No, but he stared at it a lot," said Kafsky.

"Is there a possibility he's meeting someone here?" asked Solomon.

"We've been here the whole time he has and no one has approached him. I don't think he'd order pancakes for a pay drop, do you?" asked Harris.

"I don't think so either," I agreed. "We should talk to him before he leaves. This might be our only opportunity."

"He'll recognize us," said Harris.

"You two wait here. Solomon and I will go. He doesn't know us. Solomon, can you act quiet and menacing?"

Solomon narrowed his eyes and flexed his bicep. It had the opposite effect of quiet and menacing on me.

"Is McTavett gay?" I asked. I didn't want Solomon to have the same effect on him.

Harris and Kafsky flashed each other a look. "I think he's married with two kids," said Kafsky. "Why?"

"Just wondered." I got up and Solomon followed me. We slipped into the booth opposite McTavett. He stopped stabbing his pancakes at random and looked up.

"Can I help you?" he asked.

"I'd like to buy a tank," I said, nodding at Solomon. "And he wants to make sure I get one."

"Um, I, uh..."

"You are Sergeant McTavett?" I asked. He nodded.

"Then I have it on good authority that you have a tank and I happen to be looking for one."

"I don't have a tank. I don't know what you mean or who you are but I don't have what you want." McTavett gulped and gazed out the window, alarm spreading across his face.

"But you know who does." I let that sink in.

"I think you've got the wrong guy."

I produced the photo on my cell phone that I snapped of the mystery man dressed up in Simmons' uniform and lifting the keys in the warehouse and pushed the cell phone over to him. Alarm deepened on McTavett's face and he started to rise, hurriedly throwing a couple of crumpled bills on the table. As he did, I saw the tattoo on his forearm, unmistakable in the bright sunlight.

"Sit," growled Solomon.

McTavett sat.

"This is you wearing Simmons' uniform while he suffered from food poisoning. You took the keys for the tank, loaded it onto a tank transporter and took it off base. You drove to Montgomery and dropped it off. I want it. Where is it now?"

"Listen, lady..."

"Don't 'listen, lady' me! I'm not talking about a purse on sale here. You've got a choice right now. You tell me where that tank is or I go to your superiors at Fort Charles and I tell them everything I know and then you'll spend the next few years missing your wife and kids and wishing you'd made a deal with me in the first place."

"Who the hell are you?" McTavett asked, his face paling rapidly.

"Doesn't matter. All that matters is the location of your tank. Whatever you were paid to steal and deliver it, I'll double it."

"I wasn't paid anything."

"Cut the crap. We know you took it. We're giving you a better offer."

"No, that's just it," said McTavett, his face crumpling. Tears pricked his lower lids. "Oh, shit! I'm done for anyway. I didn't get a penny for taking that tank. They've got my wife and kids. If I didn't steal it, they said they would kill them." He turned his cell phone towards us and pressed his thumb on the screen. A video began to play. It looked like it was being shot from a car window. Across the street, a young woman pushed a buggy with a small child inside. Ahead of her, a small boy on a bicycle turned around and rode uncertainly back towards her, then stopped with a big grin on his face. "My wife and kids are in North Carolina visiting her mom. Someone sent this an hour ago. It's the fourth video I've gotten. They're watching them. They haven't stopped watching them all week. So, if you want a tank, I can't help you. I can't sell it. I can't make any deals. I dropped it off and I'm supposed to keep my mouth shut until it's moved or my family is dead."

Solomon and I exchanged a glance. I took back my cell phone, pulled out my business card and laid it on the table. "This could be your lucky day," I told him. "We're private investigators not bidders on stolen weaponry."

McTavett blinked and wiped his eyes with the back of his hand. "You're not?"

I leaned in. "Seriously? Do I look like I buy tanks?"

"The woman who wanted it doesn't look like she buys tanks either," said McTavett.

"I think you'd better tell us everything," said Solomon.

"I'm not telling you a thing until my family are safe. For all I know, they're watching me too and they can see me talking to you." He glanced nervously out of the window, his eyes roaming the parking lot.

"We're just a couple of friends who dropped by to meet you," I said. "But I will tell you there's two Army personnel in here who are genuine buddies of ours and they're pissed at what you've done."

"I really didn't have a choice." McTavett's shoulders sagged and he flopped against the backrest of the maroon booth. "I didn't want to set up Simmons but I had to in order to get the tank and I had to steal it. Please, you have to help me."

"Write down the location of the tank and then we'll secure your family," said Solomon. He produced a pen from his pocket and grabbed a napkin from the stack.

"How can I be sure?" asked McTavett.

"Because you don't have a choice," I said. "We'll help you out of this mess and we'll make sure your family is safe. I think you can assume your career in the Army is over."

"I don't care. I just want Josie and the kids to be okay."

I tapped the back of the photo. "Write the location and then tell us everything you know."

CHAPTER SEVENTEEN

Solomon and I sat in his SUV a block away from the partially derelict building McTavett identified as the location where he unloaded the tank. He told us he'd driven it into the warehouse and gotten out of there as fast as he could so he didn't have much intel on the identity of the woman who approached him, or for whom the tank was intended. That left us with the problem of finding out.

Fletcher and Flaherty sat in the back of the vehicle, silent and stone-like. Delgado escaped being roped into the operation because he was still on leave and Solomon refused to interrupt his time away. I thought that was great although I was pretty sure Delgado would be peeved when he heard how much fun he missed out on. Not that there was any fun yet.

"It's been an hour, boss," said Fletcher. He glanced out the window at the silent street. No cars had passed by in ten minutes and among the parked cars, one was a burned-out wreck, two looked like they'd been stolen and dumped, and the other three were older models. I assumed they probably belonged to workers in the nearby warehouses, half of which appeared empty. It wasn't an especially nice part of town. "No one has come in or out and my butt has gone to sleep," he added.

"You should wiggle your cheeks," said Flaherty, stopping when Fletcher shot him a look. "Fine, don't take my advice but you'll regret it."

"We're too conspicuous," I pointed out. "Someone is going to notice this vehicle soon and wonder what the hell we're doing just sitting here. We can't even make out for cover." I gave a pointed look into the back seat.

"I am not making out with him," said Fletcher, pointing to Flaherty.

"Your loss," said Flaherty.

"We need to get closer," said Solomon just as his phone rang. "It's my buddy in NC," he said as he answered with a curt "Hello?"

We waited patiently while Solomon spoke succinctly, then hung up.

"What's happening with McTavett's family?" I asked.

"My buddy has eyes on the family and his men are placed in strategic positions within the vicinity. They're combing the area for whomever is watching the family and feeding those videos to McTavett to keep him scared. They think they've spotted the perp in a truck parked a little way down the street."

"And?" I wanted to know.

Solomon raised his eyebrows and for a moment, I doubted how much I wanted to know before my curiosity overcame me. I made a motion with my hand for him to spill.

"Once they're sure they are the only operatives in the area, they'll take him out temporarily..."

"Temporarily?" I interrupted.

Fletcher leaned forwards. "Duct tape and into the trunk," he said, his voice more menacing.

"Really?" I asked.

Solomon shrugged but didn't deny it. He continued, "They'll make sure no other operatives are in the area before they remove the threat and monitor his comms. Meanwhile, my buddy's team will move McTavett's family to a secure location until the tank is recovered and they're safe from further retaliation."

"What if they're never safe? What if there's payback for losing the tank?" I asked.

"We can assist in relocation if that's what McTavett wants."

"So they lose their whole lives regardless of us recovering the tank?"

"Better than losing their *actual* lives," said Flaherty. I couldn't argue with that although it seemed harsh that all McTavett did was try to protect his family and in doing so, may have irrevocably changed all of their lives forever.

"Who would kill kids?" I wondered out loud.

"Plenty of people," said Solomon. "For some, no one is off limits."

"I think we should tell Major McAuley," I said, referring to our old friend. "We should loop him in on the situation."

"Let's find the tank first, then we'll talk to him," said Solomon. "Fletch, Flaherty, you two take the west side. Lexi, you and I will take the east. Keep a low profile, don't engage with anyone, no firearms, no casualties. Get eyes on the tank, snap a photo to verify it's there, and hightail it back to the car."

"We should move the car," said Fletcher. "Lexi is right. Someone will notice it soon."

"Or burn it," said Flaherty. "We don't know who is here and we don't want to risk hightailing it on foot. We could be sitting ducks if we inadvertently piss someone off."

Solomon fired the ignition, pulled into the street, made a U-turn and traveled back the way we came. After a few left and right turns, he swiftly tucked the SUV into a moderately sized building that looked like it might have once been an auto shop but had long been stripped of all its tools and clientele. As we climbed out, a scruffy man shuffled in the shadows.

"This is my house," he grunted as he sniffed the air.

"I'd like to rent a parking space for an hour," said Solomon, producing a few bills. "That cover it?"

The man reached forwards, stretching his thin body before snatching the money. "That'll cover it," he said.

"Not a scratch," warned Solomon.

The man glanced over the vehicle. "You coming back for it?"

"Yes, and I mean it. Not a scratch. I'll match what I gave you if you make sure no one touches it." Behind him, one of my colleagues cocked his gun.

The man blinked and shuffled back into the shadows. "Not a scratch," he rasped as he left.

Solomon reached into the trunk and pulled out four Kevlar vests, handing one to each of us and putting the last vest on himself.

"Really?" I asked, gulping as I put it on. I didn't need an answer.

"Precautionary measures. Let's go," said Solomon.

"Where are we?" I asked.

"Behind the warehouse," he said.

"How do you know that? You can't even see it from here."

"We don't need to," chipped in Fletcher. He pointed to the alley at the side of the building that we walked towards. "It's through there and half a block south."

"I don't even know which way south is. How does everyone else always seem to know the direction of the compass points?" I wondered.

"Built-in compass," said Solomon. "Remember, these could be ex-military contractors and they'll be armed. They're keeping a low profile but they'll be watching everything. Look up, around you, and keep your heads down. This is purely reconnaissance. We're not engaging."

"I knew the direction because I looked at the map on my phone," said Flaherty softly in my ear. "Also, these two have been here before, just a month back while on a stakeout."

"I feel better now," I decided.

Solomon put a finger to his lips and picked up the pace. The four of us jogged the length of the alley, paused to check the exit was clear, then turned, concealed inside the shadow of the building as we powered forward. Fletcher and Flaherty peeled off and slipped through another alley, quickly disappearing from view. Solomon and I proceeded cautiously, reaching the warehouse a little more than a minute later. Just like the front of the building, it looked empty. The windows were dirty, the doors closed, and no lights illuminated the inside. If the tank were still there, the thieves were keeping a very low profile.

I tapped Solomon's shoulder and pointed to the camera over the door. He nodded and looked upwards, then pointed. Fletcher leaned over the roof, gave the thumbs-up, and disappeared. "No snipers on the roof," said Solomon. "Let's go."

We jogged forwards before darting across the strip of road separating the two buildings. The blacktop had cracked badly and thick weeds grew between the cracks. We ran to the warehouse and moving quickly, reached the first window.

"I'm going to boost you up and let you take a look," said Solomon.

"Are you sure?"

"You could boost me," he said as he cracked a smile.

"Maybe next time."

Solomon cupped his hands together and I raised my foot, anchoring it in his hands. He launched me up like I was a feather and I braced myself against the flat wall of the building. "I think this is an office," I said as softly as I could. "I can't see anything except a couple of desks and an old mattress. Let me down."

Solomon lowered me and I placed my hands on his shoulders so I could drop to the ground with a light thud. "We'll try another window midway," he said.

Midway along the building we stopped and he boosted me up again. "It's another office," I told him, squinting through a cracked window. "But I think someone's been in there recently. I can see takeout coffee cups and there's... Get me down!" I hissed as the door opened.

A man in a black jacket and cap entered just as Solomon quickly lowered me, my heart thudding. "We're in the right place. He's armed with a semi-automatic and... oh, shit!" I squeaked as my cell phone rang. I searched my pants pocket for it and pulled it out as it began to trill louder. Now was not the best time for Francesca to call. I hit the "decline" button on the screen. A moment later, it rang again and I frantically fumbled for the silencer button.

"Lexi," whispered Solomon, shaking his head.

"I know," I whispered back, my face reddening. "I didn't think."

"I hear footsteps," he said, grabbing my hand and pulling me after him as we darted across the blacktop. We paused at the building, then Solomon pulled me after him to a narrow alley opposite and pressed me into a doorway. "Pull off your Kevlar," he said as he tugged on the straps of his vest.

"Why? What if they shoot?"

"They'll definitely shoot if they see us wearing them," he said. He tossed his vest into the doorway behind me and I threw mine after it. He pushed me backwards, ruffled my hair and pulled out my blouse, partially unbuttoning it.

"Really?" I asked, confused. "Is now the time?"

"I am not hot for you right now," he said, then paused. "Okay, maybe a little." He untucked his own shirt, covering the gun at his hip and pressed against me, kissing me hard. I had no idea why he was doing what he did but I was damn sure I liked it.

"Hey! You!" yelled a voice behind.

Solomon detached from me briefly but didn't look their way. "Wait your turn," he grunted. "I paid my money."

"What?" yelled the voice.

This time, Solomon tossed a look over his shoulder. "I said I paid my money. I've got fifteen minutes. You can wait until then and she's all yours."

I stilled, waiting nervously for the shot that didn't come. Through the mess of hair, half covering my face, I could see two men in black fatigues and t-shirts, handguns cocked and ready. I inched my hand to my hip, reaching for my gun. Solomon's hand looked like it was on my hip but I could feel his fingers, knowing he was already in position to grab his gun if the ruse went south.

"Finish up and get out of here," said the man, his face barely moving. If he were disgusted or intrigued, I couldn't tell. Hopefully, he wasn't reaching for his wallet. "Don't come back," said the man after a long moment. "This is private property."

"Fifteen minutes, man," grunted Solomon, turning back to me as he added, "Can you give us some privacy?"

The footsteps receded.

"I'm a prostitute?" I whispered, raising my eyebrows. "Really? I mean... really? That was the best cover story you thought of?"

"There was no way they'd believe I was."

"You couldn't think of anything else plausible?"

Solomon rocked back and looked down at me. "Can you?"

I thought about it. "Nope."

"We'll give them two minutes to clear out, then grab the flak jackets and head back to the car. We can't risk being seen again by going back but the others might have found something. I'll alert them so that they're aware that we almost blew our cover." Solomon reached for his phone but didn't move away from me, ensuring I was still trapped in the doorway. He tapped out a message and the moment it was sent, he grabbed our flak jackets, tossing one to me. We pulled them on and took off at a run. I followed him, weaving between buildings until we were suddenly at the auto shop. The car was there, but Fletcher and Flaherty weren't. Neither was the skinny man. Solomon and I climbed into the front seats and waited. A few minutes passed and the rear doors opened before our colleagues climbed in.

"Found it," said Fletcher. "Got a great photo to confirm too. What happened to you guys?"

"Two guards on patrol stumbled across us," said Solomon. I waited for him to mention my cell phone ringing at an inopportune time but, to my relief, he didn't. "They didn't suspect anything but told us to clear out. Show me the photo." He held his hand for Fletcher's phone and looked at the screen, then turned it to me.

"That's a tank," I agreed. It was parked in the warehouse. I could see two men sitting at a table next to it. Coffee cups, guns, and a stack of cards lay on the table.

"We counted four guards," said Flaherty.

"We got three. One inside, two on patrol. That only makes seven total. Probably less if we saw the same guys."

"They're not heavily armed but I don't think they're expecting a gunfight," said Fletcher.

"All the same, we're not engaging," decided Solomon. "This is definitely not our fight. The moment they know it's over is when they'll do anything they can to maintain control of the prize. We have people we can reach out to help."

"You mean Mitch," I said. I first met Major Mitch McAuley when Solomon and I went undercover as a married couple to investigate a strange case at Fort Charles. We helped him solve a troubling case and he helped me again recently when I needed to plunder Solomon's past. He was good man: solid and reliable. Much as I wanted to avoid throwing my buddies into further distress, there was no denying they needed the help.

"I do. It's time to call it in. Lexi? This is your case. What do you want to do?"

"I'll call Captain Harris and Sergeant Major Kafsky with the good news."

"You call this good news?" asked Fletcher with a gruff laugh. He leaned between our seats, his forearms resting on the top, then shot a glance to Solomon's window. "Someone wants you, boss."

The thin man stood at the window, his face blank. Solomon rolled it down and handed him more money. "No scratches," said the thin man.

"Anyone else come looking around here?" asked Solomon.

"No one. No one comes round here at all now. There're bad men over there." He jerked his head towards the warehouse.

"You don't say," said Solomon. He fixed the man with a look, adding, "We were never here."

"Never saw you," said the man. He stepped back and vanished.

Solomon's phone vibrated. He took one look at it and said, "We should go." Without waiting for an answer, he rolled up the window and reversed out of the abandoned auto shop. When we were on the road, I called Harris.

"Do you want the good news or the bad news?" I asked.

"The good news?" Harris said, his voice hesitant.

"McTavett was on the money with the location. We verified it."

"He's with us now. He wants to know if his family is okay."

I glanced at Solomon. He nodded, adding, "I just got news that his family was taken to a safe house and the perp watching them has been detained. We'll put McTavett in touch with his family when the tank is retrieved."

I relayed that information and Harris said, "Give me a minute." I heard some muffled voices before he came back on the line and said, "McTavett wants proof."

"We'll have his wife call him in the next few minutes," said Solomon.

I relayed that again and Harris passed it on. "Thanks," he said. "What's the bad news?"

"The tank is under armed guard. We think as many as seven but that's not confirmed. I don't know how you're going to get it out of there without help but we have an idea."

"Are you going to team up with us?" Harris asked hopefully. "This is like being back at boot camp all over again but less fun."

"We're going to talk to a friend of ours at Fort Charles. Someone with authority."

"Lexi, you can't do that. Our careers will be over!" said Harris.

"Not necessarily," I said, "Besides, what choice do you have?"

Harris was silent for so long I had to check the call was still connected. Finally, he said, "Do what you gotta do. Kafsky and I appreciate everything you've already done to help us."

"I'll call you soon." I hung up, then immediately dialed Major Mitch McAuley. I liked the man. He was fair and loyal and even though it was a big favor, if anyone could help my buddies, he was it. I just hoped he would hear me out when I told him what happened.

"Lexi, hi," he said answering his personal cell phone. "Now is not a good time. We have a situation at the base."

I paused, a disconcerted feeling hitting me in the chest. "Does it have anything to do with a missing tank?" I asked, knowing that if the answer was no, I just raised one helluva question.

"Aw, crap," groaned McAuley. "How in hell do you know about that?"

"Because…" I grinned as the car sped away, "I know exactly where it is."

CHAPTER EIGHTEEN

"A prostitute?" said Lily. "Did I hear that right? Solomon pretended you were a prostitute?"

"Yup."

"Like... an expensive prostitute?"

"No, a streetwalker."

"An expensive streetwalker?"

"More of the bargain basement variety."

Lily paused, then said, "Rude."

"I know." I sighed.

"A high-class hooker would have been much better."

I frowned. "Do you really think so?"

"Yeah. There was one time Jord and I..."

"Don't tell me!" I cut in before she told me exactly what kind of shenanigans she got up to with my brother. There were some mental images a person just couldn't unsee and I didn't need to spend every family dinner for the next decade re-seeing them.

"You never let me tell you stuff anymore!"

"If I married your brother, would you let me tell you stuff?"

"I wish I had a brother," Lily said wistfully.

"I gave you mine. And you got three extra brothers-in-law out of it and I'm about to give you another brother-in-law."

"Sweet deal," said Lily. "Can I give Serena back?"

"She's non-refundable."

"I suffer for you."

"You are truly the best friend I could have."

"Which is why you're going to take me to a late lunch," said Lily. "I'm not working today and Poppy wants to see her favorite aunt."

"You just said that to get me to take you to lunch."

"Did it work?"

"I'll see you at Sushi Delights in an hour?"

Lily squealed. "My favorite!"

I looked up as Solomon walked in wearing black fatigues. "Gotta go. Get that baby ready for squishing," I said.

"What about Poppy?" giggled Lily before she hung up.

"What's with the camouflage?" I asked my fiancé.

"We have a meeting with Mitch about the tank takedown," he said, "then I'm volunteering for the first watch while they get everything they need to into play."

"The Army can't do the surveillance themselves?" I asked.

"Mitch and his immediate superiors want all of this kept on the down-low. That means as few personnel knowing about it as possible to avoid any embarrassing leaks."

I nodded, understanding perfectly. "No one wants their stolen tank making the front-page news."

"Heads would roll," agreed Solomon. "So the whole team is watching the warehouse in short rotations. I'll take the first three hours, then Delgado. I need you to take the one after."

"No problem. Is Delgado cross about participating?" I wondered.

"Not one bit. He even sounded thrilled."

I laughed, then checked my phone and set an alarm for six hours hence. "Why are we doing such short shifts? Not that I'm complaining."

"The thieves will be on high alert for anyone watching, especially if a deal is going down soon. They might panic when they realize McTavett's family are gone and their man missing. I can't think that they would want to keep that tank in the warehouse any longer than necessary and it makes sense they'll move it at night when there are less eyes to notice a vehicle of that size. I want to make sure my people aren't around for too long and I want us all to take different positions. I'll be watching from the street. Delgado will hide in one of the abandoned buildings. You're getting the car."

"Each of us alone? Is that wise?" I thought about the weapons the guards were toting. Given that they were professional mercenaries and I was a wisecracking former temp, I figured their aim was probably better and faster than mine. I didn't want a bullet-shaped hole in me. I had the starring role in a wedding!

"None of us will be alone. I've assigned team members from the risk management department to key support locations. We'll all be in radio contact at all times and there will be a backup van hidden a block away. Plus, the Army will take up strategic positions less than a mile away. The moment they're ready to roll in, we all get the hell out."

"This sounds dangerous."

"You can bow out if you want. I don't want anyone doing anything they're uncomfortable with and you've done enough already to help your buddies. We can take it from here."

I thought about it. Then I thought about how it would look if the boss's fiancée did bow out. I would look weak and it might seem like I was currying favors. I spent my whole private investigative career avoiding scenarios like that. This wouldn't be the time to start.

"I'm in," I said.

"Let's run through the plan," said Solomon, starting for the boardroom. A moment later, the office doors opened and the rest of our team strolled in, along with several members of the risk team. They all made a beeline for the boardroom.

I grabbed my notepad and pen and followed him in.

~

"Huuurrrr-sushi-hmmm-mmmmm," groaned Lily as she chopsticked a shrimp nigiri into her mouth. "I love it. I love Poppy being asleep. I love you."

"Love you too," I said as I reached for another delicious piece of sushi. Lunch and Lily's company were exactly what I needed to get my mind off the challenging plan Solomon so eloquently delivered to the team earlier. It wasn't enormously complicated but very risky.

246

All we had to do was get in and out of the area without raising any suspicion about unusual movement in vehicular or foot traffic.

Given that the tank was hidden in an area few people frequented, that in itself posed a problem but Solomon had already thought ahead and outlined a plan. For me, it was going to be easy. I just needed to drive in, park on the block he designated and hunker down for a couple of hours while monitoring the road for tank movement or anything else unusual. If someone stopped by my car and asked me what I was doing, I would say that my radiator had overheated and I needed to wait for it to cool down. If I were offered a tow, I would politely refuse, claiming a family member would collect me if the engine didn't restart quickly. It was easy enough a ruse to swallow and if it wasn't believed, there would be operatives nearby to assist me if anything went wrong.

So far, I wasn't worried. That is, not terribly worried. I was mildly worried since watching mercenaries wasn't the safest job, but the only thing worse than that right now would be if the nature of the job got back to my mom and dad. Then I would never hear the end of it. Even worse, one or both of my parents might insist on joining me.

"You look worried," said Lily. "Is it the wedding? Is there a problem with the dress?"

"Everything is fine with the wedding. There's nothing left to arrange. The dress is almost ready to be picked up and all we have left to do is the rehearsal dinner." That was exactly what Francesca told me when I returned her ill-timed earlier call.

"I can't wait. I'm so excited."

"I changed your bridesmaid dress to neon orange," I said, teasing.

Lily stopped chewing and her eyes widened. "Okay," she said.

"Crushed taffeta."

"Ohh," she whispered as she gulped.

"There's a hat too." I couldn't help myself.

A tear slid from Lily's eye. "Uh-huh?"

"It's straw. It has a big ribbon bow and..."

Lily swatted me with her chopsticks and laughed in relief. "Now I know you're kidding, but before that I was prepared to wear neon orange."

"I would never do that to you. Even I know the limitations of friendship." We both eyed the last piece of sushi and I wondered if Lily was thinking the same as me: did those limitations extend to that piece?

"Let's halve it," said Lily.

I nodded and she roughly chopped it in half, then we both dunked our shares in soy sauce and ate happily. Just as I swallowed, I looked up and waved at the tall blond woman walking towards me.

"I thought it was you," said Faye Wendell. "You remember my husband, Steve?"

How I could forget? But I politely replied, "Of course. It's so nice to see you both again."

"I never said thank you," said Steve. "You really made us get our heads on straight. Without you, I don't know if we'd both be here together." He wrapped his arm around his wife's shoulders and they beamed at each other.

"The waiter just signaled that our table is ready," said Steve.

"I'll be right with you, honey," said Faye as Steve walked away. "Lexi, it was great to see you again."

"You too, Faye," I said.

Faye rubbed her tiny bump. "He's right. We really owe you a debt of thanks."

"I was glad to help," I told her. "How's the pregnancy?"

"It's going great. Steve is thrilled. I just wish I could eat all the food here. My doctor said no shellfish."

"It's only a few months of sacrifice," said Lily. She pointed to Poppy fast asleep under a thick blanket the color of pink cotton candy. "Then you get one of these."

"Well, isn't that one perfect?" cooed Faye. "I meant to say thank you when I saw you at the bar. Have you changed jobs?"

"The bar?" I frowned.

"Lily's. We went to a party for Steve's friend, Big B. Or Bryce as everyone else calls him. We only stopped in for a few minutes to wish them well but I saw you were busy."

"I'm not working there," I told her. "I was just helping out. Lily owns the bar. Your husband and Bryce Maynard are friends?"

"Yes, he's the one that got my husband all jumpy about marriages and gold-diggers. If you ask me, he's kind of a jerk but I can't pick my husband's friends. If I did, Bryce would be last on the list." She gave a little shudder.

"You really don't like him, huh?" said Lily.

"Oh, don't get me wrong. Bryce can be great fun to be around but there's something about him... His fiancée is great. Perhaps she'll curb some of his less pleasant behavior. She's a little meek so maybe not but she seems sweet. I really don't know her all that well so I could be wrong. I'm glad he found someone although I don't like the way he treated Jessica or the way he talks about her. No matter what he says, it just isn't Jessica. I've known her too long." Faye stopped for a breath. "Sorry, I'm rambling."

"Jessica, his ex?" I asked. "She's a friend of yours?"

"She is. That is, she was. We weren't close but we were social. I haven't seen her in a few months and things were kind of awkward when they broke up; then it just got too long to call and say hi."

"I've been trying to get in touch with her. Do you happen to know where she lives?" I asked.

"Sure, of course, but what do you want to get in touch with her for?"

"It's related to a case and her name came up. I know you wouldn't normally give out someone's personal details but it could be important..." I trailed off.

"Is it one of her legal cases? I know she takes on some tough defenses. I don't want to get her into any trouble."

"Oh, no, it's nothing like that," I assured her. "I think she might have witnessed something that I need to clarify. You're welcome to call ahead and tell her I'd like to have a word with her."

Faye tilted her head, contemplating me for a moment. "I know you and I get a good feeling about you and you helped me," she said, "I'll give you Jessica's address and I'll tell her you're going to come by. She'll talk to you." She reached for a pen in her purse and wrote the address on a napkin. I recognized the address as a nice apartment building in Chilton, not far from where Solomon and I formerly lived.

"Thank you," I said.

"No, thank you. You've given me an excuse to call her and I was really looking for one. You'll have to excuse me. My husband is waving frantically and I think that means he just shared our good news with more people." She patted my shoulder, gave one last adoring look at Poppy, and hurried to rejoin her husband.

"Let's never lose touch," said Lily.

"It'll never happen."

"Or fall out."

"How can we?"

"I took your Prada purse and I damaged it. What? Now seemed the perfect time to tell you!" squeaked Lily as my face fell.

"The black one?" I asked.

Lily nodded sadly.

"That's yours," I told her. "Your mom bought it as a birthday present."

Lily's jaw dropped. "Oooh. Well, lucky for you," she said, visibly happy again. "Dessert?"

"Absolutely!"

"Do you want to come over later?"

"Not if it involves alcohol. I'm on cocktail hiatus until the wedding." I decided that when I'd awoken on the couch, I was almost one hundred percent certain I could stick to it... unless faced with temptation. If faced with temptation, I would be screwed.

"Sounds awful, but no, I thought we could make dinner and eat outside. We could use the grill."

"I will have to take a raincheck. Solomon wants me working an op later."

"Anything interesting?"

"Just surveillance," I said, since Solomon had given me strict instructions not to tell anyone, not even Lily. Often, that meant I told Lily as soon as I could but in this instance, it was probably a good idea to leave her out of it.

"Are you watching that ass, Bryce?" she asked.

"No, someone else. As soon as I finish with that, I'll need to interview this Jessica. I've been looking for her and I want to hear her perspective. If what she has to say matches my hunches, it'll be even more compelling evidence to present to my client so she can help her friend."

"Do you feel bad that you might bust up a relationship?"

"I've thought a lot about that and if it's a bad relationship, and he's lying to her, then no, I don't feel bad at all. Plus, look what he tried to do to me! He's a creep!"

"Would you believe someone if they came to you and told you Solomon was a bad guy?"

That was a much harder question to answer. I had been told, several times, to be careful around Solomon, that I didn't know him nearly well enough and few people did. Yet all that had changed in recent weeks when Solomon got shot and I had to investigate his past life. I found out things he'd hidden and he turned out to be an even better man than I thought he was. A man of morals and I admired that. "The evidence would not only have to be compelling but also contains the element that

I already knew he had a bad side before I was told he did," I said.

"I hope your evidence stacks up when you tell your client," said Lily.

"That's why I'm being careful and not rushing into it," I said as my cell phone rang. I reached for it. "It's my client," I said, then hit "answer." "Hi, Jas."

"Lexi, hi, can you come over?" asked Jas. She paused and I heard distant shouts. "They're fighting. I mean, Julia and Bryce are fighting and it sounds awful. I can't make out what they're saying but Julia isn't answering her phone or the door. I'm really worried."

"Have you called 911?"

"No. Do you think I should?"

"Yes," I decided. "Call the police now. I'm on my way over." I hung up. "I'm sorry. I have to run," I said.

"It sounds bad."

I nodded. "Could be. My client is worried and I'm going to run over there and check up on her."

"Do you want me to come too? I can be your backup."

"Not with the baby," I decided, "but I appreciate your offer."

I left money for the check and hurried to my car, driving as fast as I could and with as few traffic violations as possible to Jas's apartment. I pulled up at the curb and she buzzed me in. When I stepped off the stairs onto their floor, she was already waiting for me.

"Where are the police?" I asked, noticing the lack of official presence.

"The dispatcher said they'd send someone but no one's gotten here yet."

"Has Julia answered the door yet?"

Jas shook her head. "I didn't try. They've only just stopped shouting but I thought I should wait for someone else."

"Let's try now that there're two of us," I said. I stepped past Jas and rapped on the door. I didn't expect it to open but a moment later, it did.

Julia stood in the hallway wearing a blue print dress and a cardigan a size too big. Her eyes were red, her cheeks flushed, and a strand of hair had escaped from her ponytail. She pushed the strand behind her ear and glared at us. Behind her, Bryce came into view until he stood immediately behind her.

"I should have guessed. If it isn't the meddling neighbor," he snarled. Then he saw me and flinched, just barely. "And you? If you're going to complain that we wouldn't give you a job, you'll need to take it to HR."

I wasn't expecting that and it stopped the words in my throat. "Wouldn't give me a job?" I spluttered.

"That's right. Your skills aren't up to it. Stick to the bartending. Maybe if you took a few night classes and applied again..." he shrugged.

"Working for you is the last thing I'd ever want to do," I snapped.

"What's going on?" asked Julia looking from me, then over her shoulder at Bryce.

"She begged Vincent and me for a job and we thought we'd help her out by letting her swing by the office. What a mistake. Unskilled and totally unsuited and then she tried to offer her services in exchange for a job, if you know what I mean. I kicked her out of the office." Bryce rolled his eyes.

"I did not!" I snapped. "And you did not... Anyway that's not why we're here. Are you okay?" I asked Julia.

She squared her shoulders, her jaw set stiffly. "I'm fine."

"I heard shouting," said Jas softly. "I was worried about you."

"Just a lovers' tiff," said Bryce. "Oh man, you called the cops! Jas, you are one helluva psycho. The sooner Julia moves out of this building, the better."

Jas and I turned, seeing the two officers approaching us. I knew one of them since he was buddies with Daniel. He gave me a nod and indicated we should step back.

"We got a call about a disturbance," the officer started. "Everything okay?"

"Just these two busy-bodies wasting public money," said Bryce.

"You okay, ma'am?" he asked Julia.

She nodded quickly. "I'm sorry about this, officer. Everything is fine. Really."

"Mind if we step inside?"

"C'mon in, officers," said Bryce. "Let's get this cleared up."

The officers stepped through the door, and Jas started to follow them. "Not you," said Bryce, jabbing a finger at her. "You've done enough damage. Julia realizes how jealous you are of her and she and I aren't going to put up with you any longer than we have to."

"What do you mean?"

"We're selling. We're buying a new place," said Bryce.

"We can help you," I said softly to Julia. "You don't have to do anything you don't want to do."

"I'm not," said Julia. "But I have to deal with this now." With that, she shut the door in our faces.

Jas turned to me. "What the hell was that all about?" she asked, her face as stunned as I felt.

"Let's go," I said. "The police are here. Julia is safe and there's nothing more we can do here tonight."

CHAPTER NINETEEN

Ten minutes later, I was on the sidewalk outside Jas and Julia's building. There was nothing else I could do and I'd already assured Jas of the same. With the police in the apartment, and Julia refusing there was an issue, we were at a crossroads. Jas opted to stay at her apartment in case another fight broke out, or the police officers knocked on her door, but except for briefly explaining the real story about what happened at Bryce's office, I didn't have much else to tell her. All I could think about was the conversation I had with Lily. It was one thing for Bryce to spout those lies so easily, but the evidence I needed to provide for Julia to show him as the man he truly was would have to be more compelling.

I pulled the napkin from my pocket and looked at Jessica's address. If I needed persuasive evidence, I had one last shot to get it.

Hopping into my car, I drove directly to Jessica's apartment. It was nearly five, so there was a small chance Jessica would finish work soon and be on her way home. If she was home, great. If not, I would stake out her apartment for as long as I could before I had to join Solomon's detail. If I couldn't speak to her today, I would have to return early tomorrow and catch her before work.

Short of nabbing Bryce in a honey-trap, and I was sure he would be extra careful for the next few weeks, and there wasn't much else I could do. I was pretty sure Bryce wouldn't fall for the pretty girl ruse anyway. It was sheer lack of foresight that meant I hadn't thought to record my ill-fated meeting with him.

Jessica's building was significantly higher end than the building I just left. Planters with fresh green foliage and a small, gold-edged canopy framed the glass door and the name plates were polished brass. I hit number four and waited.

"Yes?" came the voice through the speaker.

"Jessica Collea?" I asked, reading from the napkin Faye gave me.

"This is she."

"My name is Lexi Graves, I'm a private investigator with the Solomon Detective Agency. Can I come up and ask you some questions?" I inquired. Often it was best not to be so honest in case no one wanted to speak with me, but Jessica was a lawyer and Faye had probably already called her so I thought the direct method would work better. Plus, I didn't have a lot of time to come up with a ruse.

"Regarding?"

"I've been retained by a friend of a lady who is engaged to Bryce Maynard," I said and waited. I didn't miss the sharp intake of breath that was audible over the speaker.

"I thought he was done harassing me. I don't want anymore to do with him," she said, an edge of anger seeping into her voice.

"I'm not here because of him, more *about* him. My client is worried about her friend and I thought you might be able to help."

"I don't see how. No one would believe me anyway."

"I would," I said.

I waited, wondering if she would ignore me. Then the buzzer sounded and the door clicked so I took that as my cue to enter. Ignoring the small elevator, I jogged up the stairs and stepped onto a carpeted hallway with the walls painted in a soft blue. Picture windows at both ends allowed plenty of light. Two apartments occupied this floor and Jessica had the rear one. She was waiting for me at the door, a roll of brown tape in her hand, but that wasn't what surprised me. Instead, I couldn't help zeroing in on her heavily pregnant belly. "Thanks for seeing me," I said, offering her my hand. She shook it firmly and stood back to let me enter.

"I'm not sure what good it will do," she said, shaking out her dark brown shoulder- length hair.

"You're moving?" I asked, as we walked past several card boxes and into a spacious living room.

"I am. I'm taking maternity leave and I'm using the time to transfer to my employer's Detroit office. My family lives there," she explained. "They'll be able to help with the baby."

"Does your husband have family there too?"

"It's just the two of us," said Jessica, patting her bump. She stopped and looked at me with a surprised expression. "You don't know, do you?"

"Know what?"

"This is Bryce's baby."

I stopped, shocked. "His baby?"

"Yes, it is, no matter what he says to the contrary. I know he's told everyone I cheated and I'm trying to pin it on him, but this *is* his baby. As it happens, he's done me a favor by refusing to acknowledge it. I can leave the state without him causing a fuss about custody rights."

"I had no idea."

"Well, he is everyone's favorite guy, isn't he? Why would everyone's favorite guy abandon his pregnant girlfriend?" She held up a hand, not that I had an answer. "Let me tell you. It's because he's an asshole. I got tired of his crap but I tried to make it work, especially since we were pregnant but then I couldn't do it anymore. He screamed at me to get an abortion because a baby would cramp his style and I needed to think about his future. Shame he didn't think of that when he wouldn't wrap it up, if you know what I mean?"

I nodded, still stunned.

Jessica sighed and dropped onto the cream leather couch. "When I wanted to keep the baby, he laid into me, saying I must have cheated anyway. I went ballistic. I screamed at him. I threw a glass cup! He made out I was a psycho who was abusing him! That's how he gets us, you see?"

"I don't understand."

"Bryce is so charming. All he has to do is tell his next woman how badly treated he was by his ex and she just laps it up. I know I did! I thought he was wonderful. So generous and thoughtful and kind. He even encouraged me to cut my hair because he liked it that way. Thankfully my hair grows fast. I felt so bad for him that his ex called him names and falsely accused him of abuse. Then, one day, everything he said about her, he started saying about me, and I realized it was all a big lie. That, and he never paid me back for loaning him the money for his car. At least I got out before he convinced me to sell my apartment so we could buy a house together. Together! He doesn't have two cents to rub together. He blows it on booze and a good time and probably that woman I caught him messaging. Two years I wasted on that useless guy." Jessica stopped and blew out a breath. "I'm sorry. I don't know where that all came from. Now you're going to think I'm crazy too."

"I don't think you're crazy," I told her as I joined her on the couch. I did, however, recall Ruby mentioning Bryce's ex did throw him out. Now I remembered how Bryce said he caught his ex messaging another man. If everything Jessica said was the real story, I could see why she tossed him out. "I believe you and I believe he treated you very badly."

Jessica huffed. "No one else believes me."

"Did you tell anyone?"

"Of course. I told his buddies, Vincent and Oliver, about his drinking but they don't see it. How could they? They only see him at happy hour at the bar, or at a barbecue, or a party. Everyone's drinking! They don't seem him passed out in the hallway and if they do hear about it, it's a funny little story. Ha-ha! And if we had a fight, he'd just spin it as me being a bitch. In the last few months, it got really bad and I was so ashamed that I withdrew from all my family and friends until I was alone. I was so embarrassed by his behavior I couldn't be around anyone, but then he spun it that I was a cold bitch who hated his family and friends and they hated me."

"That must have been awful."

"It was but you know what got me through it? This baby." Jessica smiled for the first time as she rubbed her bump again. "We're going to have a new start and we're going to get through this. You're won't try and stop me, will you?"

"No, I think you're doing the right thing," I said.

"Good. Because if that jerk ever tries anything again, I will sue him for harassment."

"Has he harassed you?"

"Not recently. I guess he's too busy slating me to the new girl. They got together about two weeks after we broke up. Did you know that? I think he already had her lined up, ready to feed his ego, just like he did to me when we met."

"She is why I'm here. My client is a friend of his current partner and very worried about her."

"Her friends *should* be worried about her. He'll do to her exactly what he did to me, and to the ex before me, and who knows how many others? He's not a good man."

"I think that's obvious," I said with a pointed look at her bump.

"I'm glad you said you believe me but I'm not sure if it matters anymore. I'm leaving in a few days and I don't want any trouble. I want to have my baby in peace and enjoy those first weeks as a mom. If I make any complaint, Bryce might try and ruin everything to get back at me. Besides, what can I even complain about? If every man who was pegged an asshole went to prison, there would be no free men on earth!"

I laughed and Jessica did too. Her face relaxed and her eyes softened. "I know a few good men and I'm sure you'll meet one eventually if you want to," I told her. "I won't ask you to make an official complaint but it might help if you could tell his current girlfriend what went on. Perhaps if she heard it from you, she might realize he's not the man she thinks he is."

"I don't know. I'm not sure it's a good idea." Jessica shook her head.

"I can't think of a better person to tell her who he really is."

"I can think of two good reasons. One, he'll already have painted me as a bitter psycho ex who can't be believed. He does that to his exes. Second, he might get back at me by going after my baby. I'm sorry, I can't risk it. If you'll excuse me, I need to finish packing and I'm physically uncomfortable enough as it as. I'm sorry I can't help you."

"Of course," I said, recognizing my cue to leave. I followed Jessica to the door. "Thanks for seeing me and good luck with the move and the baby. And the new job."

"I'm calling it the trifecta of stress, but thank you." She paused with one hand resting on the door and the other on her belly. "I'm sorry he's putting another woman through his crap. I hope she gets out of it before it's too late."

~

A glance at my wristwatch as I got into my car confirmed I had just enough time for a bathroom break and to pick up a sandwich and some snacks for my surveillance shift. I could easily have driven the few blocks from Jessica's apartment to Solomon's house and used the facilities there but I just couldn't bring myself to do that. Instead, I drove to a cafe and picked up a gourmet roast beef and pickle sandwich, a pack of chips, and a freshly-made, overpriced soda.

Following Solomon's directions, I drove over to my designated spot near the tank's concealment and pulled up behind another parked car. That car was empty but it was outside a business that looked like it was in operation. My car would blend right in and there was the potential that I could be a customer or an employee.

My cell phone rang as soon as I shut off the engine. "Hi," I said.

"Hey," said Solomon. "Good spot."

"You can see me?"

"I see everything."

"How many fingers?" I asked, holding up three. There was no point looking around for Solomon. Wherever he was, he would be well concealed.

"Three," said Solomon. "I expected something ruder."

"It never crossed my mind. I am a lady."

"Do you have a good visual for the warehouse?"

"Yes, so long as no one parks a truck in front of my car. I can see the doors and the courtyard. I can't see any movement."

"I don't expect you will. I expect everything to remain quiet."

"How come you're here? I thought you were taking the shift after me. Did something change?"

"Nope, just some reconnaissance."

"Any word from the Army?"

"They're putting together their team. The takedown will probably be in the early hours of the morning when our thieves least expect it."

"And when the last businesses here are closed. No witnesses," I added.

"Exactly," agreed Solomon. "I'm taking off. That sandwich looks good."

"I'd offer to share but we don't want to attract attention. Suspicious sandwich sharing could raise alarms."

"Don't worry, your sandwich is safe. There will be eyes all around but don't look for anyone. If you do see anyone, make a note and I'll fire them later."

"Harsh."

"Practical. I'll check in with you soon."

I turned on the radio and unwrapped my sandwich, taking my time to eat it, then I munched through the bag of chips and finally slurped the soda. I raided the glove compartment and door pockets for something sweet but all I came up with was a melted chocolate bar that didn't look too appetizing so I put it away until I got really desperate. Mostly though I street-watched. After a half hour, two guys walked out of a nearby business and got into the car in front of mine and drove off, leaving me feeling more conspicuous. Fifteen minutes later, a truck with closed panel doors pulled in front and completely blocked my view of the warehouse.

That left me with a choice: drive off and find somewhere else to park, risking someone with a sharp eye looking out of the warehouse and wondering what I was doing bunny-hopping the car along the street; or hope the van moved soon; or get out and take a walk, continuing my reconnaissance on foot.

After some umming and ahhing, and no sign of the van moving, I slid over to the passenger side and climbed out, the van concealing my movements from view. I locked the car doors, prayed the car was still there and in one piece when I returned, and took off at a slow pace. I walked to the next block and turned the corner, taking a few paces before I stopped. I leaned my back against the wall and drank my soda, looking for all the world like I had nowhere better to be, which was true.

From my new standing viewpoint, I could see directly onto the warehouse courtyard. As I waited, two guards came around the far wall, passing by the doors and disappearing around the near side. I checked my watch, waited, and ten minutes later, they came around again. Neither looked armed but I had no doubt they could reach weapons harnessed at their hips or shoulders in seconds. They also might smell a rat if they came around a third time and spied me still standing there. I had to move.

Pushing up from the wall, I looked around. There were no cars on this block and no areas for easy concealment. I could walk back to the street and onto the next block and back again but that would fall under suspicious movement. It was probably best that I headed back to my car and hoped the van would move imminently.

I almost reached the turn when a movement caught my eye from a partially opened doorway. Someone was moving inside but was it one of Solomon's guys? Curious, I stepped into the doorway and levered the door open, waiting for hinge squeaks that never came.

Inside, I had to blink to adjust my eyes to the gloom. Yes, there was someone at the window with a telescopic lens pointed at the building opposite. I paused, my breathing shallow, as the man shifted into the light. It wasn't one of Solomon's men but I did know him.

"What are you doing?" I called out.

He whipped around, his weapon drawn. "Jeez, Lexi! You scared the shit out of me," snapped Maddox.

"That's the second time you've pulled a gun on me."

"Don't make it a third! I might actually shoot you!" He sheathed his gun and breathed out heavily.

"Point taken." I walked over, careful where I stepped since the building had obviously been left in a hurry by its previous occupants and paper and furniture were strewn everywhere. Plus, it smelled like a litter tray and I did not want to step into anything unsavory.

"What are you doing here?" we both asked at the same time.

"After you," said Maddox.

"You first," I said. "I found you so I get to ask first."

Maddox narrowed his eyes. "Are you following me?"

"No!"

"You do know it's a crime to follow a federal employee?"

"I do now. Damn. Is it really?" I wished I hadn't known that but then ignorance didn't make it legal so perhaps it was best that I did know. Then I could take steps in the future to avoid looking like I was doing something criminal even if I were. "Hey, don't evade the answer. Who or what are you watching?"

"The building across the street," said Maddox.

"The warehouse?"

"No, the one on the right. It's part of the case we're building."

"From that place where you never were?" I asked, thinking about the dumpster dive I'd previously taken.

"I'm struggling to follow that confusing question, but yes."

I approached the filthy window and peeked out. Not only did Maddox have a very good view of the building opposite but also of the warehouse. That made it a great vantage point for me, but also a big problem. We could hardly share viewpoints but the problem was bigger than that.

"How long have the FBI been here?" I asked.

"Since yesterday. Why?"

"Just you or anyone else around?"

"Just me and my partner. He's out getting us some food."

"We might have a problem," I said. "A very sensitive problem."

"Something to do with why you're lurking around the 'hood?"

"I'm not lurking. I was casually strolling, but yes. You're watching that building—" I pointed across the street then redirected my pointing finger to the warehouse "—and I'm watching that one. I'm not the only one here too. We're working a joint op with another agency and the neighborhood is crawling with our people."

Maddox set the camera on the table pushed against the wall. "How sensitive are we talking?"

"Major issues if word gets out. How sensitive is yours?"

"Millions of dollars of sensitive. There's an art forger who uses that building. I'm this close to nailing him," said Maddox, holding up his thumb and forefinger and squeezing them together until barely any air separated them.

"Both of us have operational issues. We need to get a handle on this."

"I can't pull out," said Maddox.

I chewed my lip. "Neither can we. Can you look the other way?"

"I only have a vested interest in catching my guy," he said. "But I can't leave my post. I'm happy not to record anything unconnected to my case but I can't just leave."

"My op goes down in the early hours. It might scare off your guy."

"I have enough to move in on my guy but the Feds turning up would probably cause issues with your op. We're at a conundrum," said Maddox. He sighed. "Dammit!"

"What if there was a coordinated takedown? Can you nab your guy as we take ours?"

"It's possible. Who's the other agency you're working with? A local crew?"

"Think national."

"How national?"

"It begins with 'a' and ends in 'y'."

"Shit. What are you into?"

"It's better you don't know." I thought about it some more and all I saw was danger. "Our op will probably involve an exchange of gunfire."

"What the hell have you gotten yourself into?"

"Remember that tank I was looking for?"

Maddox raised his eyebrows and looked back to the warehouse. "It's in there?" he asked thumbing at it.

"Yes, it is, and the Army wants it back. We're just here to monitor movement until then."

"Please tell me you're not going to be involved in the takedown?"

"I'm not. I promise."

"I don't think my bosses want to be involved in this either and gunfire will definitely scare our guy off. We'll pick him up quietly elsewhere and raid the warehouse in the morning. I need to discuss it with my partner and my boss, then I'll confirm it to you."

"Thanks," I said.

"Thanks for telling me what we stumbled into here so we don't get caught in the crossfire. You know the worst time for something to go wrong is just as it starts to kick off. That's when people panic, mistakes are made, rash judgments meted out. We can avoid that now."

"I'd better go," I said. "You should secure that side door."

"My partner was supposed to have secured it on the way out. You can be sure I'll have something to say when he gets back. I'll call you very soon."

"I'm here another couple of hours. I need to alert Solomon and the Army too. They don't want unknowns in the area and it would be best if they know your location so no one accidentally targets you. Is that okay?"

"It's fine," said Maddox, "but as far as paperwork goes, none of us knows squat about each other. I'll tell my chain of command there's another agency operating in the area and you tell yours, but I'd appreciate it if you don't give out any case details."

"Got it," I agreed, then I reached over and hugged him, feeling pleased when he squeezed me back. "Keep safe," I told him.

"You too."

Seconds later, I was out on the street and by the time I got back in my car, the van had gone, leaving me nothing to do but watch my surroundings and make a couple of phone calls.

CHAPTER TWENTY

Solomon had assured me he would negotiate the situation between the Army and the FBI and didn't seem overtly worried. Nothing further happened during my shift and by the time Solomon called to say I could go home, my butt was dead and my legs in desperate need of a walk. However, I couldn't just leave, knowing what was about to go down. That would be like leaving a birthday party before the cake was served. Just plain silly. So, instead of going home, I pulled back my position and parked my car where the Army TAC team had grouped to wait for the go signal before heading up to the roof where Solomon was positioned.

I had no intention of participating directly in the tank's recovery but I was pretty sure it would be an event I didn't want to miss. I wasn't the only one with that idea. By the time night fell, leaving a dark, overcast sky with barely a hint of moonlight, Delgado, Fletcher and Flaherty were all waiting too. For me, it was half about distraction from thinking about what to do with my disaster of a case and what I should tell Jas, and half for the excitement. I figured it was excitement for everyone else. It wasn't every day that the Army conducted a covert mission in town to recover millions of dollars of stolen equipment.

"Heard the Feds are getting a piece of the action tonight," said Delgado. He hunkered down next to us and raised a pair of night vision binoculars to his eyes.

"Where did you get those?" I asked.

"Private stash. Wait. You don't have any?" he asked, checking my empty hands.

"No."

Delgado looked over at Solomon. "Wedding gift," he said. Solomon smiled but didn't say anything. "Christmas present?" Delgado persisted.

"Is that what you got Serena for a wedding present?" I wondered. Then I wondered if that was just the kind of wedding or Christmas present I would enjoy. I would be able to see all kinds of stuff at night. I wouldn't have to put the lights on for a midnight kitchen raid. I could witness some interesting things on night surveillance, although possibly it wasn't the kind of stuff I'd truly enjoy seeing. Maybe I'd enjoy the night vision binoculars if they were accompanied by a pretty purse.

Delgado pulled a face. "Not if I want to live."

"I will find out what she wants for Christmas," I said.

"No need. She's dropped seventeen well-placed hints so I have a list. Married life," he finished with a sigh.

"You love it," I told him.

Delgado grinned. "I do. I got a wife and a step-daughter thrown in. Life is sweet."

Fletcher and Flaherty looked at each other and rolled their eyes. "If you two become as insufferable as this guy when you marry, we're going to leave," said Fletcher.

"That so?" asked Solomon.

"It's bad enough when Lexi flutters her eyelashes at you when she thinks we can't see."

"I do not," I said. I waited for them to huff and turn away then fluttered my eyelashes at Solomon. He blew me a kiss.

"Revolting," said Flaherty without turning around. "Totally unprofessional. Pass me those binoculars. I want to see."

Solomon turned back to the roof edge. "Any movement?"

"None. I just don't want to look at all this loved up mush any longer," said Flaherty.

Solomon's cell phone vibrated and he answered with short acknowledgments then hung up. "That was Maddox. The Feds picked up their target two blocks out. There are still two agents in the building across the street but they've moved to a more secure upper level of that building hopefully out of the range of any gunfire. They are waiting for the call."

"What are they so interested in across the street?" asked Delgado.

"Not our pay grade," said Solomon.

Since it wasn't my pay grade either, I kept my mouth shut.

"We're only here for the fireworks anyway," said Fletcher.

"Hunker down. We're in for a long wait," said Solomon.

We passed the time, watching and talking softly until Solomon's phone vibrated again. "It's a go," he said after glancing at the screen. A moment later, several armored vehicles rolled past, fanning out as they reached the courtyard and disgorging heavily armed soldiers. Several soldiers carried a battering ram that they used to bash through the doors. When the doors were pulled back, splintered and useless, there was a small exchange of gunfire and loud shouting.

A few minutes passed, then six men were marched out and made to kneel in the courtyard. Their arms were already secured behind their backs.

"That it?" said Fletcher. "I expected more."

"Disappointing," agreed Flaherty.

"That's all they needed to do," said Delgado. "I don't see any casualties and the fuss was kept to a minimum. This was a good op."

Solomon nodded. "The danger's over. It's always just when they're about to breach that's the most dangerous time."

"Does this mean all the players are in custody?" I asked.

Solomon shook his head. "These men are hired mercs at the most. The major players are elsewhere."

"What now?" asked Delgado. "Are we out?"

"We are," said Solomon. "I offered our services to help track down the buyers but Mitch declined. They want to take the investigation in house from here. It's time for us to go home."

"See you tomorrow, boss," said Fletcher. He and Flaherty took off, jogging across the roof and disappearing through the doorway into the stairwell.

Delgado, Solomon and I followed them and jogged down the stairs. All the vehicles were gone except for one, and our own personal cars. A couple of Army personnel were monitoring portable screens and laptops and Major Mitch McAuley stood nearby. He walked over, his hand outstretched and shook our hands. "I owe you," he said. "Both of you."

"Happy to help," replied Solomon. "There's no debt here."

"We'd all have our heads on the block if it wasn't for your help. I won't forget this."

"What happens to Captain Harris and Sergeant Major Kafsky now?" I asked.

"They weren't involved in the theft but they should have stepped up sooner when they noticed the tank was gone. There will be some flak but they won't lose their jobs," said Major McAuley.

"Thank you. And McTavett? He doesn't deserve to lose his job either."

"He will lose his job since he was involved in the theft, even though it was under duress, but I think I can get him an honorable discharge. There will be nothing on his record so his future job prospects won't be severely impacted."

"Thank you," I said because I knew things could be far worse for McTavett. I was fairly sure he would be pleased to have his family home safe and that he was no longer on the job that put them in so much jeopardy. Avoiding prosecution was a lucky bonus.

"I can only swing this because of your help. We have the tank secured and it was a good resolution to the problem and no harm was done. We'll dress up the paperwork as if this was our sting op from start to finish."

"I'm sure everyone concerned will agree to that," I said.

"You're moving it tonight?" asked Solomon.

"Soon. We've intercepted intel that the buyers are due to pick it up the day after tomorrow so as soon as we have them in custody, we'll arrange to relocate the tank. Until then, we'll secure the warehouse and transport the hired guards we have in custody to Fort Charles for interrogation. You don't have to worry about us getting in the way of the Feds either," said Major McAuley.

We shook hands again and Solomon and I walked over to our cars. "This is a good thing," he said. "You might want to break it to your buddies first that they're off the hook."

"They'll be relieved to hear it."

Solomon leaned against my car and folded his arms. "How's the other case? Wrapped up?"

"Not yet. I told my client about Bryce attempting to coerce me and she was as appalled as anyone would be. I have a lot of information but no concrete evidence. I'm at a crossroads. I can tell my client everything I know, but it's all hearsay. I don't think hearsay will help her friend leave a man who is no good for her." It wasn't the result I was looking for but I wasn't sure how much further I could go.

"Sometimes we have to realize that some cases don't end all neatly wrapped up or happy."

I thought about Julia and how sad and strained she looked when confronted by Jas and me and the police officers. Jas sent a text to say things remained quiet at Julia's apartment, which was good news, but I wondered how long it would continue. What happened to Julia if Bryce encouraged her to sell her apartment and move away from her friend? "I wish this one did."

"Let's go home and get some sleep. Things might be clearer in the morning."

"Race you," I said.

"I have a bigger, faster car."

"In that case, I'll just see you at home." I pushed up on tiptoes and kissed him on the lips.

"How tired are you?" asked Solomon.

"Not one bit. I'm wired."

"Drive safe," he said and winked. "We'll celebrate the end of this case at home."

"It wasn't even your case," I pointed out.

"You don't want to celebrate?"

I smiled. "Oh, yes, I do."

~

I woke late with Solomon's arm wrapped around me, hugging me against his smoldering hot body. I closed my eyes and refused to be properly awake for another five minutes. When I felt Solomon stirring, I squeezed closer and snuggled up to him.

"I'm so lucky," I mumbled against his chest.

"Did you just say I'm yucky?" he asked sleepily.

"No. Lucky."

"Yes, I am." He kissed the top of my head and tightened his grip around me.

I sighed. I really was lucky, we both were. We loved each other. We were kind and honest and we barely argued; and when we did, it was respectful and calm. We looked out for each other and I knew Solomon always had my best interests at heart. Our relationship seemed to be the direct opposite of Julia and Bryce's.

"Why the sigh?" asked Solomon.

"Life couldn't be better."

"It can only get better."

"I don't need it better than this. I have everything I want."

"I can think of some more things I want."

I wriggled so I could see his face properly instead of a wall of chest. Not that I minded staring at his chest. "Like what?"

"A family. Maybe a dog."

The family I knew about. The other thing was new. "You want a dog?"

"It has been a recent thought."

"Anything else?"

"To decide where we're going to live post wedding."

"Ahh." I snuggled down again. I knew that topic would come up again in conversation.

"We do need to decide. Do we stay here or do we go back to the Chilton house? Or do we sell them both and buy somewhere else entirely?"

I blinked. "Sell our homes?"

"It makes sense. We could buy somewhere together. Somewhere new."

"Oh."

"You don't like the idea?"

"No, I do. I just hadn't thought about it before. I've always wanted to buy this house. It's my dream house."

"It's a small dream house," pointed out Solomon.

"And your house is perfect for us and we can grow into it," I continued. "But you were shot there..." I trailed off.

Solomon took in a deep breath and blew it out again. "I know. It's not a problem for me. I think we should do that counseling. We can get through it."

"Marital counseling?"

"Trauma. You mentioned therapy after your wild night in with Lily."

I thought about it. "Okay," I decided. "Let's get married, do the therapy and then we can decide."

"Perfect," said Solomon. His cell phone on the nightstand began to ring. He leaned over and checked the screen, then answered. When he hung up, he said, "I have to go. My client thinks his office is bugged and wants a full sweep. I think he's paranoid but he's paying for it."

"Go," I said, giving him a playful push. Solomon didn't move an inch.

"Are you heading into the office?" he asked.

"Not this morning. I'm going to hang out here and type up my report and think about what to do next for my client."

"If it's about the Army case, we agreed there would be no reports. No paperwork."

"The other case," I corrected.

"It is completely acceptable to tell your client you can't help any further," said Solomon.

"I want to do more. I want to get irrefutable evidence that shows Julia exactly who Bryce is. So far, all I've got is an unidentified woman connected to Bryce who says he's a cheat, a pregnant ex who loathes him, my own claim of him asking for sexual favors, and everyone else who think he's a terrific guy."

"Conflicting reports."

"I know mine is true. If I'm telling the truth about him, the other women probably are too. He's definitely not the guy he makes himself out to be. I'm sure of that now." I rolled onto my back and sighed.

"Are any of them willing to go on the record?"

"I am. The pregnant ex doesn't want to jeopardize her position and I don't know who the other woman is. What should I do?"

Solomon rolled onto his back, shoulder-to-shoulder with me, and stared up at the ceiling. Then he dropped his head to the side and looked at me. "Go with your client and tell Julia everything. It's up to her what she does with the information you give her. Even if she believes you, she might want to stay. She might not be ready to leave."

"That's sad."

"We don't get to pick how our cases turn out."

"What if he hurts her? They had a fight yesterday and the police were called."

"She still has to make that decision. It is her choice." Solomon pushed back the covers and swung his legs out of bed. He walked over to the closet and pulled out jeans and a shirt. "You'll do the right thing," he told me. "You invariably do."

I kept that vote of confidence in mind long after he departed to debug his client's office. I took my time in having breakfast and was on my second cup of coffee when my cell phone rang.

"Hi, Harris," I said.

"Lexi, we don't know how to thank you," he said. "Me and Kaf are here and wow... it's been an unreal few hours."

"Is the tank home?" I asked.

"Not yet but soon. They caught someone else in connection to the theft."

"You're welcome," I said. "I'm glad I could help."

"Apparently, McAuley is likely to get a full commendation for cracking the theft ring."

"That so?"

"Yeah. Someone in the Army turned rogue and brokered the sale. The official report is being dressed up as a sting designed to catch the unscrupulous thieves and that we all had our parts to play. In reality, we got yelled at something bad but Kaf and I are officially off the hook so long as we maintain the story."

"I am happy to hear that."

"McTavett is going to lose his job but I think we can fix him up with something on the outside. He's had enough anyway. Poor guy has spent the last few days utterly terrified."

"This is a good result," I told him, smiling.

"If it hadn't been for you... Thank you again, Lexi."

Kafsky thanked me too and they hung up. I took my coffee and laptop into the living room and sat down to work. I typed up everything I knew about Bruce Maynard and then read it all, altering and adding to it as

I needed. When I was satisfied, I printed the document and slid it into a manila folder. Solomon was right. Once I handed over the information I gleaned over the course of my investigation, I had to let it go.

I called Jas, ready to tell her exactly that.

"I don't know that I can give you good news," I told her, disappointed that I didn't have anything better to say. "I want to give you my report and I think we should tell Julia together. The only evidence I have is hearsay so he could easily talk his way out of it."

"Maybe he won't," said Jas. "Julia was here earlier. She knocked on my door this morning and told me the police being at her apartment yesterday really opened her eyes and she'd been thinking about it and she realized she's had enough."

"Really?" I couldn't keep the surprise from my voice.

"Yes. Bryce stayed over so she's telling him now."

Something niggled at the edges of my memory, but I couldn't think of what worried me. "I'm glad she's come to the decision herself," I said. "Perhaps giving her the report later will fortify her resolve and she'll realize that she made the right decision."

"I think so too. Can you drop it off? Anytime is fine. I said I'd work from home today in case Julia needed any support."

"I'll drop it off soon," I said. When I hung up, I held onto my cell phone, a frown furrowing my forehead. Someone told me something recently but what was it? And why did it seem so important to remember now? I got up and paced the floor, forcing myself to think.

Like a bomb, it burst into my head. Maddox said it: *The worst time for something to go wrong is just as it starts to kick off.*

Solomon said something similar too: *It's always just when they're about to breach that's the most dangerous time.*

That reminded me of some material I once read about women leaving relationships. It was the moment they left that was often the most dangerous period, especially if the abuser realized his victim had her mind made up and intended to defy him.

I had already seen how explosive Bryce's behavior could be. If Julia was ending her relationship now, she might be in serious danger.

I grabbed the folder from the coffee table and shoved it into my purse. Snatching my keys, I raced for the door. I got to Jas and Julia's building in under fifteen minutes, hurrying upstairs. I paused at Jas's door, listening for sounds from Julia's adjacent apartment. Soft, muffled sounds came from inside, then a whimper that cut off abruptly. My instincts fired. Something was very wrong.

I banged on the door with my fist. "Julia?" I yelled.

"What's going on?" asked Jas, opening her door. She blinked when she saw me. "Lexi? I didn't expect you so soon. Is everything okay?"

"Something's happened," I told her, as I resumed pounding. "If you don't open the door right now, I'm calling 911," I yelled.

The door opened and Bryce stuck his head out. His hair, usually so neat, was ruffled out of place and his tie was askew. "Get lost," he growled, his face red and his eyes bloodshot.

"Where's Julia?" I demanded.

"She's busy." He made to push the door shut but I wedged my foot in the way.

Behind him, there was movement, then Julia stumbled into view. Her hair was a mess and blood streamed from her nose. She held her arm awkwardly and her eyes were red and wet with tears.

I didn't stop to think. I pulled back my fist and, packing all my weight behind the movement, punched Bryce hard in the face. He dropped, astonished, clutching his nose. I stepped past him, grabbed Julia by her unhurt arm and hurried her into Jas's apartment where Jas slammed the door shut behind us. Behind us, Bryce yelled obscenities.

"You're okay now," I told Julia as she began to cry again in choked gasps. I flexed my aching hand and raised my cell phone to my ear, ready to call for the police and an ambulance as I took in the odd way she held her arm and the deep finger marks around her throat. Jas wrapped her arms around her friend and Julia shivered. "You're safe now," I told her, my back against the door. On the other side, Bryce continued his litany of threats. "You're going to be okay."

CHAPTER TWENTY-ONE

"I really appreciate you visiting," said Julia. "You didn't have to." We were sitting in her living room a few days after Bryce's attack and it was nice to see Julia smiling. A large bunch of flowers sat on the side table but the television still had a big crack down the middle and needed to be replaced. Jas thoroughly cleaned the blood off from where Julia told us he shoved her face first into it, but things would be much better after the set was replaced.

"You can press charges," I said.

"How? No one actually witnessed anything. It'll be what he said versus what I said. As far as it appears, I stumbled and fell onto the TV and that's when I hit my nose and made it bleed and I also banged my arm on the way down. He'll make me sound like I'm hysterical. Even the police didn't have anything to hold him on."

"You don't know that."

"I do. Bryce sent me an email."

"He did?"

"Yeah." Julia reached for her laptop and opened it, then pushed it towards me. "That bastard has made it sound like I'm some kind of crazy psycho klutz."

I read it, and was appalled. It was a nice email on the surface. Bryce expressed his wish that she recover quickly and suggested she replace the rug that caused her to stumble and maybe even tidy up a little more so she wouldn't fall over anything else. Then he claimed to be shocked that she would say he intended to hurt her in anyway because he loved her although he couldn't see any future for them now. It was as though he just dumped her.

"I haven't replied to it. I don't know how to respond," said Julia.

"I'm not sure you should reply," I said.

"But if I don't, does it seem like I'm accepting what he said as the truth? Yet, if I do reply, it could be seen as an effort to start a conversation and why would I do that if I'm afraid of him? It's truly a no-win situation." Julia sighed.

"You can insist the police prosecute him," said Jas. "We saw you when he opened the door. You were bleeding and we both saw the marks around your neck. We can be your eyewitnesses." She looked to me for confirmation and I nodded.

"But you didn't actually *see* anything. It's my word against his. He's so convincing." Julia reached for a tissue and dabbed at the tear that rolled from her eye. She tucked the tissue in her hand and adjusted the blanket over her knees. "I fell for it. I believed everything he told me and then he did this to me."

"You weren't the first. You shouldn't feel bad about believing the man you loved," said Jas. "I thought he was terrific in the beginning too."

"You saw through him faster than I did."

"At least you did see him eventually," I said. Between us lay the file I compiled. I hadn't the heart to give it to Julia the day she'd been taken to hospital but she read it now. What she thought of it, however, was a mystery. She read it silently while Jas and I sipped hot tea and then she closed it and placed it on the coffee table.

"I hate that he'll probably get away with this," said Julia. "I hate that I believed him when he said his exes made stuff up. Lana. Angie. Jessica. How could I believe that many women were lying about the same man? I would have done anything for him. I even had my hair cut because he said he liked it short better. I don't even like it this way!"

"I can put you in touch with a lawyer. Even if you don't want to pursue it with the police, you can have a notarized statement kept on file just in case he ever tries anything again. I can ask a couple of friendly detectives to scare him off too," I suggested. "But I think you should reconsider filing charges. You have the hospital report. That's your evidence right there."

"I'll think about it." Julia reached for her mug and sipped. "This is the most liberated I've felt in weeks," she admitted. "I didn't realize how wound up I was all the time. Bryce's behavior become so slowly abhorrent that I didn't even realize how bad it really was. It seemed like his behavior was normal. All the horrible things he said his exes did, he accused me of and I knew I wasn't doing any of them. I'd tell him to stop and he'd say he never said things like that. I knew he did. I couldn't understand it. Then he would buy me flowers or take me to dinner and everything would be wonderful, but only for a little while."

"It's called gaslighting," I told her. "Bryce messed with your reality. He made you doubt yourself."

"Is that really such a thing?"

"It is," I confirmed. "And the escalation of abuse? That's from normalizing bad behavior."

"What's that mean?" asked Jas.

"He pushes the boundaries of what's okay. When no one calls him on it, he continues and then that escalates to something else. Then, that becomes normal so he escalates again."

"The drinking. The name calling. The pushing... I was the only person who saw it." said Julia. "It's going to take me a long time to get over this. I thought I had everything I wanted in Bryce and really, I had nothing. He wasn't the great guy I thought he was. He was a total phony."

"You have everything. You have a lovely home and friends and family who care about you. He's the one with nothing," I said. "One day, I'll tell you about my ex-fiancé and we can laugh about the lucky escapes we've both had."

"I think that's some way off," said Julia. Then she smiled. "But I'd like that."

"And I'll be there every step of the way," said Jas. She reached out to Julia and they held hands, smiling at each other. Then Julia began to cry again and so did Jas and I felt my eyes getting wet. So it wasn't exactly the outcome I was looking for, but Julia was safe and that was the best thing.

"I have to go," I said, checking my watch as a knock sounded at the door. "I have my rehearsal dinner to get to."

Jas went to answer the door and when she returned, several of her friends were with her.

"So there is life after the crazy ex?" said Julia hopefully as her friends fanned around her, fussing and exclaiming endearments.

"A better life than you can even imagine," I told her as I stood to leave. "Just you wait and see."

~

I was the last one to arrive for the rehearsal, which was fine, because if there was one time in my life I could legitimately be a diva, it was for anything to do with my wedding.

Solomon waited at the altar and next to him stood Delgado in best man duty. Both were in jeans and t-shirts and I could hardly imagine them in their finery tomorrow.

Solomon's sister Anastasia and Lily were there, along with Chloe and Rachel, my two older nieces. My younger nieces, Victoria and Poppy, would both be dressed in flower girl dresses but since they couldn't walk, they would be held inside the congregation. Garrett's son, Sam and Daniel's son, Ben were pageboys and they didn't crack one joke or pull a single prank as we practiced walking the aisle. I never saw them looking more serious. Garrett's oldest son, Patrick opted to be an usher but mostly he made googly eyes at Anastasia and I couldn't blame him. She looked stunning even in her jeans and button-down shirt.

My parents didn't need to be there but they came anyway. The only person really missing from our families was Solomon's brother, Damian but he was in witness protection and couldn't join us. I wasn't sure Solomon would want him there anyway although he hadn't mentioned Damien much since we last saw him. Perhaps that was a topic for therapy too.

"How are your nerves?" asked Lily after the celebrant directed us to walk through our positions and timings while she checked to be sure we were happy with the readings.

"I feel okay," I said. "I don't feel nervous at all."

"Wait until everyone is watching you tomorrow," said Mom.

I sucked in a breath. All those eyes on me? I wasn't sure if I loved or hated the idea.

"It'll be fine," said Lily. "If it looks like anything is going south, I will trip and fall, drawing all eyes on me while I flail around."

"You would do that for me?"

"If I really have to but I'd prefer not to," she said, "but of course I would embarrass myself if I had to and it would be so bad no one would even remember what you did in error."

"Is your dress ready?" asked Mom.

"Yes, it's hanging in the closet."

Mom gasped. "Solomon will see it!"

"He won't. Plus, we're staying in a suite at the hotel tonight and he's staying elsewhere so there is no chance he'll see it before the wedding. Are we going to the dinner? I am so hungry," I gasped as I felt the first hunger pangs forming.

Solomon stepped over and took my hand and after we thanked the celebrant, we walked out, trailing family members behind us. A small convoy of us traveled over to the restaurant where we booked our rehearsal dinner. Before we got out, Solomon looked over at me.

"You're quiet," he said. "Overwhelmed?"

"No, not at all. Okay, maybe a little bit," I admitted, "Mostly I'm just excited."

"What's on your mind?"

"I took that file over to Jas and Julia. She read it."

"And?"

"And nothing. She's not sure about pressing for prosecution but if she did, she would be right to. Her concern is not being taken seriously and Bryce talking his way out of it. The jerk already sent her an email completely changing the narrative. He said it was her fault for being clumsy. I'm not sure a prosecution would get anywhere."

"Covering his bases," said Solomon.

I nodded. "I wish I could have done more."

"She's safe?"

"Yes."

"And because she chose to be, not because of your investigation."

I nodded again.

"That's a good result." Solomon squeezed my hand. "You did a good thing. You kept investigating even when you weren't sure there was anything there. You got the information she can reflect on if she ever thinks of going backwards."

"Bryce had me fooled too. He had everyone fooled. He seemed like a really good guy. How does she ever trust a man again?"

"Same way you did," Solomon reminded me. "Slowly."

"I told her life would be better than she could even imagine. Was I wrong to do that?"

"Nope. That's hope. Everyone needs hope."

My mother rapped on the window and signaled us to follow. "Let's go to dinner," I said. "This is our last night as single people."

"I'm sure food tastes the same after marriage."

I laughed as we got out the car and followed my parents inside, ambling towards the room we'd reserved for the dinner. Our actual reception would take place in one of the other function rooms but Francesca assured us a smaller room would do just fine for the rehearsal. "I just need to freshen up," I said, heading for the restrooms off the lobby. As I emerged, I started to cross the lobby towards our private room, but when I saw Bryce in the restaurant adjacent to the lobby, I stopped dead.

I couldn't miss the perfectly slicked hair or the charming face but now that I'd seen the repulsive man beneath his handsome veneer, it all slipped away and he totally disgusted me. He wasn't alone. Sitting across from him was a pretty woman, the pair of them laughing as they ate. Then he raised his glass and they toasted something. Before I could think better of it, I made a beeline for them.

"You're unbelievable!" I snapped as I came to a stop next to his table.

"And you're the chick that punched me in the face because I wouldn't give her a job," said Bryce. He reclined slowly in his chair, assessing me with a cool expression that showed I hadn't rattled him. A small cut was etched across his nose. "No means no. You need to understand that. Stop harassing me."

"I punched you because you attacked your fiancée," I said, loud enough that the neighboring tables could hear.

"Careful, I think you just admitted to assault." His smile mocked me.

"Do you know what kind of man you're sitting with?" I asked his companion.

"My girlfriend is a wonderful woman who knows exactly what kind of man I am," he said, answering for her as the woman frowned, looking between the two of us.

"Girlfriend? It's been less than a week."

"Kendra and I met a month ago and it was love at first sight." Bryce reached for her hand and she beamed at him. "I knew I had to be with her. Thanks to her, I've got my self-respect back. I know what it's like to be truly appreciated and respected now."

"Oh, bullshit!" I scoffed.

"Honey, why don't you powder your nose?" he said, giving Kendra's hand a squeeze. Without a word, she pushed back her chair and got up. As she stepped around me, she gave me the filthiest look she could muster and narrowly avoided stepping on my toe.

I leaned over him and pointed my finger in his face. "How long do you plan on keeping up this charade? I know what you did to Julia and I know what you did to Jessica too."

"I didn't do a thing. It's my word against theirs and who's going to believe them?"

"Maybe Kendra will." But even as I said it, I knew she wouldn't.

Bryce saw my dilemma and a nasty smile spread across his lips. "Kendra believes she rescued me from that horrible relationship and who am I to correct her? She's been a wonderful shoulder to lean on this past month and she knows she's got it made with me."

"You think flowers and dinners can hide your real nature?"

"I'm giving Kendra exactly what she wants. I gave Julia and Jessica that too. It's not my fault they lost out on me. I'm a real catch."

"They found out who you really were."

"Haven't you heard? I'm a great guy. Everyone loves me. Ask anyone. My boss. My parents. My buddies."

"One day, people will realize."

"Will they? No one wants anything to do with Jessica. I hear that psycho is leaving town and good riddance. No one will believe Julia's hysterics either. She's always been highly strung. All I had to do was tell Kendra what she wanted to hear. No one will believe the word of my psycho ex-girlfriends."

"You discredited them all along."

Bryce smiled again, slimy and satisfied with his devious nature. "I just said my truth and no one saw anything different. I'm just the poor guy with bad taste in women. Now if you'll excuse me, my lovely date is back and we'd like to enjoy our dinner without the likes of you hanging around. Before you think about saying a word to her, consider this. That kind of behavior plays into exactly what I told her about Julia. All you're doing is reinforcing that my exes spread lies. I'm the real victim in all this."

He had me stuck because he was right. If he discredited Julia so much, then anything I said would just be viewed as malicious mischief by Kendra. Yet, if I said nothing, she might end up being the woman he attacked so badly, he killed her.

I pulled a business card from my pocket and walked away, anger filling me. Halfway, I intercepted Kendra. "I know you don't believe anything bad about Bryce," I said as I pressed the card into her hand, "but call me if you ever need help."

She turned it over and looked at it. "I don't need any help," she said.

"Keep it anyway," I said, stepping around her and walking away, knowing I was leaving her with a horrible man but hoping that for a little while, his behavior would be good and she would be safe. I couldn't persuade her to come with me, even if I wanted to, but maybe she would keep my card. And maybe she would wonder why so many women were scared of him.

Solomon waited at the entrance to the dining room, his arms crossed. "Who was that?" he asked.

"That is the man that assaults women," I said.

"Not a man," he said. "Are you okay?"

"Yeah, I just want to get out of here." Before we left the lobby, I waved to Garrett who had just arrived and I called him over. He unlinked his hands from his two younger kids, and handed them off to his wife.

"What's up?" he asked.

"See that guy over there in the window?" I said. "That's Bryce Maynard. There were two calls into MPD about him in the last couple of weeks."

"You had me look into him," said Garrett.

"His ex-fiancée, Julia, is too scared to prosecute but he left fingerprints on her neck and fractured her nose, among other injuries. The hospital and the responding officers witnessed them too. Can you help her see through all the criminal proceedings? He can't get away with this." I eyed Kendra again; how happy she appeared as he reached over and demonstrated what she would look like with shorter hair. "She's in danger and she doesn't know it yet."

"I'd be happy to help. Let me get things rolling," said Garrett.

"Do you want to skip the dinner? We can get takeout if you prefer?" asked Solomon.

"No, I want to be here, with you."

"Then let's go celebrate. There's nothing more you can do here."

I took his hand as we turned away and I didn't look back.

CHAPTER TWENTY-TWO

"Oh, Alexandra." My mother stepped back, her hands cupping her cheeks as she sighed. "You look beautiful. You look just like a young me. Doesn't she, Lily? Just like me!"

"Like twins," said Lily diplomatically. She stepped to one side so the photographer could snap a series of shots.

I turned back to the full-length oval mirror the hotel supplied and checked my reflection. The dress was as perfect as the last time I tried it on in the bridal salon. The alterations to the skirt meant it swept the floor perfectly, allowing my blue heels to peek out as I walked. The bodice was beautifully fitted and the jeweled sash was the perfect finishing touch. My hair was swept up and my makeup the perfect blend of natural but not my normal natural; just a really good version of natural. My eyelids were dusky and my cheeks glowing while my lips had the faintest hint of pink. I adjusted my birdcage veil and Lily fussed with it to make sure it was just so before she handed me the colorful bouquet.

"Did I mention my dress has pockets?" I said, demonstrating again. "I can carry lip gloss and all kinds of important things."

"Fabulous," agreed Lily.

"I think we're ready," said Mom. "Take my arm and I will walk you downstairs."

The bridesmaids waited in the lobby under my Dad's and Anastasia's watchful eyes and everyone clapped when I stepped off the last stair. I couldn't help smiling and blushing.

Mom rushed outside and then back again like a blue whirlwind. "The cars are waiting," said Mom. "Anastasia, Lily, and I will take the little girls and we'll see you there." She squeezed my hand and her face crumpled. "I'm so glad someone is marrying you," she said, squeaking with pleasure before rushing outside.

Dad rolled his eyes. "If you think that was bad, you should hear what Grandma O'Shaughnessy said to your mother before our wedding."

"I'm sure she'll tell us later," I said.

"Doubt it. Your brothers are under strict instructions to get her drunk, and then swiftly cart her away to her room as soon as her eyelids begin to droop."

"Smart plan."

"It's either that or she'll start putting curses on people."

"Ah, just like Garrett's wedding," I said.

Dad offered me his arm and I wrapped my arm around his. "It's not too late to run," he said softly, leaning in so only I could hear.

"I'm not running."

"We can drive."

"No!"

Dad beamed. "I didn't think so but I had to check."

The car carrying my mother, bridesmaids, and flower girls departed and the chauffeur waited by the door for us. I slid onto the back seat of the car, careful to tuck my skirt around me so it didn't catch in the door. Dad hurried around the other side and hopped in. "I could get used to this," he said as we moved off. "It's nothing like your mother driving."

"Don't give her any ideas. She might sign up as an Uber driver."

"Would that be so bad?" Dad wondered. "Lexi, I'm really happy for you. I want you to know that."

"Thanks, Dad."

"I like Solomon. He's a good man and I believe he will always be good to you. That said, if it ever goes wrong, you can come home."

"Thanks."

"There's no shame in our family, we're just family. We stick together. We'll stick by Solomon too, for as long as he's a member of our family. He's one of us now, but you're my baby girl."

"Dad, are you crying?"

"No," he spluttered and squeezed my hand harder.

We were silent a while as the car navigated towards the venue. My mind was full of making sure I didn't put my elegant heels into mud, or trail my dress through grass or step on the hem since we opted for an outdoor wedding. If I strictly focused on those details, I wouldn't think quite so much about Solomon waiting for me. The thought of him at the rose arch made my heart race but in a good way.

I was busy thinking about how handsome Solomon would look in his suit when the car spluttered, jolted, and lurched to a stop at the side of the road.

"What happened?" asked Dad, leaning forward to talk to the chauffeur.

"It's the engine. Again," the chauffeur sighed.

"What do you mean *again?*"

"It's not the first time this has happened," he explained.

"You didn't mention that when we paid for the car!" said Dad.

"Ahh," said the chauffeur as he hopped out before Dad could blow a gasket of his own. We waited while he popped the hood and a plume of smoke filtered out.

"This is not good," I said.

The chauffeur ducked his head through the front window. "So, this car isn't going anywhere," he said. "I'm going to call a tow truck."

"You want us to get to the church in a tow truck?" yelled Dad in a rare occasion of losing his cool.

"Can you maybe get someone to pick you up? We could call back the other car."

"Call the other car," I said, "get them here as fast as they can."

The chauffeur stood outside and opened his cell phone. "Cell phone's dead," he called.

"Use mine," said Dad. He pulled his phone from his pocket and thrust it at the man.

"Great. Do you have the number?" he asked.

"No!" we both yelled.

"Do you have your phone in your dress?" asked Dad.

"No, I gave it to Lily!" I turned to Dad. "What are we going to do?"

"We're six blocks away," said Dad.

"I can't walk one block in these heels."

Dad patted my leg. "We'll figure something out. I'll call Garrett or Daniel."

"They left their cars at the hotel and got cabs."

"Then Jord."

"He and Serena left their cars too and carpooled."

"What about Delgado?"

"He's the best man!"

"I'm going to check the situation, then I'm calling a cab," decided Dad. He got out of the car and went to speak to the chauffeur. I sat in the back like a frou-frou princess and waited, hoping that someone had a brilliant idea as traffic whizzed past us.

A low rumble made me look up and blink. Then I rolled down the window. "What are you doing here?" I asked when two uniformed men approached the window.

"Moving the tank," said Harris. He looked me over and nodded approvingly. "You look nice. Going somewhere special?"

"I was until the stupid car broke down. My dad is calling a cab."

"Cancel it. We'll take you. Where are you going?" asked Kafsky.

"In the tank transporter? It's six blocks and the last part is a narrow street. It won't fit. Plus, how am I supposed to climb up into the transporter's cab?"

"I got something smaller," grinned Harris. "Can we borrow the ribbons from the car?"

Dad appeared next to him. "Who called the cavalry?" he asked.

"Not the cavalry. Just the regular Army, sir. Me and Sergeant Major Kafsky here wanted to attend the wedding but we couldn't get leave. It's a good job we happened to be passing by. We're going to get you and your daughter to the wedding."

"How?" asked Dad.

Harris tapped his arm and they turned around. When Dad looked back, his smile spanned one side of his face to the other. "Best. Day. Ever," he breathed, his eyes wide.

"Oh, no," I said, shaking my head. "No. No. No."

~

"A tank?" said Lily when I hopped down onto the pathway leading to the gardens where our ceremony would take place. "Why didn't you tell me you were ditching the car and arriving by tank? I would have come!"

"It wasn't planned."

She pointed. "It has ribbons!"

"Pilfered from the car."

"There's a bow on the gun."

"Also improvised."

Are your friends special forces?"

"They're something," I said. Practical jokers, friends, and two people I was currently very grateful to.

"That's right. Very special forces," said Lily. "Very special forces got you here."

I looked around at the audience who had gathered to see what the commotion was about. The jaws of my nephews had dropped to the floor along with most of the adult males. A couple of them were inspecting the tank and a lot had their cell phones out, snapping shots. I was sure I would have some trouble convincing people that these were not shots suited to social media. "Solomon can't see this," I said. "I can't explain it. That is, I can explain it but I don't want to. It's not classy. No bride in the world has ever arrived at her wedding by tank."

"Except you," said Lily, still staring at it. "No one will ever forget this."

"I'm going to start right now!" I decided. "We have to get it out of here before Solomon comes to see what the fuss is about."

"We told him to wait in the garden but he's going to hate missing this. I am thrilled I got to see it," said Lily. She waved to Harris and Kafsky. Grinning, they waved back.

"Get another photo," said Dad, posing proudly against the tank. The photographer obliged him and I had to wonder how many photos she had taken of me emerging from the vehicle.

"Told you we'd get you to your wedding on time," said Harris. "I would hug you but I think you're lucky to still be clean as it is."

"I can't thank you enough," I told him.

"Consider it my gift. I'm just sorry I can't stay and watch but someone might complain if this doesn't turn up on time," he said, knocking the tank side with his fist. "Have a great wedding, Lexi. You make sure you tell Solomon that he's a lucky guy."

We waved as the tank took off at a slow rumble, then quickly picked up speed until it was gone, carefully maneuvering onto the main street and back to the tank transporter that had followed us most of the way.

"That was some entrance," said the man at my side.

"You made it!" I gasped. "I didn't know if you would come."

"Wouldn't miss it," said Maddox. He wore a dark blue suit and a pink rose was tucked into his lapel. "You look beautiful. Gorgeous. Sensational."

"Thank you."

"I suppose you had to nail it for your first wedding. You're a knockout."

I raised my eyebrows, unsure if he could see the movement from the other side of my veil. "My first wedding?"

"Sure," grinned Maddox. "You might have gotten it perfect for this wedding but it's only a practice run, right? You're going to knock it out of the park when we get hitched."

"You're terrible," I told him.

Maddox winked and reached for my hand, squeezing it, then he dropped it and kissed my cheek through the thin veil before he took off around the corner. I watched him go and didn't call after him.

"Ready?" said Dad, offering his arm again.

"Ready," I said. I glanced over at the wedding planner, Francesca. She still gawked at where the tank had been and didn't move. "Francesca?" I called. "Are we ready?"

She finally blinked and moved. "That was a tank," she said.

"Yeah," I sighed. "It was."

"I wonder if I can hire that," she said before she seemed to snap to attention. "Oh, yes. Yes. We're ready. Places, people!" She began to fuss around us, organizing the flower girls, the bridesmaids and finally, Dad and me. She spoke into her headset and a moment later, the faint sounds of music sprang up. She adjusted my veil, gave me the thumbs-up and indicated the flower girls should begin walking.

We followed the path around the side of the building, stepping onto a rose petal strewn carpet that led between two blocks of chairs towards a curved rose arch. It couldn't have been a more romantic setting. Francesca provided everything we'd asked for and in the middle of that hot summer's day, I felt my heart soaring. I walked forwards, holding onto my dad's arm as I looked around, seeing all the people who turned up to celebrate our wedding and support our marriage, smiling as I passed them.

Occupying the second and third rows were my brothers and their wives, except for Lily who was ahead of me. In the middle of my brothers was Maddox. He smiled warmly and I returned it, happy that he was there amongst all the people I cared most about. A couple of steps and I was past them and arriving next to Solomon.

He leaned forwards and whispered softly in my ear, "A tank?"

"You heard?"

"I'm impressed. If I'd thought of it, I would have gotten a tank too."

"His and hers," I said and I finally giggled, the tension seeping out of me when we held each other's hands. So what if I'd arrived by tank? Arriving on time was the best thing.

"Are we ready?" whispered the celebrant, leaning towards us.

Solomon and I looked at each other and nodded before turning to the celebrant. "Ladies and gentleman," she started, her voice strong as it carried across the crowd, "we are here today to celebrate the marriage of Alexandra Graves and John Solomon."

The celebrant continued with a short speech before she began the ceremony, indicating when we should speak and then calling for the rings. Delgado stepped forwards and dropped a ring into each of our palms. I turned over the platinum band in my fingers before I slid it onto Solomon's finger and we repeated our vows to each other.

"You may now kiss the bride," said the celebrant as a collective cheer went up.

Solomon smiled. "At last," he said and he kissed me.

Lexi Graves returns in *In the Line of Ire,* out now in paperback and ebook!

When Private Investigator Lexi Graves receives an expensive bag from her new husband, she's delighted... for all of five seconds. That's exactly how long it takes her to realize it's a fake. Then another fake bag turns up, along with an outraged mall manager that is desperate to find the culprit before the mall's impeccable reputation for selling quality goods is tarnished. When the initial investigation takes a murderous turn, Lexi knows she has no time to lose.

Going undercover would be easy if Lexi could convince anyone to talk. Then the FBI and Solomon Detective Agency collaborate to track down the culprits, and Lexi is further tasked with exposing the master mind behind the recent flood of fake goods. The counterfeiters, however, are smart enough to cover their tracks and the suspects are all seemingly innocent. Yet, one of them is a murderer... and ready to strike again.

If you enjoyed *Very Special Forces*, you'll love *Deadlines*, a spin-off from the bestselling Lexi Graves Mysteries, out now in paperback and ebook!

Shayne Winter thinks she has everything she ever wanted: a job as chief reporter at the LA Chronicle, a swish new apartment in a fabulous neighborhood, and a Californian-cool lifestyle just waiting to reveal itself. But on the first day of her new life, it all goes horribly wrong. The apartment is less 'young professional' and more 'young offender', the only furnishing a handsome squatter with roving eyes. Even worse, Ben, her predecessor at the Chronicle, has returned to claim his old job, leaving Shayne nothing but the obituary column and a simple choice: take it or leave it.

Her first assignment should be easy: write up the accidental death of washed-up former child-star Chucky Barnard and file her column. Yet when Shayne interviews the people close to Chucky, his sister claims Chucky had everything to live for and his untimely death could only be murder.

Convinced this could be the perfect headline to put her life back on track, Shayne vows to find the truth, convince a reticent homicide detective to investigate, and bring a killer to justice, all before Ben grabs her story and the killer makes Shayne his or her personal deadline.

Love mysteries? Try *Jeopardy in January,* my new standalone mystery, out now in paperback and ebook!

Sara Cutler loves her job as head librarian of the public library, an integral part of the historic heart of the picturesque mountain town, Calendar. The combination of old books, quirky clientele, and endless reading is nothing less than perfection for Sara. So when she discovers a body in the rare books section that threatens to destroy her quiet existence, along with the imminent demise of the library, Sara vows to find the killer.

She never expects to receive any help from Jason Rees, the handsome, big city developer whose only objective is to get rid of the library. Sara assumes he is counting on the murder to serve as the final death knell his firm needs to demolish the library. However, that doesn't prevent him from falling head over heels for the very woman with whom he's clashing.

When news arrives that the dead woman was nothing that she appeared to be, the whole town is instantly enthralled by the concept of having an actual jewel thief in their midst. Even more puzzling is: where did she hide her stolen treasure?

All Sara must do to save the library is simply solve the murder, find the hidden jewels, and convince herself not to succumb to the one man she would rather see run out town. It doesn't take long before she realizes that amateur sleuthing isn't as easy in real life as it is in the stories she loves to read.

Made in the
USA
Columbia, SC

80125110R00190